The Church of Black Sparrows

By Alan Cork

CRANTHORPE
MILLNER

D1596923

ISBN 978-1-912964-49-9 (Paperback)

www.cranthorpemillner.com

First Published (2020)

Cranthorpe Millner Publishers

To Joyce Doris DesBois, the mother I never knew

Chapter One
The Bad Shepherd

It was the end of the line. The train stopped just before the buffers. The impeccably dressed, white-haired young man stepped out of the train and looked around him with barely concealed disgust. The unmanned railway station was deserted and depressing. It was raised up on the railway bank with what remained of Blacksparrow Lane on one side and the small river that merged in with the River Thames on the other.

The railway bank was overgrown with nettles, brambles and bushes with vicious looking thorns. He was watched with suspicion from among the brambles. An urban fox.

The man bared his teeth and snarled at the fox which turned and fled into the brambles.

No one else got off the train. The name of the station, Blacksparrow Halt, was written on signs attached to the railings on both sides.

He looked down from his elevated position on the platform. Behind him were the remaining inhabitants of Blacksparrow Lane, lucky enough to live on the end of the road that had not been destroyed.

Ahead of him was rubble and wasteland surrounded by a high metal fence with spikes on top. The fence stopped at the edge of the Thames.

There were two ways down: a steep flight of cement steps or a gently sloping, winding pathway for the less mobile. He chose the steps.

He was a man who rarely used public transport. His chauffeur-driven Rolls Royce took him everywhere. But he wanted to experience the journey that the ordinary plebs would have to make.

When he got to the bottom of the steps, he found himself confronted by a beggar.

"Can you spare some change for a homeless man?" the beggar asked. He had been sitting but stood up to face the new arrival. He was dressed in a stained and torn overcoat. His hair and beard were long and straggly. His teeth were brown. He held out a shaking hand that had long fingernails.

The white-haired young man winced at the smell of stale alcohol and unwashed body odour.

"Go away and die, maggot," the young man spoke coldly.

"Show some sympathy, please, sir. You look like a wealthy man. I lived there for many years as a tenant. My wife died, my children left and then they, some massive property developers, came along and bought out all the properties there." He waved his hand at the metal fence. "They kicked us out of our homes and then flattened them. The council gave me temporary housing for a while but then even they kicked me out. Those greedy developers destroyed my life. Please help." He grabbed the young man's arm.

2

"Don't infect me with your filth," the young man thrust him away with such force that he fell over on his back.

The beggar made an attempt to get back up.

"Stay where you are or I will slice you in half like the rotten twig you are," threatened the young man, feeling inside the deep pocket tailored into his jacket. He was looking around him for the sign of any witnesses or CCTV cameras. They were alone but modern surveillance cameras were much harder to spot these days.

"I will report you to the police for assault," the beggar whined.

"Look at you. Who are the police going to believe of the two of us?" The young man shrugged.

"Who are you?" the beggar sobbed.

"I am the man who made you homeless. My name is Felix Hoad. Remember it and take it to your grave. My name will be remembered. Yours will not. The only reason I am letting you live is because I have something much more urgent to deal with." The white-haired young man strode away, snarling as his bespoke black leather shoes became covered in dust and dirt.

"My name is Pringle, remember it," the beggar croaked after him.

Felix Hoad stopped at a padlocked door in the metal fence. He produced a key and unlocked the padlock. He opened the door and stepped through into the wasteland.

The day had started out badly but now it was going to get so very much worse.

This was the day when, for the first time, Felix Hoad would finally be confronted by someone or something that was even more evil than himself.

Few people are either completely good or completely evil but Felix Hoad was an exception. Nothing else mattered to him except the growth of his own power and success and nothing was allowed to get in his way. He really had no conscience and everyone he dealt with knew this. Either they obeyed him or they suffered the consequences.

He was, however, always very careful to cover his tracks.

He was driven by greed, perverse desires and a need to constantly seek out answers to life's mysteries that were always just out of reach.

Even as a child he frightened adults with his cold lack of fear. His own mother, whom he eventually killed, described him as being born without the fear gene.

He embraced dangerous sports, hang gliding, scuba diving, speedway, potholing, cave diving, jumping off mountains or out of aeroplanes, always trying to challenge his high tolerance to fear stimuli.

He enjoyed controlling and manipulating lives of others. His biggest high was always in destroying the lives of others.

He had never married or formed a long-term relationship because for him sex and death were intertwined. For him the ultimate climax was murder.

His father had been a butcher and had taught him the art of cutting up meat in the hope that he would take over the family business. He became adept with the butcher's cleaver but had no interest in using it as his father did.

When he was ready, he used his personal cleaver, a modern smaller and lighter version, to chop his father up and distribute the pieces amongst the meat he parcelled up and sold to their customers. As far as the world was concerned his father had just run away, deserting his wife and son, never to be seen again.

When he was a poor butcher's son he lived in old t-shirts and jeans. He worked his way up the crime ladder working as a collector of protection money for some East End gangs – continuing to collect for himself even after the gangs broke up, learning at a young age how to intimidate people. Now he was rich and successful, he had his suits handmade with the finest silk. He always had what was called a poacher's pocket sewn inside his bespoke jackets. The poacher's pockets got their name from originally being a deep inside pocket in which poachers would conceal and carry dead grouse, chickens or rabbits. But for Hoad this is where he carried the butcher's cleaver that went with him everywhere. The pocket went all the way down to the bottom of the jacket and easily concealed the vicious weapon.

So Felix Hoad could be said to be completely evil and when he did not get his own way there was Hell to pay.

Just then Felix Hoad was very impatient and angry because his biggest project yet was falling behind schedule for reasons he did not understand. He was head of a property development company which bought derelict land and buildings cheap by forcing out the original owners and tenants and then turning the area it acquired into desirable buildings.

There was a hold up in the demolition of a site he had taken over in Blacksparrow Lane in the Docklands area of London. His lieutenants had been unable to get to the bottom of the hold up or provide him with any suitable explanation so he had to find out for himself.

He looked around at the derelict Blacksparrow Lane site. Hoad strode around the abandoned bulldozers and cranes looking for the workmen.

He paused to take in his surroundings, suddenly aware of a different atmosphere. There was a cold wind blowing dead leaves and litter around the levelled ground and half demolished houses.

It was unnaturally quiet for an area so close to central London and the River Thames. It was summertime but it could have been autumn in Blacksparrow Lane. There were a few straggly trees that seemed dead or dying. The grass and plants were brown and dead on soil that was too black. There were no living things in that bleak, desolate land.

An old church remained upright amidst the rubble of demolished buildings. On the top of it, he saw a sign of some life: some black birds were regarding him coldly from the roof. One even perched on top of the tall steeple staring downwards, like a sentry.

People said the name Blacksparrow Lane went back centuries, having got its name from big, black sparrows that it was said could only be found there. It made no sense to Hoad, surely only sparrows can be brown or grey? He stared at the birds again and wondered … but no, it wasn't possible.

He surprised himself by shuddering. What was that? Not fear, surely?

"Hey!" a loud shout snapped him out of it. He turned and saw where it came from, a gathering of nervous workmen. He strode towards them.

Hoad was tall and perfectly formed. His pure white hair grew long and lank around his pale face. His chiselled jaw was covered by a white beard and a white moustache grew under his large, aquiline nose. His eyes stood out, dark and cold, surrounded by white lashes and eyebrows that were so white you could think they were dyed. His sensual lips were too full and pouty, almost as if they had been Botoxed, but that was not his style. His teeth, so white and regular that you wondered if they were false, were clenched in barely concealed rage.

A man broke away from the other men and approached him, almost shaking with fear. He was middle-aged and dressed in overalls and a hard hat.

"Mr Hoad, I am Johnson, the foreman. I was told you were coming-," he started.

"Mr Johnson, you are about to be sacked and when I sack someone, I make sure they never work again," Hoad hissed at him while Johnson cowed away. "You have put us behind our deadline. You would not believe how much money I am losing every day we do not get this project started."

"I am so sorry sir but it is the church. The men were not happy about demolishing the church-," Johnson spluttered.

"Are you telling me that this gang of morons are frightened to knock down an old church?" Hoad asked. "They don't look a very religious lot to me," he ran his eyes over the motley crew of ugly, hairy men. Hoad was a staunch atheist himself and considered all religions to be peasant superstition.

"Our gang is made up from workers all over the world so they do not have any one particular religion. I am a Born-Again Christian, myself. It is more the

7

building itself they are afraid of. There was also a weird cranky old woman making a protest…" Johnson was embarrassed.

"A one-woman protest stopped you? Get me in a crane with a wrecking ball and I'll flatten the building myself," Hoad snarled.

"There is something odd about the church," the foreman started to explain. "I know because I'm a local man. For years it could never get a regular congregation. People always felt uncomfortable in the building."

"Churches are not supposed to be comfortable," Hoad snapped.

"They were either too hot or too cold in the church and it always smelt bad," the foreman added. "The Church of England gave up on it. There was so much vandalism and sacrilege. In the end it was deconsecrated and sold off. It has been empty for years."

"It must be alive with vermin," Hoad said.

"You would think so but even the rats and insects stay away. Not even a cockroach would enter that church…" the foreman trailed off.

Suddenly Hoad's deadline seemed less important. "Now you have me intrigued. Are you telling me that the men believe the old church is haunted?"

"I wouldn't say that. It's just something about the building that makes them uncomfortable."

"That's it. I have to see this building myself," Hoad said.

"Do you want to go inside?" the foreman asked.

"Absolutely."

Johnson looked extremely uncomfortable and some of his men laughed at him.

8

"Then I will go with you even though the place gives me the creeps. Kruk will come with us." The foreman gestured at one of the men, a grinning giant who held a sledge hammer. "Kruk is from Poland and nothing scares him. Damn good workers these Poles. Put our English layabouts to shame."

Kruk nodded and grinned wider still. Hoad suspected his English was poor and he had no idea what they were saying.

"We will need these." Johnson produced three torches. "Although you won't be able to light up all the darkness inside. We are going somewhere profane."

"I don't believe in ghosts." Hoad just chuckled.

The three of them climbed over the rubble of flattened buildings till they came to the church, still upright and untouched among all the destroyed homes, its spire rising to the heavens.

There was an old wooden sign that should have read: 'The Church of the Good Shepherd' but someone had crossed through the word 'Good' with black paint and written above it, in the same black paint, the word: 'Bad'.

"The Church of the Bad Shepherd, aye. I like it. At least the local graffiti artists have a sense of humour," Hoad commented.

"I am surprised that any of the local vandals know how to spell," Johnson murmured.

Hoad went up to the entrance and tried the wooden double doors but they were locked.

"I keep it locked for safety's sake but even the petty criminals round here won't break into this place because of its unsavoury reputation. I couldn't stand being inside it myself. I always felt I was being watched and there were all sorts of weird noises. In the end I locked the doors for good. I'm not embarrassed to say that in a spasm of panic, I threw the keys in the river. But it didn't end there. The place is full of secret tunnels and bolt holes and that creepy woman still managed to slither her way in and out."

"So are you suggesting we go in through a tunnel?" Hoad scoffed.

"No, we can go through the front door." Johnson gestured to the mighty Kruk, warning Hoad to stand aside.

Kruk strode up to the doors and swung at them with his sledgehammer. It took just one blow to smash through the locks. Kruk kicked the doors open.

Hoad walked in first followed by Johnson and Kruk.

They had a torch each and switched them on, looking around them.

"Welcome to Blacksparrow church," Johnson said.

If Hoad had thought it was eerily quiet outside, it was nothing to the uncanny stillness inside the church.

There was also something else.

"Jesus what a foul smell," Hoad said as he breathed in the stale, tainted air.

"It smells like a farmyard. The animal stink reminds me of an Inner-City farm I used to visit as a child," Johnson said.

"Goat," Kruk spoke for the first time. "It is the smell of goat."

The church was in surprisingly good order. Not a cobweb to be seen. Hoad ran the torch beam over the rows of wooden pews, the high vaulted ceiling, the altar and pulpit and the ornate, stained-glass windows that carried different images of saints, still visible under the dust.

"Holy Mother of God," Johnson exclaimed suddenly.

His torch beam fell on the wooden cross behind the altar and the thing that had been rammed on the top of it.

It was the decapitated head of a goat. Blood had trickled from the head and down the cross where it had dried.

"We must call the police." Johnson was visibly shaken.

Hoad went over to the goat's head and examined it closely. There was no doubt it was real. Its long tongue dangled out its drooping, open mouth. Two huge horns curled out of its skull and a pointed beard jutted under its chin. The head had been forced onto the pointed top of the cross by the severed neck.

Hoad turned to Johnson. "No need to call the police. It is made of plastic," he lied. "It's an artificial joke head with glass eyes and fibreglass hair. What looks like blood is red paint."

"That's a relief," Johnson wiped the sweat from his forehead. He had bought the lie.

Suddenly loud organ music bellowed out, deafening them.

Hoad swung his torch beam over to the source of the cacophony and spotlighted the huge organ with shiny metal pipes jutting up to the roof. As soon as his torch touched on the organ something leaped off the seat and scuttled away into the shadows. He couldn't see who or what it was. It had just been a blur and now it was gone.

"Who's there?" Hoad called.

The three torch beams began sweeping round the huge church.

Hoad was aware of something perched on the rail of a gallery that looked down on the church from under the ceiling. He first thought it was a statue of some sort.

But then it moved.

He began to raise the torch beam to see what it was. As he did so he felt a twinge of anxiety, almost fear.

Fear! He almost laughed out loud. Just for a moment he thought he felt a twinge of fear but then he dismissed the unfamiliar emotion.

"Felix Hoad, have you come to worship?" a woman spoke to him, her shrill voice echoing throughout the church ceiling.

He shone the torch on her.

The woman squatted on the railing of the upper gallery, her long thin legs bent double. She seemed well balanced and unconcerned by the height, not using her hands to hold on.

She stared down at him through two prominent eyes above her sunken cheeks. She had a great, pointy nose, like the beak of a hawk. Her greying hair was pulled back into a tight bun held in place by a number of long steel hair pins with different coloured beads at the end. It was hard to judge her age. Her face was wrinkled and haggard but she leapt about with the agility of a teenager. She jumped backward off the rail onto the walkway, straightened up, and glided along the gallery to the wooden staircase at the end. She began climbing down it towards them. She was tall, thin, nimble and dressed in a tweed suit, black stockings and flat shoes. It seemed that the woman could find her way around in the pitch dark without a torch. She had the eyes of a creature of the night.

"You are trespassing, ma'am. I have warned you about that before," Johnson spoke to her with a trembling voice. Then to Hoad he said: "This is the woman I told you about. As if we didn't have enough problems without her creeping and slithering around in the darkness and freaking out the men."

"So you are the one-woman protester? Was that you on the organ and if so, how did you get up to the gallery so quickly? You can't be in two places at once," Hoad grinned at her as she dropped to the floor and walked towards him.

"Who says I can't?" her voice was shrill and grated inside his head.

"How did you get in here in the first place?" Hoad asked.

"This church has many secret passages going back centuries. You could get lost in its twisted and ancient depths …"

She stopped in front of him.

"You know my name but I am afraid you have the advantage of me," Hoad said to her.

"Mrs Harriet Milverton. I have been following your career with interest. You are a wicked man," she smiled at him.

"And I suspect you are a wicked woman, Mrs Milverton. Is there a Mr Milverton?" Hoad asked.

"Oh he died," was the brief answer.

"Why am I not surprised?" Hoad then asked her: "Why on earth do you want this empty, derelict, unused old church saved from demolition?"

"Oh it is not derelict or unused. It serves a different faith," she said.

"I knew it," Johnson was getting more agitated. His face was shiny with sweat. "Blasphemy, Devil worship, Black Magic!" he shouted at her.

There was a rumbling sound in the ceiling and dust and grit showered down to the ground. The altar shook briefly and the cross with the goat's head stuck on it toppled forward, crashing onto the dais.

It was too much for Johnson. "Bloody heathens. I have to get out. I'll wait for you outside," he turned and ran, sobbing and praying to himself, outside through the great double doorway.

"What a ridiculous little man." Hoad watched him go with a barely concealed sneer. "Who believes in the Devil in this day and age?"

"You would be surprised," Mrs Milverton said. "Every believing Christian, Jew or Moslem must believe in Satan. Beelzebub is part of their religion and a big part of our world's culture and history."

"And what do you believe in?" Hoad asked her. He had been hellbent on getting this project moving again and fast but what she said caused him to pause. If there had not been a witness, he would have smashed her head in and hid her body so that when the church was demolished she would be found under the rubble having died because no one knew she was inside. But now he was eager to know more.

"It's complicated," she said.

"Try me."

"Well among other things I head a circle of Neopagans. We pagans were here before most of the other religions."

14

"And who is your God?"

"Some Neopagans worship the Great God Pan, the Horned God. As Christianity was imported to this country it latched onto the existing Pagan religion and the image of Pan evolved into your traditional image of Lucifer."

"Ah, that goat's head…"

"My real religion is the old religion, the first and the original. All the other religions are the invention of man and a mere thousand or so years old."

"Why this church?" Hoad persisted, his eyes alight now with interest. Darkness had always fascinated him. "What has it got to do with all that hocus-pocus?"

"Now that is an interesting story." Mrs Milverton gave a cold smile. "Being next to the River Thames, one of the earliest major harbours for international shipping, the church has been a magnet for different races and different religions for centuries. This area was where many early immigrants first set foot on British soil. It was into diversity in a big way long before the rest of the world caught up it. So this church ground has been used by many religions. Not just branches of Christianity, either. This was also a melting pot for the worship of older, darker beliefs.

"This was a centre of alchemy, voodoo, paganism and old magic but those early necromancers were just the scientists of their day. They were experimenting with what we now call genetic engineering, cloning and DNA, long before the world had names for them. The flocks of big black sparrows that were only found round here were said to be a successful result of one of their many experiments with all forms of life. The ability to create life should not belong to God alone. Those

15

alchemists knew then that each person's blood was individual and carried their unique biological signature. When you signed a pact with the Devil with your own blood there was no going back.

"This present church was built in 1880 but the nave and tower were built during the reign of Edward III in the 14th century, and a church stood on the site for a thousand years. Before Christianity, the people of England were Pagans and many of our old churches were built on Pagan sites. When this church was badly damaged by a flying bomb in World War Two some people said that it was the hand of God rather than the Germans that directed it. The church was restored but the congregation stayed away after reports of continuous vandalism, desecration and sacrilege. The church made most people feel uncomfortable and the air was always foul no matter what they tried to do. The Church of England eventually sold it off for development and it was de consecrated."

"Thanks for the history lesson but I can't see it being any different to hundreds of churches up and down the United Kingdom. I see nothing special about this one," Hoad shrugged. "It is in my way. It has to be demolished right now."

"Wait. I want to show you something," Mrs Milverton said. "Follow me."

She led Hoad and Kruk to one side and through a door into what looked like a vestry. It was cramped, dark and dusty. She lifted up a mouldy rug from the floor and pointed down to the floor.

The floor was stone but carved on top was a double circle overlaid by a five-pointed star.

Hoad looked at it closely. "A pentacle?" He noticed narrow cracks down the middle and on the edge of the pentacle. "Look like it can be opened. Has it ever been opened?"

"Not in modern times. I don't think this place should be destroyed until we see what's underneath it." Mrs Milverton looked at him.

"I'll get someone with a jack hammer," Hoad straightened up.

Kruk however gestured for them to stand aside and approached the stone floor with the sledgehammer over his shoulder. He said something in his native tongue and then swung the sledgehammer down on the floor with all his might.

The whole church seemed to vibrate with the blow.

"Careful. You could bring the whole building down on us without a bulldozer," Hoad warned.

Kruk just grinned and swung the hammer again. The church shook and quivered and dust and grit fell upon them.

"I think the building is going to collapse before we can get that open," Hoad said.

Then Kruk struck the floor a third time and suddenly cracks began snaking over the stone floor. All three of them sprang back in case the floor opened up and swallowed them.

The floor with the pentacle on it was breaking up and great slabs of stone were cascading into the darkness below. There was a lot of crashing and deep rumblings, and dust billowed out of the widening hole. When it settled the three of them moved closer to the hole and peered in. All they saw was the start of a stone spiral staircase that wound down into blackness.

17

"It could be dangerous but I am not going to leave it unexplored," Hoad said. "I'll lead the way."

So with the torch shining the way, Hoad began climbing down the steps, followed by Mrs Milverton and Kruk.

Round and round and down and down the spiral stone staircase they went, into the deep dark earth.

It became harder to breath. The air was foetid and low on oxygen from being sealed underground for so long.

Kruk was grunting and seemed to be swearing in his own language. Hoad swung the torchlight on him. The big man was no longer grinning and fearless. He looked scared and angry. In contrast Mrs Milverton seemed happy, her eyes glittering with excitement in the dark. Hoad turned the torchlight back to where he was going and persevered, hoping Kruk was not going to be the next one to panic and flee.

"Jesus, we are going underneath the Thames," Hoad panted.

"To the centre of the Earth," Mrs Milverton spoke calmly.

"You are sure it is not to Hell?" Hoad said.

"I thought you did not believe in Hell, Mr Hoad," Mrs Milverton said.

"You should know that I am impervious to fear," Hoad told her. Then he continued, proudly, "I was skydiving once and my parachute failed to open at 13,000 feet. I calmly cut open the parachute as I fell and managed to release it just before I hit the ground. During all this my heart rate remained steady and my only thoughts were on how I was going to get revenge on the skydiving company who had failed to check my parachute."

They seemed to have been descending the spiral staircase into pitch blackness forever. Hoad lost track of time.

Then the steps ended. Hoad stepped out into a huge, cavernous room. He swung the torchlight around. There were statues, pillars, pews and a high, domed ceiling. There was a lot more to explore; a complex of chambers, catacombs and passages spiralled deep underground.

"It is another church built under the original church," he said as Mrs Milverton and Kruk joined him on the floor.

"Oh I think you will find that this is the original church," Mrs Milverton said. "This is a temple to the true God."

It was so still and silent. And yet the air was vibrating, like the beating of a giant heart.

The air was really bad now and Hoad was feeling faint as he gasped like a fish out of water.

Again that unfamiliar feeling he thought must be fear niggled at Hoad. Perhaps it was that thing people called claustrophobia? They were alone and trapped deep underground after all.

The torch shone on what looked like a stone pond or bath sunk into the floor. It was filled with water that was strangely black and still.

A suit of armour stood against the wall, holding a battle-axe.

"How old is this place, I wonder?" Hoad asked.

"We could be in what was once a Neolithic tomb expanded on by different generations of seekers," Mrs Milverton said.

"Seekers after what-?" Hoad started as his torchlight swept the chamber.

Then he froze and was certain this time he felt real fear as two large eyeballs goggled back at him.

His torchlight had illuminated the figure of a man crouching in the dark.

Behind him Kruk let out a terrified bellow.

Evil stared at them.

The man that stared back at him was from a different century. His giant boulder of a head was supported on a long scrawny neck that jutted out of the high-winged collar of a Victorian suit. A huge Adam's apple jutted out like a growth half-way down the long neck.

Now there were sounds but Hoad was not sure if they were real or in his head. Lots of soft whisperings hummed all around him as he looked, transfixed, at the abominable figure.

Mrs Milverton let out a gasp behind him. "Quincy Pitt!" she hissed.

The ancient man caught in the torchlight did not move. He was frozen in time. He seemed alive but in fact the menacing Victorian who stared at them was just a very old sepia photograph. The antique photo was surrounded by a gilt frame which hung from a hook on the top of an upside-down crucifix, which was fixed on top of an altar.

A pair of golden candelabra stood either side of the picture.

The large, old picture showed a spindly old man in a Victorian frock coat and high-winged collar, crouching forward and glaring out of the portrait with eyes that were luminous orbs in a mummified face, half-hooded by leathery eyelids. Black hair covered the abominable, overlarge head and grew down the protruding cheekbones.

The nose was prominent, with an edge like a blade. The great dome of a skull would have indicated great intelligence and intellect to a Victorian scholar of defunct phrenology, while the shrivelled lips drew back on teeth that were more like the fangs of a wild animal, with broken and jagged edges.

Both hands, on the end of long thin arms, were wearing stitched leather gauntlets but there was something strange about the right hand.

"Note the right hand has an extra finger. Five fingers and a thumb in all. The hand of Quincy Pitt!" Mrs Milverton announced.

"Who is Quincy Pitt?" Hoad asked.

"He was a Victorian scientist, inventor, icon and inspiration to many powerful figures of the 19th century," she answered.

"Never heard of him," Hoad said.

"Not many people have," Mrs Milverton studied the picture in awe. "He was an early cult leader. His followers were the rich and powerful elite of Victorian society who swore an oath of secrecy."

"I need to have a closer look." Hoad moved forward. "It looks like an example of early photography from the 19th century, taken on a glass plate using a magnesium flare."

"Stay back!" Mrs Milverton held up her hand and then pointed to the floor.

A circle drawn in chalk on the floor completely surrounded the altar. Placed around the chalk line were various sealed bottles and jars. They were either filled with a murky liquid or fine powder.

"An old magic circle reinforced with different potions. I'm not sure if they are there to protect the picture or to protect people from the picture," she added.

It was then that Kruk went berserk with terror.

"Bad, bad! Must destroy!" he screamed.

He was a powerful man and flung them both aside with little to no effort. With his sledgehammer he began smashing the bottles and jars.

As he did so, fumes long-sealed inside the glass containers began leaking and flowing into the already poisoned air. The bubbling liquid spread over the floor around the broken glass and flowed into the powders, which turned into wisps of smoke that rose upwards.

Those faint whispers suddenly turned to loud, mocking laughter in Hoad's head. The picture of Quincy Pitt really looked alive and moving now. The eyes were becoming larger and larger until they bored into his brain.

The mouth was yawning open, revealing more of those beast-like teeth.

And as the poison filled their brains and lungs, so sanity left them.

Hoad found himself ripping his clothes off. He looked across at Mrs Milverton. She was doing the same, tossing aside her tweed suit to reveal a gaunt and emaciated skeletal body. They were both naked, obeying an order that only they could hear.

They dropped onto their hands and knees and knelt before the altar.

Kruk on the other hand was going completely feral.

Now he had smashed all the bottles and jars he turned his wild eyes on the portrait.

"Die, die," he bellowed and ran at it with the sledgehammer raised above his head.

"Stop him!" Mrs Milverton screamed. "It must be preserved at all costs."

They threw themselves at Kruk from either side and brought him down before the hammer could reach the portrait.

"Get off me!" Kruk rolled on the floor and tried to throw his two naked attackers off.

Mrs Milverton pulled a steel hair pin from her bun and held it by the bead at the end. Then she plunged it behind Kruk's ear and into his skull.

He yelled and screamed as blood spurted from behind his ear but it did not slow him down.

Hoad reached for one of the gold candelabra from the top of the altar. He swung it down at Kruk's head with all his might.

Blood gushed from Kruk's head but Kruk, still bellowing like a stuck pig, kept fighting to get at the portrait and smash it with his sledgehammer.

Mrs Milverton grasped the other candelabra and hit Kruk with it, this time between the shoulder blades. He was in pain but still he tried to rise to his feet and smash the picture.

Hoad scrabbled for his discarded jacket and reached inside the deep pocket. He pulled out the butcher's cleaver and held it up, glinting in the dark. Hoad then ran at Kruk and swung the cleaver at his face. It struck his chin, the blade splitting his jaw.

Mrs Milverton had extracted another steel hair pin from her bun and this time she jammed it up Kruk's nose and into his brain.

But Kruk was strong and nothing seemed to slow him down. He was badly wounded and in pain but still he fought back with the strength and fury that comes with madness.

Mrs Milverton began continuously pounding the back of his head with the candelabra while Hoad tried to extract the sledgehammer from Kruk's hands. He was pulling his fingers back from the handle, breaking them one at a time.

Suddenly the last finger cracked back with a bellow from Kruk and Hoad pulled the sledgehammer free and tossed it aside.

Hoad stood up, staggering, his naked body covered in blood. He was sick and giddy with all the poisonous fumes he was breathing in and barely able to stand.

Kruk was getting up, bleeding from a dozen wounds and with two steel hair pins embedded in him, but still as strong as a bull.

Hoad raised the cleaver and smashed it down on Kruk's head.

Amazingly with the top of his skull cracked open exposing his brains, which were dribbling down his face, Kruk still fought back, and stood upright before them.

Mrs Milverton was on him, striking at him with the candelabra in a frenzy again and again.

Kruk was laughing now. A bloodcurdling , crazy laugh. Then all three of them were laughing as the toxic fumes penetrated their minds.

Hoad stabbed him full in the face with the cleaver. Kruk's face turned blood red but still he did not fall.

He swung the cleaver at his chest and sliced it open with one blow. Kruk stood before them now with not just his brains exposed but his intestines dangling from his open torso.

They were all standing in a spreading pool of his blood.

And he continued to laugh, a maniacal sound that echoed round that huge underground chamber.

Hoad continuously hacked at him with the cleaver till at last Kruk toppled forward and slumped to the ground. Hoad did not stop. He swung the cleaver down on him over and over again as his body collapsed and was still. Bones cracked and shattered and blood splattered over Hoad's naked body.

With a last blow from the cleaver, Hoad took his head off.

Then he and Mrs Milverton sunk to the ground, naked, dripping blood and gasping for air.

"Kruk will make a suitable sacrifice for burial in the foundations," Hoad said.

"You know what we should do now?" Mrs Milverton prompted, running a decrepit hand up his blood-soaked am.

Hoad looked at his own muscular, toned, well-endowed body and then at her cadaverous body with a grimace.

"We are two of a kind, Mr Hoad," Mrs Milverton continued, smiling, a grotesque leer.

Despite himself he found his body responding. His heart raced, the blood lust and madness thundered through him as he allowed her to fall on top of him.

The torches turned off and almost pitch blackness descended except for two pinpricks of light from the watching eyes of Quincy Pitt in the portrait. The two killers had dark, loveless and bloody sex in front of his image.

Their cries echoed throughout the chamber as the copulated and then they fell still.

After a while, without speaking, their breathing calmer now, they switched the torches back on, went to the dark sunken bath and immersed themselves in the black water. There were living things in that water. They slithered and squirmed round Hoad, nibbling at him and sucking the blood and fluids from his flesh. He was not bothered.

They heaved their naked bodies, now washed clean, out of the water. They dragged the bloody remains of Kruk over to the bath. Mrs Milverton extracted her steel hair pins from the severed head, washed them and returned them to her bun. Then they tipped what was left of Kruk into the black water for those unknown slithering things to feed on. They watched the swirling and splashing water for a while. Kruk was being devoured.

Then they dressed their still wet bodies in their clothes. Hoad washed his cleaver in the water and returned it to his poacher's pocket. With that they began the long painful trudge back up the stone spiral staircase. The further away they got from the poisonous fumes the more their sanity began to return.

Hoad turned to Mrs Milverton and said, "The church above goes but what is down here will stay."

"This is just a small part of it. There is so much more to explore in these chambers and deep under them," she said.

"I want to explore it all. And I want to know more about Quincy Pitt."

"I will teach you. Call me Harriet."

When at last they burst out of the smashed door of the church, they were gasping for fresh air. Slowly, sanity returned. But Hoad's new obsession remained.

A very anxious Johnson was waiting for them, his men grouped behind him.

"Where is Kruk…?" he began.

"He bottled out. Ran out the back way in terror," Hoad grinned. "I expect he is still running."

"Oh dear… Well, I don't suppose we'll see him again. He was an illegal immigrant who worked for cash so there is no record of him in this country. No income tax, no notice period, no employment laws."

"Now the rest of you can all fuck off," Hoad raised his voice to speak to them all. "This church *will* be demolished but not by you. By professional specialists who know how to raise it to the ground but leave what is beneath intact."

"You can't get rid of us just like that," Johnson blustered.

"Oh, but I can. Most of you work off the books. You are all fired. Pack up and go!" Hoad shouted at the shocked crew.

"I'll sue you," Johnson threatened.

"I wouldn't recommend that otherwise you might end up being part of the foundations of my new tower." Hoad delivered his threat with a cold smile, a smile that told Johnson he was not bluffing.

Johnson lowered his eyes, afraid to look at Hoad.

Mrs Milverton gripped Hoad's shoulder. "I will be in touch," she said.

"How will I find you?"

"Don't worry. I will find you." She smiled and wandered off through the dirt and rubble. The workmen backed away from her as she passed them.

Hoad pulled out his mobile phone and called for his car and chauffeur. "I'm not going back to Blacksparrow Halt again. I've taken in enough of the local ambience."

*

That was the start of it all – long before Ronan Bell became involved and the unholy madness and terror really began. Everything led on from there: Ronan's

28

fight for life, justice and his own sanity, all those bizarre deaths, the all-powerful multi-national corporation that seemed to have a psychotic life of its own, the buildings that housed unspeakable evil, something abominable from Victorian England awakened in the 21st century, the creation of the tower, Ronan being forced to question everything he thought he knew about life and death, and finding and losing love.

But let Ronan tell the story in his own words.

I love old things. Better still, I love finding old things that are worn, broken and neglected and making them like new again. That is why I object to being called an antiques dealer. I always tell people that I am an antiques restorer.

My name is Ronan Bell and I run my antiques restoration business down in Surrey. I do not have a shop. I am not a retailer as I keep telling people. I have a workshop where I bring dead and broken antiques back to life. My business is known as Ronan's Restorations. Making treasure out of trash is my motto.

I am in my late thirties, a country lover rather than a townie but being in Surrey keeps me in touch with both town and country. I live near Box Hill, one of the high points of Surrey and a great place to climb when I want to be alone and rise above life's petty problems. I don't know whether I should describe myself as single or married. My wife walked out on me because she said I was too boring and I had no money but we never officially divorced, as far as I know. I'd have had to sign something.

I am not a good businessman. I buy old, damaged goods and do them up with the intention of selling them for a profit. However once I have restored them, I am always loath to part with them and hang onto them instead of selling them.

Anyway it is partly because of my passion for damaged goods that could be turned into valuable antiques that I was at the auction.

A local Surrey recluse who was said to be wealthy, Rodney Scobey, had died and he had left behind a bit of a mess, both financially and in his private life. Something about how he lived and how he had died was being investigated by the police. That is why he was only said to be wealthy – it seems his wealth was something of an illusion.

While I say he was a recluse this was also not quite true. We never saw him day to day, but he was always holding huge gatherings of strange people. These people came from all over the country, if not all over the world, to attend his exclusive parties. Some said orgies rather than parties, of course. There was all manner of wild rumours surrounding those parties but I did not like to think about it. My wife was often in attendance. She had been one for wild times and the good life while I had been the homebody.

Rodney Scobey had died without a next of kin or a will and now his many creditors were demanding a share of his estate. So everything he had was being sold off at auction at his former home, Grimoire Priory.

It was a big, old, grey stone house with tall turrets, tall chimneys and dark windows hidden in the middle of an overgrown and tangled woodland area that was completely surrounded by a high wall except for the iron gates to the long drive. The gates were unlocked for the auction and I drove through. The drive was in darkness, even in daylight, due to the overhanging trees. There was a stone pond in front of the house filled with dead leaves, stagnant green water and a naked female statue which was wrapped around an inoperative fountain in its centre.

It was the first time I had been there and I found the house and its surroundings oppressive. It was the sort of place people went to hide away in and do secret things that they did not want anyone else to know about.

The accountants and liquidators who were sorting out the mess left by the late Mr Scobey had brought in a firm of professional auctioneers to sell various items. A catalogue had been distributed before the auction and I knew what I wanted.

I parked my white van in the front. My van was hardly fashionable or any good for impressing women but great for collecting and transporting antiques of all shapes, sizes and weights. You could get full sized statues, leather sofas or giant wardrobes and sideboards in there. It also served as an advertisement for my business as I had my Ronan's Restorations name and phone number painted on the side.

I think the van was the final straw for my wife. She was a sports car girl not a white van mam.

I paused to look into the stone walled pond on my way to the house. The dark green water seemed very deep. There was a sudden ripple in the slime which released a bubble of foul air. I was not sure if the disturbance in the filthy water was from a fallen leaf or something swimming in the depths of the pond. I hurried away in disgust and joined the small crowd trooping through the open front door.

Before the auction began, we were allowed to wander around to view the various items with a glass of wine in hand. There was a good turnout. These auctioneers knew what they were doing. There was nothing like a few free drinks to get the customers over-confident and uninhibited, bidding more than they had planned.

There was a lot of fine old furniture and paintings. Laid out on a huge table were plates, vases, clocks, tableware, statues, ornaments, and books on display, with numbered cards next to them, all up for auction. There were more than a few oddities from all over the world among the collections for sale. These included iron manacles, whips, thumbscrews, ornate daggers with serrated blades that looked as if they could slice through concrete (the catalogue told me that they were Thugee daggers from India and I thought the Thugees only strangled people), gold chalices covered in strange designs, a huge coiled snake preserved inside a corked bottle of wine, shrunken heads and some really graphic, explicit paintings of the sort you would never put on display if you had children or elderly relatives visiting your home. There were fine, old leather-bound books. Carved wooden idols, carved elephant tusks, stuffed and mounted birds, snakes, and tigers were other highlights.

A silver swastika lay on the table. I was disgusted at that but the catalogue told me that the swastika had been around for thousands of years before the Nazis. The hooked cross as it had been known had been seen as a symbol of good fortune. It was only insane men who had made it into a symbol of cruelty and evil.

However none of these weird exhibits excited any particular interest in me.

It was just Lot 99 I had to have.

And there it was. A statue of Pan the Horned God with cloven hoofs, hairy chin, furry legs and an overlarge dangling penis, playing his pipes. The Greek God of the wild, shepherds, pastures, flocks, and woods. It had been carved in a dancing mode and there was a particularly disturbing leer on its face. It stood about six-foot-high on its pedestal and seemed to have been carved out of a hard wood such as mahogany.

This one had fallen into neglect and disrepair. It was chipped and had lost its colour and shine. I could bring all that back.

I had tried to get my wife Estelle to talk about what went on at this secluded house but all she would say to me was that Grimoire Priory contained a carved wooden statue of Pan and if I ever had the chance I was to acquire it. "The house is full of gold and priceless works of arts but according to Scobey the statue of Pan is worth more than everything else. Its value cannot be measured. It must be preserved for what is at its core. Make sure it does not fall into the wrong hands," she'd pleaded.

It was a very odd thing to say but Estelle did not make a lot of sense towards the end. However once I saw a photo of the Pan figure, I just had to have it.

Don't ask me why that ugly, evil-looking thing appealed to me and don't read any significance into the overlarge penis. I am neither interested in penises nor do I have any hang up about the size of my own. I am basically heterosexual, even if my track record with the ladies has not been good. I just wanted this grotesque statue because I could never refuse my wife any request and it provided just the restoration challenge I enjoyed.

I also liked to turn something ugly into something beautiful.

We sat on rows of chairs while the auctioneer sat looking down at us from a stage with a table on it. Some of my fellow bidders were familiar faces from other local auctions – collectors, dealers, and agents for the rich secret bidders. The auctioneer banged the table with his gravel.

"Ladies and gentlemen, welcome," the auctioneer began. "I have been authorised to auction off many of the treasures of Grimoire Priory formerly owned by Rodney Scobey and seized on behalf of his creditors. They have been put up for sale for this one day only. This is a rare and exciting opportunity to acquire many unusual and valuable antiques from around the world that have been kept under wraps in this property for years.

"Let us start with Lot 1, an iron chastity belt still in working order …" The auctioneer pointed to the contraption with barely concealed disgust.

Yes, as I was interested in Lot 99, you can guess that it was a long and tedious auction. Many items did not meet the reserve price set by the sellers and were passed over unsold. It seemed to take an eternity before the auctioneer came to Lot 99. And because it was such an ugly and neglected item there did not seem to be much interest in it. Oh joy!

The bidding for Lot 99 was brief. Only one other person showed a slight interest but lost interest when I raised my bid to £200. The auctioneer slammed his gravel down and pointed to me. "Sold to Mr Bell!" Pan, the God of the wild, was mine!

I stayed for a bit longer and thought I would take a look around the house before leaving. However I found that large parts of the house were cordoned off with yellow tape and uniformed policemen standing guard.

I looked over the tape through one of the opened doors and saw a taped outline of a body on the floorboards. There was chaos: overturned tables, smashed jars and cages with their iron bars buckled or ripped apart.

"Come away, sir," a uniformed policeman gently grabbed my shoulder and moved me aside. There was something familiar about the middle-aged policeman. He had a pious face with very bushy eyebrows.

"We've met before?" I asked.

"Yes, you helped us identify some stolen antiques, Mr Bell. I'm Police Constable Peace. I was also on duty when you reported your wife missing."

"Of course, I remember you, PC Peace."

"Between ourselves, sir, we first thought you had done away with your wife. The spouse is always the first suspect but you didn't strike me as a killer. I can always tell. You have puppy dog eyes and weak body strength," Peace said. "Then obviously we later discovered that Mrs Bell had made the decision to run away and she didn't want you to know where she was."

"Yes … but, you *do* know where she is? Can't you tell me?" I pleaded.

He shook his finger at me. "Sorry, confidentiality is my watchword. Marriage huh?"

"You and Mrs Peace…?" I prompted.

"Oh no we have been together more than 25 years and we are happily married. We met in the church we still attend. We are God-fearing people although I have to play it down in the station. Political correctness rules if you understand my meaning. My wife is not happy with me being here with Satan and all his works, I can tell you."

I looked around at the chaos and asked, "For God's sake, what on earth happened here? What happened to Mr Scobey?"

"You really do not want to know," the grim-faced policeman answered. "And believe me, God had nothing to do with it. If it had been up to me, I wouldn't have allowed this auction to go ahead. Such a secluded place … ideal for any dark deeds that require privacy. This house should be burnt to the ground and everything in it. Then its remains and all the earth around it should be cleansed by a service of exorcism. I tell you - none of us wants to stay on guard duty after dark. Give us murderers and serial killers to deal with any day rather than patrolling Grimoire Priory. When the sun goes down, there are vile things that come out of the undergrowth in the woods all around here. I need to get myself straight into our church after a day here… Anyway, I mustn't talk about what we've found here. My lips are sealed."

I ignored that. The man found his outlet in gossip.

"Was that Rodney Scobey?" I asked pointing to the taped outline.

"No. That one died of a drugs overdose. I think that drugs played a big part in some of the loathsome things that went on here. No right-thinking people would have had any part in it."

Since PC Peace was being so frank, I felt that I could push my luck. "There have been rumours of strange deaths here but as no one was ever charged I didn't know whether to take them seriously. Can I see where Rodney Scobey died?" I asked.

"I could lose my job. This is a secure crime scene."
He hesitated.

"My wife was part of what went on here. I'm just looking for some answers," I insisted.

"Well … I think they are wrapping things up here which is why they allowed the auction. Maybe if I showed an outsider this, it might help me to cope with it." Peace lifted the tape and let me through. "But this must be between us. Hush hush. No one must know that I have let you in here…"

He took me through to an adjoining room. There was a wooden door at the end with a four starred pentacle carved on it. He opened the door and led me through.

There was a lot of dried blood on the floor and another tape outline.

"That was where they found Scobey and he was pretty badly messed up." Peace pointed to the outline.

The room was filled with trestle tables covered with steel cages, aquariums, fish tanks and bell jars. The glass containers were smashed and the steel bars to the cages were buckled and torn apart.

"What was going on here?" I persisted.

"I didn't tell you but it looks like he was doing some animal crossbreeding here. We can't find out what he was keeping in these cages and tanks. We found them like this. All busted open and empty," Peace grimaced.

"Did they not find any DNA evidence to give them an idea what they contained?" I asked.

"I can't discuss it and I don't want to discuss it. I could lose my job." PC Peace was firm. "There is a lot of pressure to keep everything that went on here under wraps and out of the press."

"Cover ups have a way of getting uncovered."

"We must go now. I have shown you more than I should. Time to leave." He escorted me out of the crime scene. "What you have seen and what I have told you is between you, me and these walls."

I shook his hand and assured him that I would be the soul of discretion.

However I made a mental note that I could revisit PC Peace should I feel the need to learn any more confidential information.

I went back to the auction room where there was a sudden noisy intrusion.

A man burst into the main hall, huffing, puffing and wild eyed. He was dishevelled, dark haired and had a strange, blue, handlebar moustache that had been gelled into curls at each end.

When he heard that they were on Lot 126 he let out such a loud sigh of despair that everyone turned and looked at him. He then rushed over to one of the auctioneers' helpers and looked as if he was going to make a fuss.

I went and paid and tried to pick up my statue of Pan. It was too heavy. I put it on a trolley to wheel it out to my van.

It was while I was wheeling Pan out to the drive that the man ran up to me, panting and sweating.

"Mr Ronan Bell?" he asked.

"Yes." I paused and looked at him.

"My name is Samuels. I came here on an errand to buy Lot 99 for a very important client. Unfortunately, I was delayed and missed the opportunity to bid. I can now make you an offer for the statue. I understand you paid £200. I will give you £1000 for it here and now. You will make £800 for doing nothing."

"Thank you, Mr Samuels, but I have to decline," I said. "The money is not important to me. Buying

40

neglected and forgotten antiques like this is a labour of love for me. It is probably a reproduction and you will find other copies if you search hard enough."

"Two thousand pounds!" Mr Samuels doubled his offer without hesitation. Then as he saw me hesitate: "Ten thousand pounds!"

I was tempted. I could do with the money. I was thinking of accepting but then Samuels made a mistake. He pushed his sweating face into mine and snarled at me through clenched teeth: "I will make you a better offer. Give me the statue and you get to live to the end of this day."

His eyes were unfocussed. I could not smell alcohol on him so I suspected his erratic behaviour and dilated eyes were down to drugs. This probably explained why he had been late for the auction. Maybe it also explained why he did not realise that dying his moustache blue was ridiculous.

I had become expert in detecting when someone was on drugs during the latter years of my marriage.

I also saw fear in his eyes. He was terrified, not of me, but of failing the person who had commissioned him to buy Pan.

"Goodbye, Mr Samuels. If you make any more threats like this I will fetch one of the policemen from inside." I was firm. I don't give in to threats. I opened my van doors and wheeled Pan inside the rear of my van.

"No, wait-," Samuels shouted as I slammed the doors shut.

He chased after me as I ran to the front of my van, got in and started it up.

"Stop. What do you want for the statue? I can get it for you, whatever you want. I know that money is not the only commodity for everyone. Boys, girls, drugs that will light you up like a Christmas tree. You just have to ask," he shouted through the front door windows of my van. "My principal will be so very unforgiving that I missed out on Pan. Stop. I am begging you."

I ignored him and drove away, shaking him off as I gathered speed. I watched him run after me in the rear-view mirror. He pulled out a notebook and began writing in it. He was taking down my contact details painted on the side of the van.

I was glad to leave Grimoire Priory and make my way home. I still felt uncomfortable, however. The creepy and oppressive feeling that place had given me would not go away.

There was a small window in the partition behind me that gave me a view into the rear of the van. I turned my head to check it out.

The wooden eyes of the horned God looked back at me above its leering smile.

I nearly crashed the van with shock. I turned my gaze back to the road. It was stupid I know but I could feel that damn statue glaring at me all the way home.

I was glad to get to my home. It was a modest cottage with a workshop and yard next door, isolated and without neighbours. It was ideal for my one-man restoration business. I kept the tools of my trade in the workshop; lathes, paints, preservatives, and my sandblaster for blowing the layers of filth off stone statues and the outside of buildings. It was here that I polished, painted, glued, carved, and brought old antiques back to life.

My current project, this for a paying customer, was a Victorian four-poster bed which stood in the middle of the workshop awaiting my attention.

I pushed Pan into my workshop on my trolley. He was heavy. It was a pity he could not walk on his own goat's legs. I shoved him in a dark corner but he still seemed to be watching me so I threw a sheet over him and went next door to cook for myself and have a black coffee. I do not like milk, it makes me heave, so tea and coffee are always black for me and I never have cereal.

My home is furnished with all sorts of things I have restored. A huge grandfather clock ticked away in one corner while a stuffed grizzly bear posed with its claws out in another corner and a grand coffin with brass handles was propped against the wall.

There was a fluffy cat basket and a cat bowl on the floor, a reminder of my wife's Siamese cat, Mr Gilgeaous. Don't ask me where she got its ridiculous name from. Yes and she had to have an expensive pedigree Siamese cat, not a cat she could have had for nothing from the local cattery.

At least she had taken Mr Gilgeaous with her when she left. The cat gave me the creeps. It would not eat cat food. It had expensive gourmet tastes. It ate better than I did. And it did not meow like normal cats. As is common with Siamese cats it almost seemed to be able to talk in its throaty growl.

I did not like it and it did not like me, which was odd as normally I'm an animal lover. The cat was an appalling snob, just like Estelle. Good riddance. I planned to chuck out that basket and bowl, seal up the cat flap in the front door and lay the ghost of creepy kitty.

My bedroom is full of clutter – junk which I prefer to call collectables and artefacts that I bought in charity shops, auctions, and car boot sales. Another reason my wife had got fed up with me. But it was junk that I felt had the potential to be turned into something desirable. For that reason, I had taken to sleeping on my couch downstairs. It was a firm leather couch and I slept better on it than I did in my bed.

I had bizarre, disturbing dreams. My estranged wife Estelle was in them somewhere. She was trying to tell me something but couldn't because she did not have a mouth. She clawed at my chest with long fingernails. There was a scraping and scratching noise that made me wake with a start.

It took a moment for my eyes to adjust. It was dark but moonlight streamed into the room.

I heard the hypnotic sound of pan pipes. My heart nearly stopped. He was playing his pipes and calling to me!

As I gradually came to my senses, I realised that what I could hear was the wind whistling through the open front door.

Suddenly the face of Pan jolted into the moonlight, staring at me through wooden eyes.

Pan, the horned devil, was rasping across the floor as he moved towards me.

I leapt off the couch, stood up and watched the wooden statue glide towards me, closer and closer. My front door was open and an icy draught blew in from outside.

I ran for the light switch and turned it on.

A man was behind Pan and pushing him towards me. He showed his face, a face with an absurd blue moustache.

"Mr Samuels. You have broken into my house. Now I am definitely calling the police," I said, reaching for the telephone.

I stopped when he came out from behind the statue and pointed his gun at me. His hand was shaking which probably made it more likely that he would shoot the little pistol, even by accident.

I backed away from the telephone.

"You should have taken the money, Mr Bell. I was going to have this one way or another. However you might just survive this night if you give me a little help here. It is embarrassing to ask I know…" He was drenched in sweat.

"What do you want, Samuels?"

"You are an expert in these old things. I can't figure it out for myself. Open it for me." He pushed Pan towards me.

"I don't understand. Open it…?"

"The torso is hollow and something is concealed inside. It has been carved in such a way that the opening is obscured. I need you to find it and allow me inside." Samuels rattled the statue impatiently.

"Let me have a closer look." I started examining the statue. Carved wooden fur covered its back and chest. I knocked on its chest and indeed there was a hollow sound, something I had failed to notice earlier. "Well, well, you might just be right."

"Get on with it." He shook the gun at me. "I need to discover what it contains before I hand it over."

I began feeling with my fingertips round the torso of the figure. I did not even like touching the statue. It was like touching a dead body. It made the hair on the back of my neck rise. Buying this had been one bad decision.

There were a number of symbols and circles scored out on the wood. Then I found the outline of a perfect square in its back.

"This might just be it," I said. "It is like a door." I began pressing against it and there was a click.

"Out of the way! It's mine." Samuels shoved me out of the way and gestured me to stand back with the gun.

I was happy to move away and watch him fumble and press against the back. Suddenly a door in the back of Pan leapt open as if it had been on spring hinges. We both looked into the dark aperture it had revealed.

Gingerly, Samuels put his hand into the blackness. Suddenly he jumped and cried out. "Something bit me."

He pulled his hand out in a hurry but he was holding something and handling it very carefully. It was a metal cylinder container, about two feet long, with a cap and leather strap at the end.

He put it down on the floor to look at his hand. There was a very small amount of blood coming from his hand.

"Damn, just a pin prick. I must have caught it on a nail or a splinter inside."

"I'll get you a bandage." I was being sarcastic.

"Don't bother. There is going to be a lot more blood here very soon." There was a click as he took the safety catch off his gun and pointed it at me with his trembling hand. My mouth dried up with fear. Looking into his crazy eyes I knew he was going to shoot me.

46

"Don't you want to see if you can get that open first?" I tried to distract him and gestured to the metal cylinder.

"I have no idea what it is. Yes, I might need your help again." Samuels paused, lowered his gun, and began to twirl his weird blue moustache like a pantomime villain as he went into deep thought.

Then he staggered and his face grew pale.

"What is happening to me?" he spluttered. He grasped his stomach as if he was in pain. He choked and lurched forward, dropping the gun.

"My hand is burning," he screamed.

He held up his hand and stared at it. The hand had turned dark red and was swelling and puffing up. The redness and swelling moved down to his arm and disappeared inside his sleeve. The veins in his wrist began to bulge. His shirt burst open at the wrist, the button flying across the room. His whole body convulsed wildly.

He tried to speak but choked and only vomited. He began to scamper and dart around the room. I knew he was in pain and I would like to have helped but he was too fast to catch. I felt I was watching a dance of death.

Then he ran, still convulsing, over to the wall and grasped the mantelpiece. He dribbled and gurgled through chattering teeth. His fingers drummed on the mantelpiece at high speed. Slowly the convulsions changed to a slower jerking and twitching.

"She really won't like this," he spluttered, his final words.

Then he was still, freezing into a rigid position, propped upright against the mantelpiece.

I walked over to him. He was standing upright, his body and face set hard, with his eyes bulging and his mouth fixed in a gaping, silent scream.

I did not need to touch him to know that he was dead.

Something inside that evil statue had killed him. Was it some sort of protection for that metal cylinder installed by the person who created the statue of Pan? Perhaps a dart or spring-loaded nail covered in some ancient poison that stabbed at intruders. Whatever it was it had paralysed Samuels, turning his corpse into a statue. Rigor mortis had come early for Samuels.

I was in a state of shock but decided I had to pull myself together and deal with this.

Using my knuckle I closed the door in Pan's back. Once again it became invisible to the naked eye. I pushed Pan back against the wall. I was intrigued. I wanted to check out the cavity inside Pan's back myself, but I would use a torch and wear heavy industrial protective gloves.

I picked up the cylinder. I wondered what was inside it. I think this is what Samuels, or the person who had employed him, was really after.

I instinctively felt that the statue was just a shell to protect this cylinder. That was why Estelle had said that the value of the figure lay in its core.

I would check it out later. I shoved it in a cupboard full of oddities and collectables.

I took another look at Samuels. The swelling in his hand had gone down and it had returned to its normal colour.

Then I went to the phone and dialled 999.

The police and ambulance came quickly.

A middle-aged, overweight man in a rumpled suit and with a farmery face was the first through my broken open front door.

"Detective Inspector Craven, Surrey Police," he introduced himself. "Where's the body?"

I pointed at the sentry-like Samuels.

He walked over to it. Two ambulance men came in after him.

"Wow this stiff really is a stiff," Craven said. "We don't need you." He waved the two paramedics away and waved in a small army of police, telling them to be careful where they stepped. He noted the fallen gun and was careful not to touch it.

The paramedics departed and police began cordoning off my house with yellow tape.

"Does this make my house a crime scene?" I asked.

"Yes and please do not touch anything." He looked around my house with barely concealed contempt. "This is more like a museum rather than a home. I wonder what a psychiatrist would make of your taste in furnishings. Can we talk outside?"

We went into my front garden and sat on the wooden seats while uniformed police stood guard outside. A van drew up and people in white overalls, masks and disposable gloves poured out and into my house. I'd seen enough TV to know these were scene of crime officers, here to collect forensic evidence.

"Hi, Doc. I bet you won't have seen one like this before," Craven said to one white-overalled man who carried what looked like a doctor's bag.

After a moment, one SOCO came back out and said to Craven: "Wow, a standing corpse. That is a first for me. Although there is a myth that Bramwell Bronte, brother of the Bronte sisters, died standing up just to prove it could be done."

"I want facts, not myths. What are we looking at here?" Craven asked.

"Well at first glance there are no obvious wounds. How long since he died?"

"Not long," I answered for Craven. "Minutes rather than hours."

"That cannot be right." The doctor was puzzled. "Not with that amount of rigor mortis... I would rule out a stroke or a heart attack. I suspect poisoning of some sort but I need to find out how it was administered. I will know more when I get him on the table," the doctor said. "It may be a simple overdose."

"I have an idea about that," I said.

"Leave this to the experts." Craven scowled at me.

"I am just trying to help," I said.

"This is one for the bizarre case files," the doctor said as he disappeared inside.

"Right. Now we need to get back to you," Craven looked at me.

A younger plain clothes policeman came and sat beside us, took out a notebook and pen and began writing.

"Your name first."

"I'm Ronan Bell and this is my property."

"Do you live here alone?"

"Yes I do now."

"I always think that men who live alone are a bit unnatural. Bit of an eccentric, are you?" Craven asked. "Are you gay or a kiddie fiddler?"

"Certainly not. I am still married but we are separated. There is no need to get rude and personal," I said.

He shrugged and said: "We get more complaints about me than anyone else in my department. Oh I've been threatened with the sack and sent on all these sensitivity courses," he sniffed with contempt, "but they keep me on. Do you know why? Because I get results. I will always get to the truth. I need to know everything. Who, what, where, when, and start at the beginning. Who is the dead man and what is his connection with you?"

"I met the dead man for the first time today. He told me his name was Samuels. I don't have a first name. He wanted to buy the wooden statue of Pan I had bought at the Grimoire Priory auction but I refused to sell it to him. He was buying it for a third party, he said. He became very agitated when I said no. Anyway I brought it home and put it in my workshop. I had gone to sleep. He must have broken into my workshop and stolen the statue but then broke into my house with the statue and woke me up."

"That seems unnecessarily complicated. Why did he not just drive off with the statue once he had it?"

I chose not to mention the secret compartment. Well, he hadn't asked. So much for always getting the truth. "I think he intended to kill me. That was his gun."

"Why, over a wooden statue…?"

"He, or I should say they, wanted me silenced."

"How much did you pay for this statue?"

"£200."

"It seems very unlikely that anyone would kill a stranger over something worth just £200."

"Look, the man was irrational and very scared of the person who had hired him to buy Pan. He threatened me with a gun for goodness sake. I think he was on drugs. He suddenly started convulsing and running round the room, stopping where you see him now."

"Your story stinks, Mr Bell. Depending on what forensics discovers I will almost certainly bring you in for questioning. Don't go anywhere." Craven glared at me.

"I have nothing to hide," I said. Craven had not asked the right questions and had not listened to me. Life passes so many people by because they talk at each other without listening to what they have to say.

"I will be bringing you in for further questioning," Craven said. "In the meantime you cannot stay here. Your home is a crime scene and is likely to remain so for at least two days. We can put you up in an inexpensive hotel. If you go anywhere else, we need to know where you are at all times."

"I think I know where I can get a billet. Excuse me," I went off to talk into my mobile phone.

I telephoned Peter Wilde, a near neighbour and newspaper journalist. I had first met him in our local pub, The Wheatsheaf, and found I was no match for him when it came to drinking. He was however a good friend.

I told him I was looking for somewhere to stay and the reason why.

52

"Welcome, naturally, old chap, plus it sounds like you could give me the inside story on your murder victim. I could do with a scoop to put me in the good books with my bosses."

"Thank you. Will your wife be OK with me coming to stay with you?"

"Mrs Wilde will be delighted."

He never used his wife's first name. I think it was an acknowledgement that she was the boss.

"I think we may be looking at murder here," Craven was barking at the forensic team. "Leave no stone unturned."

When they wheeled out Samuel's body it was still as stiff as a board with its mouth fixed wide open.

"Will he be like that forever?" I asked the doctor.

"Of course not. Rigor mortis wears off," he told me.

So I went to stay with the Wildes for a couple of days. Her cooking was excellent and I had some decent meals for the first time in a long time. When you live alone you tend to snack rather than have set meals.

When I was given the all clear by the police to return home, I called a 24-hour locksmith to repair both my doors. I tidied and cleaned up. The SOCO team had left an unsightly mess – gloves, medical packaging, tape, all sorts.

I was exhausted afterwards, so I crawled upstairs to my bed to try to sleep. One nice feature about my bedroom was that there was a skylight window in the sloping ceiling that allowed me to look up at the stars, the sky and sometimes the moon before I drifted off to sleep. Usually, it helped me relax, but today I wasn't so lucky.

I had barely slept at all when I was rudely awakened by someone pounding on my newly repaired front door. They were persistent and would not go away.

I rose from my bed and shuffled downstairs to the door in my pyjamas and slippers.

I opened my front door on a strange looking woman.

The woman on my doorstep was tall and unhealthily thin and stared at me through two prominent eyes above her sunken cheeks. She had a pointed nose, like the beak of a hawk. Her greying hair was pulled back into a tight bun held in place by a number of long steel hair pins with different coloured beads at the end. It was hard to judge her age. Her skin was pale, almost grey, and wrinkled like the skin of a mummy. She was dressed in a tweed suit. She had skinny legs in black stockings and flat heeled shoes.

If she had asked for food, I would happily given it to her as she looked starved to me but no, that was not it.

"I tried ringing but you did not answer the phone so I came here straight from the airport," she said in a shrill, scratchy voice. There was a big Passat Estate car with darkened rear windows parked behind her. I guessed she had come in that.

"I am sorry. Who are you?" I asked, still befuddled.

"Mrs Harriet Milverton. I have been out of the country otherwise I would have been at the auction myself and not had to work through an incompetent agent and you would not have had all this trouble, Mr Bell."

"Samuels, he worked for you?" I asked. "You know he is dead?"

"Yes, yes, and he deserved nothing better. If he had not died, I would have killed him myself. I have come to purchase the carved statue of Pan from you directly without any bungling middlemen." She didn't mince her words.

"I am not sure if I need to keep it for the police."

"They have finished their forensic examination of your place, haven't they?"

"Yes."

"Well then, I will take it."

"Who says it is for sale? And I have to warn you handling it might be dangerous. Samuels cut his hand on it. It was just a small pin prick but he got ill and died just after that."

"The people who carved the statue of Pan were experts in creating deadly traps to protect its secrets. Rummaging around in protected areas would have been enough to release a poison-covered dart. I am not worried. I am immune. I have been keeping death at bay for decades. I have outlived all my husbands. I study ancient herbs, Mr Bell. I can whip up a deadly poison and its antidote in seconds. I have immunity to most diseases and I have even managed to slow the ageing process with my own concoctions. And, aided by a daily dose of Royal Jelly from African bees, the most aggressive and most deadly species of bees, you would be surprised at how strong I have become," Mrs Milverton told me.

She didn't look that strong to me – just a bag of bones that would crack and splinter under the slightest pressure. She was still a scary woman, however, and I didn't want to get into an argument with her. Also I was no longer keen to hold onto Pan. It seemed to have a deadly curse on it. I wanted the Greek God of the wild, shepherds, pastures, flocks, and woods out of my house.

I was more interested in the cylinder that Samuels had removed from it. I wouldn't tell her about that. I was going to keep that for myself.

"Tell me why Pan is so important to you?" I asked her.

"I desired the statue the first time I saw it at Grimoire Priory," was her answer. It was a desire she seemed to share with Estelle.

"So you attended Rodney Scobey's little gatherings then? I understand that the police are investigating those."

"Witchcraft is not against the law. Freedom to practise all religions is part of the British way of life."

"It was more than that wasn't it. Kinky sex, sadomasochism, drug abuse, kidnappings, animal sacrifices, even the odd disappearance of visitors to your parties. That was what I heard."

She did not want to talk about it. "Final offer - £50,000 for Pan, Mr Bell. It is not negotiable." It was an ultimatum. "If you refuse there will be consequences."

"£50,000 is fine but I need something else, not money." I tried to keep my face straight. £50,000 would solve all my immediate financial problems. "What I also need from you is some information that I have not been able to find for myself. If you can provide it then we have a deal."

"What is it?"

"An address or contact details for my wife Estelle Bell. If you attended Scobey's dubious gatherings then you would also have seen her there and may even have met her. One of your members must know where she is. I need to find her."

Estelle may have fallen out of love with me but in spite of all our differences I had not fallen out of love with her. She was a beautiful woman and many people were surprised that she had married a stuffy nobody like me. Estelle was a woman attracted to the dark and dangerous side of life which eventually had taken her away from me. And not knowing where she was and what was happening to her was eating me up.

"Wait," Mrs Milverton held up a long bony finger and then moved away, pulling out a mobile phone. She spoke into it out of my hearing, pulled out a small notebook and wrote in it.

While she was doing this, I was writing down the registration number of her car. I had to have some information on the creepy and sinister woman I was dealing with.

Then she came back into my house, pushed past me, and walked straight over to Pan to examine it.

Then she turned and spoke to me. "I have a sheet of paper here. It gives the address of your wife. Outside in my car is a case containing £50,000. We like to deal in cash. No cheques, no bank cards, nothing that can be traced. Take them both now and agree to a non-disclosure as regards me. No one must know that I bought the statue. I will leave with it and that will be the end of the whole matter. If you discuss this with anyone some really foul and loathsome things will be done to you."

She regarded me coldly and I felt the threat in her eyes.

"Agreed." I swallowed. "I will go and fetch my trolley. Pan is too heavy to carry."

I left her to go to my next-door workshop.

It took me a couple of minutes to unlock the workshop, locate my trolley and push it back towards my house.

I turned as I heard the sound of a car engine.

I was just in time to see her Passat Estate car driving away. I could just make out Pan in the back through the darkened windows.

There was no way a frail woman like that could have lifted Pan and put him into the back of the car by herself, Royal Jelly or not, I thought. She must have had an accomplice waiting to help her once I was out of the way. But I'd been certain no one was in the car when I looked at it. I couldn't figure it out.

Perhaps she *was* strong enough to carry the statue by herself? That made her even more scary. I had to try some of her African bee Royal Jelly for myself.

I had her registration number. I planned to report this as theft to the police.

Feeling I had been conned I walked back into my house only to discover a suitcase and a sheet of paper lying on my table.

An address in North London had been written on the paper in flourishing, copperplate handwriting. There was no phone number. I unzipped the case. It was filled with bundles of notes held together in paper bands.

She may have been malevolent and sinister but Mrs Milverton had kept her word. No point in contacting the police now.

I tried Directory Enquires for Estelle's North London address and found that the number was ex-directory. I couldn't phone her. A personal visit was the only answer.

My first stop would be the bank to pay some of the cash in. Only enough of it to cover my overdraft and debts, of course. Too much would be suspicious.

The suitcase with the bulk of the money and that mysterious cylinder all went up in my loft.

After I had been to my bank on the High Street, I made my way to the railway station. There was no way I was driving through London. I hated driving in cities. I was going to use the train and tube to get me to my estranged wife for the first time after more than eighteen months. I wondered what her reaction would be to me suddenly turning up.

Would she welcome me back with open arms? Or would she greet me with hatred and fury? I expected the latter. I would soon find out.

I hated London. Not the historic buildings and museums but just the overcrowding and the general unfriendliness, not to say open hostility, you get when too many people are fighting for the same space.

Estelle loved it. Surrey had been a compromise for us both. Close enough to London for her but with the peace and space of the countryside for me. Running my own business meant that location was not a problem for me. And having Box Hill nearby was a real bonus for me. It was my bolt hole that I ran to when life got on top of me.

Estelle and I had always been poles apart but in a way that had worked for us in the early days. Being opposites kept us in the middle ground and stopped us going into extremes, to start with anyway.

But then Estelle had got in with a new crowd and drink and drugs began to take over her life. Then when she got involved with the Grimoire Priory gatherings, I lost her. One day she just announced that she could not live with a "turnip-headed country bumpkin" like me anymore and left. I tried to stop her but by then she had become increasingly irrational and violent in her behaviour and I had to let her go.

Now I was on my way to see her again after all this time.

After the train journey, it was the packed and smelly tube for me. I had hoped to sit quietly and attempt some meditation to prepare me for the mood swings I expected but I couldn't even get a seat. I should have taken a taxi. I could afford to now. I had just got so used to travelling on the cheap.

Going to North London was even worse for me. There is a strong North/South divide in London. There were those who lived south of the Thames and loved it, like me, and there were those who lived north of the Thames and viewed anything south of the river, like Estelle, as inferior and to be avoided. North London snobs! Taxi drivers had invented the expression: "I'm not going South of the river at this time of night."

Now Estelle was back in her beloved North London. Her high-rise block of flats was a short walk from the underground station. I looked up at it and made a bet with myself that Estelle lived on the top floor. She liked to look down on people.

There was an intercom entry system for each of the flats. I looked down the list for Estelle's name. I almost missed it. She had reverted to her maiden name, Rivers. That did not bode well for my surprise visit.

I pressed the buzzer. No answer. I pressed it again. Still no answer.

I went through the entrance into the lobby of the flats where a concierge sat behind a desk and viewed me suspiciously.

"I am here to see Estelle Rivers," I told him.

"Yes, is she expecting you?"

"Probably not. I am her husband."

He looked at me open mouthed for a moment. Then he used his internal phone. "Hey, ma'am? There is a man here who wants to see you. He says he is your husband. Shall I chuck him out?"

He listened for a moment and then looked at me with disbelief. "Wow."

He put the phone down and looked puzzled. "She said to send you up. She is in the penthouse."

"Of course she is." I went to the lift.

How on earth had she been able to afford the penthouse in a place like this?

When I got out of the lift at the top floor, the door to the penthouse flat was open for me. I walked in. It was luxuriously furnished and French windows looked out onto a balcony and spectacular views across London.

There was a bloated, haggard woman seated on the sofa.

"Get me a drink," the woman said in Estelle's voice. "Whisky and ice."

"Estelle is that you? I did not recognise you." I was shocked.

"Just get my drink." She waved to a well-stocked bar in the corner. "How did you find me?"

"Friend of a friend," I said as I went to the bar. "Did you bring Mr Gilgeaous with you to this flat? Is he here?" I asked as I looked around nervously.

"No animals are allowed in these flats. Not even a rare breed like Mr Gilgeaous."

"He is certainly not an ordinary cat. Vain, dangerously insane, arrogant, aggressive, lazy, spoilt … he can't even meow like a normal cat. What did you do with him?"

"I gave him away to a good home."

"That cat cost me two thousand pounds." That was money I could have spent on better things, like food, council tax and the electricity bills.

"Mr Gilgeaous will be well cared for. A famous celebrity veterinary couple took him in. Rick and Zoe Leppard. You must have seen them on TV."

"Good for them but what a waste of money for me. I could never refuse you anything. That was my problem." I began fixing her drink. "You should have told me that you have been ill."

Illness was the only possible explanation for the dramatic change in her appearance. Who or what had destroyed her great beauty?

I carried the drink over to her and she snatched it greedily from me. Her hands were shaking.

"Estelle, I think you need to go to a rehabilitation centre," I said.

"Dear Ronan, as boring and predictable as ever. But I missed your stabilising influence. You wouldn't believe the substances I've drunk, eaten, and injected since I left you. You also wouldn't believe some of the pure evil things I have taken part in." She began crying silently, tears trickling down her face. "Now I just want peace, serenity and a way to wipe the memories of what I have done from my brain."

I felt I should comfort her but I could never cope with crying. I looked away and around the sumptuous flat.

"How are you paying for all this?" I asked. Then my eyes fell on a framed photograph. "Or should I ask who is paying for all this?"

The black and white framed photo was a head and shoulders shot of a man. He had pure white hair which hung down to his shoulders around his pale face. A white beard covered his chiselled jaw and a white moustache grew under his large, aquiline nose. His mouth was set in a sneer. His eyes stood out, dark and cold, surrounded by white lashes and eyebrows that were so white you could think they were dyed. I had that same sensation that I had felt from the wooden eyes of Pan – that they had been watching me – and now I felt that the eyes in this portrait seemed to be staring right at me.

"Who is this? Your latest conquest?" I asked.

"My conquest? I am his conquest. He bought me body and soul, evil bastard. That is a photo of Felix Hoad. I thought that Rodney Scobey was bad but Felix Hoad is the wickedest man I have ever known." Her voice rose to a hysterical shriek.

"Who is he?"

"City whiz kid, property developer. A rich and powerful monster who is now chief executive officer of the QPL multi-national conglomerate. Some people worship him like a god. They would murder their own mothers if he told them to. He has enough power and charisma to enslave the strongest of characters. The memories of what that man made me do are tearing me apart. If only a surgeon could cut those memories from my brain."

Estelle let out a cackle of laughter that made the hair on my head tingle. There was insanity in her laughter.

"Is he a cult leader for impressionable teenagers?"

"Oh no, many of his apostles are themselves rich, mature and powerful. His influence is everywhere, as is the influence of the QPL group. He recently became QPL's new chief executive officer following on from the disappearance of the previous CEO, Nicholas Mercer. They had been close friends; Mercer had been his mentor. Then one day Mercer was gone. He was being investigated for all sorts of irregularities, it was said. They feel he did a runner. Anyway Felix did not let the fact that his friend was missing stop him from making the most of the opportunity. There is a moral and ethical abyss at the heart of all QPL's businesses, and also at the heart of Felix Hoad, so he was the logical man to replace Mercer. Now he has followers in high places and influences everywhere."

"I have vaguely heard of QPL. Are they a newish company?"

"Nothing new about them. The origins of QPL go back to Victorian times, to the 19th century. They started out as builders but now they own subsidiary companies in many other industries, including the media. They also have subsidiaries in countries that used to be British colonies way back in the days of the British Empire. They are quietly becoming one of the most powerful corporations in the world without people realising it. Behind their respectable business front they are the criminal elite, the aristocrats of crime."

"This is getting a bit paranoid. It is the drink and drugs making you think like that. You need to come back home with me and get some professional help, medical and psychiatric," I started.

"The things that man has got away with would destroy your provincial mind." Estelle regarded me coldly.

I began to pace around the room. I had the strangest sensation that the eyes in the photograph were moving to watch me as I crossed the room. I have heard people

66

say that about paintings before, that the eyes seem to follow you around the room, but never with a photograph.

"So what are we talking about here? Is Hoad into some sort of weird religion?" I asked.

"He acknowledges no one as his superior but he bases his whole way of life and business methods on the founder of the QPL group, Quincy Pitt." Yes. Queen Victoria was on the throne when Quincy Pitt was building his empire and crushing everyone who got in his way. He was a stooped, ancient and spindly master manipulator with a sixth finger on his right hand."

"Sounds charming. So this Pitt must have been dead now for well over a century? There is no way he can influence what is happening today." I was trying to make sense of her insane ramblings.

"Don't you believe it? But you won't read anything about him in history. Quincy Pitt manipulated and controlled people and companies from the shadows and Felix Hoad operates in the identical way."

I looked again at the portrait picture and Felix Hoad stared right back at me as if he were challenging me to a fight. Those eyes were so real and so threatening!

"Are you free of him now?" I asked.

"You are never free of him. He has dumped me because I have nothing left. He has squeezed all the life and soul out of me. But his Mambo keeps a wax effigy of me with my life essence in it. She modelled it in my likeness herself. As long as she has that he and she can control me."

"What is a Mambo?"

"It's his personal assistant. Hoad calls her his Mambo. "It means Voodoo priestess."

"Is she from Haiti or the Caribbean?"

"Oh no his Mambo couldn't be more English. She is a Tweedy English spinster."

"A Miss Marple type?" I asked.

"More like a walking corpse type," she answered.

A shiver ran down my spine as I recalled the woman on my doorstep that morning. "Wait, we are not talking about Mrs Harriet Milverton are we?"

"You know her?" Estelle looked surprised.

"Friend of a friend …" I shrugged.

"It is important that you tell me how you came to meet her," Estelle insisted.

"Well when they were selling off the contents of Grimoire Priory, I purchased that wooden effigy of Pan you were so keen on. But then Mrs Milverton turned up on my doorstop and offered me a lot of money for it. So I let her have it."

Too late I remembered Mrs Milverton said that foul and loathsome things would be done to me if I discussed it with anyone.

"You fool!" Estelle screamed.

I jerked back at her outburst, raising my hands in placation. "Relax. The important thing was inside - a sealed cylinder. I have taken it out and I have it hidden safely away. I have her money but got to keep Pan's secret. As for Voodoo dolls, I've read that they only work if you let them work. So tell yourself that it has no power over you and it won't."

I took all this talk of witchcraft and Voodoo as a joke, but I could see how strongly Estelle believed in it and that was dangerous. I had to break the hold it had over her.

68

"Swear that you will keep that sealed cylinder away from them. Also get the wax effigy of me away from Mrs Milverton and free me from her," Estelle begged.

"I will make it my business to see Hoad locked up. I will protect you and report the whole gang of them to the police. I know the police are already investigating the late Rodney Scobey. You must come back to live with me and get yourself sorted out. Then perhaps we can get our marriage back on track…"

"You won't be able to break my ties with Felix Hoad that easy. You have no idea what you are up against," Estelle said and then her face crumpled and she began breathing fast. "I need fresh air."

I went over to her and helped her shaking body up. I felt that the eyes in the photograph had followed me as I crossed the room and were watching my every move.

I propelled her over to the French windows, pushed them open, and took us out onto the balcony.

We stood looking out over London spread all around us. Estelle's breathing gradually slowed.

It was windy up there and the silk curtains flapped around us.

"Look, you can see the QPL building from here." She pointed in the direction of East London, at a distant, uncompleted skyscraper surrounded by scaffolding. "It grows taller every day. It will be called Mercer Tower after the man who once headed QPL and had the idea to gather all its different companies together in the one building, its headquarters."

Some strange black birds flew around us and seemed to be attracted to the balcony. They came very close but I wasn't sure what sort of birds they were: not blackbird, not crows. Sparrows? No – too big and the wrong colour.

I waved my hand at them and shooed them away. They squawked and retreated but still hovered close by. I turned my attention back to Estelle.

"Are you feeling better now?" I asked.

"Yes. Now I would like another drink."

"No Estelle, I think that I will make us both a cup of coffee. Let us start the changes from now. I presume you have coffee?"

"You'll find some in the kitchen," she told me.

I patted her shoulder and turned away. As I walked back into the flat, I asked: "Is there anything else you would like?"

Estelle answered with one word: "Forgiveness."

"I forgive you," I said.

"Thank you."

The kitchen was behind a bar in a corner of the flat so I could watch the open French windows while I made two steaming mugs of black coffee with lots of sugar.

I was feeling optimistic. Estelle was listening to me. Perhaps now she had done it all and seen it all she was ready to settle back down with me.

I carried the mugs over to the French windows.

"This Felix Hoad should be prosecuted. Where does he live?" I asked.

When there was no answer I said: "Darling?"

I carried the mugs through the French windows and onto the balcony.

The balcony was empty.

I dropped one of the mugs which smashed on the ground.

70

For a moment everything was silent and seemed to go into slow motion.

Then the screaming of the people in the street far below reached my ears.

I peered over the edge. Estelle was a speck on the distant pavement. There was a small crowd around her and they looked up at me.

"My poor Estelle." Tears flowed from my eyes to plummet down after her.

One of those mysterious black birds perched on the edge of the balcony and seemed to be looking at me.

I threw the remaining mug of hot coffee at the bird. The mug went over the edge and the bird took flight.

I could hear the people on the ground shout as the mug fell and smashed to the ground far below.

I pulled back out of sight.

I went back inside. Now the eyes in the framed photograph were mocking me and I swear there was a smirk on the mouth that had not been there before.

I hurled my clenched fist into the picture. The glass smashed and the whole thing fell to the floor. A shard of glass stuck into the side of my left hand and blood dripped down to the carpet.

I pulled the shard out and blood continued to drip. I did not care. I stood waiting.

I don't know how long it was before the porter opened the door to the flat and let in two uniformed policemen.

"That's him!" he shouted, pointing at me. "He said he was her husband. She was terrified, the poor woman."

71

So I went through it all again. Estelle's flat was declared a crime scene and the forensics officers moved in. The pavement below was cleared and her body was taken for examination.

Someone bandaged my left hand and I was taken to a police station in North London where I was left in an interview room with a cup of tea for ages. I had to go to the Gents once but a uniformed policeman came with me and watched me. This made me realise that I was being treated as a suspect.

There was what looked like a big mirror against one wall in the interview room but I had seen enough cop shows on television to guess that it was a one-way window and that I was being observed. There was also a CCTV camera watching me in the corner. I guess I was being recorded.

A tall, fit-looking man came in and introduced himself.

"Detective Superintendent Ives." He shook my hand. He seemed too young for that high rank. "Interview with Ronan Bell." He gave the time and date. "Sorry to keep you waiting. I have been trying to get a picture of what happened. This must be difficult for you, Mr Bell. I am sure that you must be terribly upset by the

72

death of your wife. I am sorry for your loss. However we must hear your side of the story while it is still fresh in your mind."

He sat down and faced me, smiling.

"Being in London I thought I might be taken to Scotland Yard." I was trying to keep things light-hearted.

"We reserve the interview rooms there for really VIP crooks and suspected terrorists." Ives was still smiling. "So you are up for the day from your Surrey home. Tell me in your own words about today."

So I did, holding nothing back about my troubled marriage, and how Estelle had walked out on me. Then I gave him a brief outline of the conversation we had in her flat before Estelle threw herself off the balcony.

"Felix Hoad is a well-respected CEO of a remarkably successful corporation. He is the sort of man who could get a knighthood one day. So be careful about any accusations you make against him." Ives was still smiling but the smile did not reach his eyes this time.

"The higher they are the harder they fall," I quoted.

Then he suddenly asked, "This is the second suspicious death you have been involved in, Mr Bell. We find that rather odd."

"Well I guessed you would have checked me out and found out about Samuels." I tried laughing but my laughter was strained.

"So your wife ran away from you and did not give you her new address. She also changed her name. There is a familiar pattern here, Mr Bell. I have seen it many times before. The battered wife fleeing the abusive and possessive husband. She managed to escape you for 18 months before you tracked her down."

"Stop, you have it all wrong-" I began to protest.

Someone knocked on the door.

"Oh dear. Because you are a suspect in two suspicious deaths covered by different jurisdictions I am compelled to work with the Surrey police." Ives grimaced. "Here in the Met we don't like sharing our cases with country coppers. They are only good for catching poachers." Then he shouted, "Come in."

The door opened and my stomach dropped as Detective Inspector Craven ambled in.

"I have been listening, you know," Craven spoke to Ives. "We have more murders by shooting to deal with in the country than you ever do in the cities."

"Knives are the weapon of choice in the inner city," Ives responded.

Craven introduced himself for the benefit of the recording: "Detective Inspector Craven, Surrey police, and I can't remember the last time anyone was ever arrested for poaching."

"Hallo again." I nodded to him.

"Sorry for your loss," he muttered to me without sincerity. "So. Are you going to claim to be an innocent bystander for a second murder?" Ives asked me.

"My wife committed suicide," I pointed out.

"I have had the report back on Mr Samuels. The autopsy revealed that he was a regular drug abuser but that was not what killed him. He was poisoned by a variant of Curare injected into one of his fingers," Craven announced, reading from some notes. "He died of asphyxiation as his respiratory muscles were unable to contract."

"Now we are entering the world of exotic murders." Ives was smiling again. "Curare is not a drug used by drug addicts. It is a paralysing poison used on blowgun

74

darts by some South American tribes. It is an old-fashioned poison often featured in 1940s crime fiction. I trust no one tried to inject poison into you, Mr Bell?" Ives gestured to my bandaged hand. "What happened?"

"I smashed a picture frame and cut myself on the broken glass. It seems to be taking a long time to heal."

"So you had a violent fight with your wife?"

"No, no, I smashed the glass after she had jumped."

"Why?"

"I was angry and it was a picture of Felix Hoad."

"Do you get angry a lot, Mr Bell?"

"No."

"You threw a coffee cup over the balcony and nearly hit someone in the street below."

"I can explain. There was a strange bird on the balcony ..." I started but stopped when I realised how insane I sounded.

If they were playing good cop, bad cop here, I am not sure which was which. While Craven was surlier and more aggressive, Ives was wearing me down with his more probing questions.

"Are you going to investigate this Felix Hoad?" I challenged them both.

"You tell us that your wife had drink and drug problems. I am sure the autopsy will bear that out. For those reasons, any allegations she made are likely to be unreliable. Drug addicts and alcoholics suffer from paranoia and have difficulty distinguishing truth from fiction." Ives spread his hands. "Hoad is a well-respected and well-connected businessman. I really have to have a strong case before I can start looking into his affairs."

"Look, you know all this is linked to Rodney Scobey. The late Mr Scobey is under investigation," I said.

"We have closed the Scobey case," Craven announced. "We thought there had been serious crimes at Grimoire Priory when we discovered numerous blood stains but it turns out it was animal blood. As for Scobey's death it seems he did it to himself. He was so badly hacked about and torn up that it was hard to believe that it was self-inflicted but he had taken considerable amounts of hallucinogens so we cannot imagine what was going through his mind. It was suicide of a sort."

"Why was there so much animal blood?" I asked.

"Ritual sacrifices. There were some odd rites practised there. But we have freedom of worship in this country. No laws have been broken. We couldn't even prove animal cruelty. If we were able to prosecute everyone who slaughtered animals in a way we didn't approve of in this country we would have to raid the thousands of Halal and Kosher meat premises up and down the UK. We don't burn witches at the stake anymore." Craven shrugged.

"The uniformed policeman I spoke to at Grimoire Priory didn't take it so lightly," I said.

"Give me that policeman's name," Craven demanded.

"I didn't ask for it and he didn't give it," I lied. I wasn't going to lose the chatty Police Constable Peace his job just because he refused to be part of some cover up. "What about the smashed jars and cages?"

"How do you know about them?" Craven looked furious. "You are talking yourself into being arrested,

Mr Bell. You seem to know so much about what went on there that I think you must have been part of it."

"I just think that the police should not stop investigating."

"Look, that case is closed and Grimoire Priory is now being sold."

"Who would buy a place like that?" I wondered aloud.

"The rumour is that it is Marquis Thorn," Craven told me.

I had heard of Marquis Thorn. He was a publisher of sleazy tabloids. Peter Wilde, the neighbour who had put me up, worked for Thorn. Round and round we go. I was getting a real sense of conspiracy here. Peter had once been a proud journalist but now he was a burnt out alcoholic.

"It is a bad building and it attracts bad people," I said.

"Oh no, someone else has outbid Thorn for Grimoire Priory and he makes Attila the Hun seem like a softy," Ives corrected Craven. "You are right. It is a property that attracts real bad people."

"So what happens next?" I asked.

Ives leaned forward and spoke to me over steepled fingers. "We have two very suspicious deaths here, one of which has been confirmed as murder. And you alone were with both victims when they died. If we release you, we need to know where you will be at all times."

"You have to either charge me or let me go and you have nothing to charge me with. I am going back to my home and business."

"Ronan's Renovations?" Craven almost sneered as he said it.

"Yes. I provide a much-appreciated service. What about Estelle's belongings?"

"Once it is established that you are her next of kin you can have them but not at the moment while we are still investigating. Here is my card." Ives gave me a card with his contact details on. "If you remember anything else give me a ring. And don't go far; I will almost certainly need to talk to you again."

Both policemen looked unsatisfied but of the two I felt that Ives was the more sympathetic. Also the more intelligent.

Estelle's coroner's inquest was brief. In the end, the only possible verdict was: "suicide while the balance of her mind was disturbed".

Once they released Estelle's body, I was able to organise a quiet funeral for her at a local church attached to a crematorium in a cemetery.

I had the coffin closed. I did not want anyone viewing the bloated body that had smashed onto the pavement after her long fall. I wanted people to remember her as she had once been – beautiful.

During her descent into alcoholism, drug addiction and madness, Estelle had turned against her few relatives and friends, seeing them all as enemies who spied on her. She made any visitors and friends feel unwelcome. So none of them grieved for her and they did not accept the invitation to her funeral. So sad; so few people understand the horrors of addiction. It is a sickness, and Estelle was never cured.

She had also turned on my friends and driven them away. I had a sister who lived in America with her family but she did not come over for the funeral. So it was a sad and lonely affair with a vicar who did not know her trying to deliver a heartfelt sermon.

It was attended by some neighbours that I did not know very well, a couple of my regular customers and the local busybody and gossip who made herself a part of everyone's business whether she knew them or not.

My only friendly support came from Peter Wilde.

He was an older man, with an even older liver, thanks to his legendary alcohol consumption, who found himself a bit of a dinosaur in the modern world of journalism. His face was a map of broken capillaries.

He sat next to me in the pew with a comforting hand on my shoulder.

When the funeral was over, I left the chapel and paused. There were a number of strange, ugly, black birds perched around the cemetery. None of them were flying and they seemed to be still and waiting.

They looked like the same kind of birds I had seen on Estelle's balcony, though I was still not sure what species they were – too small to be crows, the beak was wrong for blackbirds, they were bigger and the wrong colour for sparrows but they were closer to sparrows than anything. There was something threatening about them and they did not move when I approached. "Fly away!" I yelled. I went right up to one before it squawked at me and flew off.

"Do you see those black birds? They give me the creeps," I said to Peter who stood behind me. "They are like the birds I saw flying round Estelle's balcony when she jumped."

"I am glad you see them as well. I thought it was the DTs for a moment," Wilde chuckled.

"Shoo," I shouted at the birds and ran at them. I pushed a branch of a tree to one side and faced Mrs

Harriet Milverton, sitting on a gravestone. She wore a large, brimmed, black hat.

"What are you doing here?" I asked.

"I am just saying farewell," she answered.

"New hat?" I nodded at her strange headgear.

"It is my funeral hat. I like to show some respect." She grinned at me, a humourless leer. "I saw you looking at the birds. They are extraordinarily rare black sparrows, Mr Bell, and should be treated with reverence. They put in an appearance for your wife. They are drawn to death."

The woman had to be mad. Black sparrows that gathered for a funeral …

"They don't look like sparrows to me. Sparrows are grey and smaller," I said.

"These are not your common sparrows," she told me. "They are uncommon sparrows. They are big and bold with black feathers and black eyes and beaks and claws that are stronger and sharper than your common sparrow."

"At least Estelle has some peace now. I want you and your ugly birds to go away and never bother me again."

"Peace possibly, but Estelle has a restless spirit which may not have gone quietly into the dark."

"Estelle said you had made a wax effigy of her. I promised her I would get it."

"No problem. Here it is," Mrs Milverton took off her hat and emptied what was inside onto the ground. It was a wax doll, about four inches tall, but smashed and broken.

"Whoops. It is in pieces because I dropped it from a great height. Clumsy me." Mrs Milverton's thin lips twisted in a grim attempt to smile.

I didn't like that. "You are not welcome here." I became angry. "This was a private funeral. Get on your broomstick and go!"

I saw the funeral director approaching and turned my back on her to shake his hand and say goodbye. I turned back to find that Mrs Milverton had gone. So had those menacing birds.

The shattered remains of the wax doll were still on the ground. I picked them up.

"What are you going to do with those?" Peter asked.

"You'll see."

They had done their work so they would have no power now. However to be on the safe side I carried the pieces of the doll into the church and took them to the font.

"Has this water been blessed?" I asked the vicar.

"Yes, it is Holy Water," he replied.

I dropped the pieces of the Voodoo doll into the water which began bubbling straight away. The broken doll dissolved into powder and turned the water in the font a muddy brown.

"What have you done?" the vicar cried, shocked to see the water so contaminated.

"You'll need to clean it up and add new water. I apologise. Here." I stuffed £20 into the collection box.

When I returned Peter Wilde was still there, waiting for me.

"Who was that scrawny crone you were talking to?" Peter asked.

"Mrs Harriet Milverton. She knew my late wife and the late Rodney Scobey," I told him.

"Mrs? So who is her husband?"

"He is dead as well. I think it was husbands in the plural and they are all dead."

"Jesus – people dying all around her. Is she the Grim Reaper?"

"She is part of something sacrilegious here in the heart of Surrey and somehow a big city whizz kid named Felix Hoad is involved. If you are still a serious journalist you might want to do some digging."

"I'd rather have a drink and you must need one after the funeral. Come on let's make to the Wheatsheaf."

I didn't need a drink. "Sorry this is not the time," I turned him down.

"Hey, I am not the hell raiser I used to be. I only drink wine these days. My body can't take the pints anymore. Plumbing shot to hell. Going to the Gents every few minutes if I drink pints. Spirits and shorts are even worse for me. They give me a headache and a belly ache so I never drink them. I am a wino these days," he explained.

"I just want some peace and quiet," I said.

So we wandered off to the Garden of Remembrance within the cemetery and sat on a wooden bench surrounded by a rose arbour. There was no danger of being overheard. The people who surrounded us were all dead and buried.

"You should know I am not a hard-bitten reporter searching out scoops anymore," Peter sighed. "The job has changed out of all recognition since I trained as a journalist. Most of our reporters don't have shorthand anymore. We all have our own concealed recorders.

83

They don't have the long training I went through. They are always falling foul of the laws of libel, sub judice and contempt of court rulings. You will hear of more mistrials now because of newspapers condemning a suspect in print before they have been found guilty or innocent. We sit at computers and rewrite press releases. The PR people are having a field day. They can get any old rubbish published. Because of staff shortages and multi-skilling stories get dropped in without checking or investigation."

"I suppose the phone hacking scandals have further discredited the press," I said.

"Oh no we have always bugged telephones but it wasn't always illegal," Peter grinned. "I just hate computers. I miss the old days of banging my story out on a manual typewriter. Now I work for the computer. It should be the other way round. The computer should work for me."

"At least you have adapted to new technology. You would have become unemployable if you had not."

"Bloody computers. They will be the death of me," Peter moaned. "There is a name for computer phobia. Many of us old hacks had it. The name will come to me shortly."

"So what about Felix Hoad? He who drove Estelle to her death. Is there a story there?"

"I have heard of Felix Hoad. He is CEO of some multi-national conglomerate but it is not one of those big corporations that are always making the news."

"Perhaps they are just good at covering things up. The name of the corporation is QPL, according to Estelle."

"QPL? I'll think about it. I hate my job these days. I am surrounded by computer nerds and vegetarians who drink bottled water and seem more interested in the political correctness of a story than its content or its truth. I have been given an official warning for being drunk on the job. When I started, journalists would have been given an official warning for being sober on the job. I would love, just once before I die, to snatch up the phone and shout: 'Hold the front page'. We used to be called The Fourth Estate. Now we are a joke. I once worked for a respected and influential newspaper. Since it was taken over by Marquis Thorn it has become just another sleazy tabloid."

"The name Marquis Thorn came up recently. He was trying to buy Grimoire Priory but was gazumped by someone, apparently, even more corrupt than him. What can you tell me about Thorn that isn't in the public domain?"

"Well he has his own private helicopter and his own helicopter pilot brought with him from South Africa. He has his own landing pad on the roof. He also keeps a hunting rifle in his office. It is said that he used to fly over herds of wildebeest in Africa, picking them off one by one with his rifle from the helicopter."

"He sounds charming. A right candidate for this gang of Satanists. Tell me, is Black Magic and Devil worship still a hot topic for your newspaper?" I asked.

"Yesterday's news." Peter shrugged. "People are more concerned about terrorists and paedophiles. They don't take all that hocus pocus seriously these days and it is not against the law."

"Well it seems to be a big part of the story here."

"Interesting. I have a contact who is a bit of an expert in all that mumbo jumbo. I may introduce you to him. I will also have a look at Felix Hoad and QPL and see what I can find but don't get your hopes up."

The next evening I met Peter at an old pub in Wapping, East London. It was called "The Town of Ramsgate", so called because in days gone by, the fisherman of Ramsgate, a Kent seaside harbour, used to take their catches of fish up there to sell them at the docks. It was a long, narrow pub with an alleyway running alongside that ended in steep narrow stone steps that went all the way down into the River Thames.

"What an unusual old pub," I said to Peter and I sat down beside him.

"How I miss the pubs of Fleet Street … but that is the past now. This is an interesting old pub with an evil past." Peter smiled as he bought us a bottle of wine to share. "See that?" he pointed to a frayed and knotted rope that dangled in the outside garden. "That is supposed to be a hangman's noose. Those steps are known as Wapping Old Stairs. They say that Judge Jeffries, the famous Hanging Judge from the 17th century, was caught there trying to flee the country and ended up being hung himself. Men press ganged into the Royal Navy and convicts due to be deported to the Colonies were imprisoned underground here. Smugglers and pirates were regular customers. The Execution Dock was nearby and the bodies of the hanged men were chained to posts in the river so you could view them from here."

"Charming. I must bring my next date here. It does seem an appropriate venue to talk about Felix Hoad and the QPL group, though. What do you know?"

"It is very interesting. QPL is a huge multi-national with its fingers in so many pies that it did surprise me how little publicity it gets. It is still a private company so it has no army of stockholders to keep happy. The origins of QPL go back to the days of the British Empire when as builders and property developers in Victorian England, QPL spread throughout the world to assist in the growth of many former colonies. They are much more than builders today. They now own companies in the business of agriculture, defence, chemicals, shipping, transport, pharmaceuticals, new technology and the media.

"However, once I started asking questions, I began to understand how they had kept things so quiet. I was warned by my bosses to back off and told that all stories about QPL have to be cleared and signed off by them."

"There has to be a big story here. Corruption in high places, drugs, sex and even Devil worship involving the rich and famous. Felix Hoad seems like a Charles Manson for the upper classes. I can't believe that your scandal sheets would want to suppress it. So much for freedom of the press."

"Freedom of the press, don't you believe it!"

"So who in your organisation is gagging stories about QPL?"

"Oh it goes straight to the very top; Marquis Thorn himself."

"So Estelle wasn't as crazy as I thought. QPL really is all-powerful. Does this mean you have to stop researching them?"

"Not really. It just means that I will have to be a lot more subtle about it."

"QPL doesn't own Marquis Thorn's media empire does it?"

"Oh no but it is possible that many of QPL's subsidiary companies are big advertisers and they could pull their entire advertising if we start to blow the whistle on them. Corporate blackmail but it happens."

"So you can't expose them?"

"I didn't say that. I need to do a lot of investigating and fact checking. We keep our own files on the rich, powerful and famous but some of them are sealed. I have just had glimpses of what could be a huge story here – a giant conglomerate that operates without ethics or conscience, driven to continuously expand and grasp more power. A psychopathic corporation led by a murderous megalomaniac in Felix Hoad. I will drag them out of the darkness and into full public scrutiny with some old-fashioned journalism. That is the other thing with today's young journalists - they feel that if something isn't on the Internet it doesn't exist. This is something big and powerful that has been flying under the radar, not just for years, not just for decades, but well over a century. I have to thank you for awakening my old reporter's zeal. I may have the opportunity to unmask something very evil that reaches into every corner of the globe." Peter grinned and gulped down his wine. "So what if the publishers I work for won't touch it. There will be others who will.

"One thing that strikes me as odd straight away. It is almost impossible to find a photo of Felix Hoad."

"I can help with that one. Estelle had a framed photo of him. I smashed the glass, cutting my hand, but it is among the boxes of her belongings that I am sorting out," I told him.

"Scan it and email it to me."

"Modern technology is not my strong point and I am not sure I know how to scan photos on my equipment."

"You probably have a bit of that computer phobia I was talking about yesterday. The name of it will come to me shortly. OK then bring the photo up to my offices tomorrow if you can. Come about lunch time and we can pop out and share some more wine."

"I'll do that but I don't want you getting any more warnings because of me."

"No worries. I have a feeling that my story will have grown a lot bigger by tomorrow and then they won't want to drive me out. Now drink up."

"Why? Where are we going?" I asked.

"It is time to meet the mumbo jumbo expert I told you about. I hope you have some protection."

"What protection do I need? Bell, book and candle. A crucifix?"

"You'll soon find out. Come on. It is close by."

We did not have our cars, probably just as well considering the amount of wine we had consumed. I had travelled to Wapping on the Overground and Peter never drove to work. Once outside the pub, Peter hailed a cab.

The journey was indeed short and the cabbie dropped us at an old single storey wooden chapel. There was nothing outside to give a clue as to the denomination of the chapel. It could have been Baptist, Methodist or Seventh Day Adventists for all I could see.

Peter banged on the huge double doors. There was no answer and all was silent inside.

He then pushed one of the doors and it swung open.

"I'm going in," he said.

"Hey isn't that trespassing?" I asked.

"It is the House of God. Its doors are ever open. Anyway after all that wine I need a pee."

So did I – so I let Peter creep in and I followed.

It was bare, gloomy and cold inside. A few chairs, rows of wooden pews and a raised dais at the end, it was lit by the moonlight streaming through its non-ornate windows. No organ, just an old piano that had seen better days.

"It doesn't look as if they get much of a congregation," I whispered to Peter.

"I seem to remember that the toilets are through there." Peter made for a door in one corner.

"So you have been here before?"

"Yes, chasing a Black Magic story that ended up on the spike. No interest in naked people dancing round an altar these days. Reminds me of a line from that movie: 'The greatest trick the Devil ever pulled was convincing the world he didn't exist'."

"The Usual Suspects."

"That's the one. Now let me find a toilet before I wet myself." Peter flung open the door.

The backroom had been turned into a bedroom. There was a wardrobe, chest of drawers and a large double bed with a naked couple on top of it making love. She was on top and bouncing up and down astride him while he lay below fondling her breasts. She was blonde and pretty, he was dark and hairy with a beard and moustache – and when I say hairy, I mean hairy all over as I could see. They stopped and looked at us. She pulled him out of her.

"Coitus interruptus," the man spoke in a booming voice with a strong Northern Irish accent. "One method of birth control approved by the Vatican. What brings Peter Wilde and a stranger bursting into my den of iniquity?"

"Would you like to strip off and join us?" the woman asked.

I was shocked.

"I am all for foursomes but only when the other three are female." The man grinned. "Anyway I suspect Peter has permanent Brewers' Droop."

"I can't carry on anyway. They've broken the mood," the woman complained.

"First I must use your loo and then I'll explain." Peter rushed for the other door waving in my direction as he went. "Meet Ronan Bell."

"Hallo Mr Bell. Peter told me something of you over the phone. Excuse us while we dress. I am Sebastian Fullalove."

He and his lady love rolled off the bed and grabbed for their black clothes that lay on the floor.

Peter returned and then it was my turn to rush to the loo. I discovered it was more than a toilet. It was a shower room with sink and mirror. It looked as if Mr Fullalove lived here.

Relieved, I returned to the bedroom to find them dressed.

He was dressed as a priest complete with clerical collar and a crucifix round his neck while she was a nun complete with wimple.

"Thank you, Father. I have to go anyway," the nun said. "I am late for Vespers."

"I don't want to incur the wrath of your Abbess again. I haven't recovered from the last time she came round here and vented her passion on me."

"What about your vows of celibacy?" I had to ask.

"Doesn't apply to me," Fullalove smiled. "I have been defrocked and excommunicated. But I still like to call myself Father and wear the uniform just to annoy the church."

"And what about-?" I nodded at the nun.

"Oh she is for real. Don't ask, don't tell." Fullalove waved at her as she left. "Goodbye Sister and may God go with you." After she had gone, he added: "Lovely lady. Used to be a lap dancer before she became a nun."

"When I said you might need protection, I was thinking that there might be sexually rampant nuns here. And I was right," Peter chuckled as he spoke to me. "As for you Father, you might lock your doors or at least put a sock on the door handle."

"Let's go and sit down and discuss your situation." Father Sebastian Fullalove shrugged and took us back into the main chapel. He said pull up a pew and really meant it, sitting us down on pews by a wooden table, and producing a bottle of red wine and three glasses from a cupboard. "Communion wine. You are ahead of me so I have to catch up. Let us celebrate the Eucharist with the blood of Christ."

We chinked glasses and drank.

"So is this still a working chapel?" I had to ask.

"No, it was abandoned and derelict but I had it converted into a home for me. I bought it with the hush money – sorry, loss of office compensation – that the church paid me," Sebastian explained. "However it is a good venue for the private counselling I carry out for those who seek spiritual guidance.

"I have been excommunicated for refusing to recant my heresy of believing in humanism and preaching it from the pulpit. I was also guilty of enjoying sex with consenting adults. Unforgivable. If I had molested children the church would have covered it up. I am from Belfast and witnessed first-hand the murderous hatred between people who worshipped the same God but with slight variations. To see someone murdered or maimed just because they were Protestant or Catholic would shake anyone's faith. I also broke the confidentiality of the confessional. I went public about a man who confessed to me that he had committed a crime that an

93

innocent man was serving time for. The innocent man was pardoned and freed but I was cast out of the church. I now earn my living as a consultant and personal advisor on spiritual matters. The man I freed from prison was grateful and gave me a handsome reward out of his huge compensation pay-out which has helped support me. The final straw was when I told a woman whose son had committed suicide that he would not go to purgatory and that he could be buried in consecrated ground. Enough about me. Tell me about this upper-class coven."

So I told him as much as I knew. The whole story, starting with me buying the statue of Pan at an auction and every single crazy consequence that followed.

When I had finished Sebastian said: "Felix Hoad's gang of ghouls sound worse than the Freemasons."

I laughed. "If he is so all powerful, I wonder how come I had never heard of him before."

"There have been people like him throughout history," Sebastian told me. "Charismatic leaders operating from the shadows who seem to put a spell on their followers so that they obey without question. I have made a study of them. Grigori Yefimovich Rasputin who brought down the Russian Tsars; Aleister Crowley who proclaimed himself The Great Beast; Charles Manson and his killer hippie family; the Reverend Jim Jones who ordered a thousand of his followers to commit suicide in Guyana in 1978; Quincy Pitt, the Victorian bogeyman; sect leader David Koresh who died with 75 of his followers following the Waco, Texas siege in 1993; 48 dead in Switzerland in a mass suicide in 1994, all members of the Order of the Solar Temple set up by Dr Luc Jouret ... and I could go on."

Quincy Pitt, that name again. I had never heard of Pitt until Estelle mentioned him just before her death.

"Rasputin is a particularly interesting case," Sebastian went on. "He refused to die you know. He was shot and stabbed many times, clubbed, beaten with chains and castrated. They fed him with chocolates and cakes laced with arsenic at a dinner in his honour. He had consumed enough poison to kill seven men but still he lived. They then wrapped his body in a carpet and threw it in the Neva River where it sunk under the ice but still Rasputin fought back and broke out of his bonds. After his body was recovered from the river three days later the conspirators who had planned his murder carried his body into the woods and set it on fire but to the horror of the bystanders, his body appeared to sit up as it burned. Some people do not let go of life without a fight and perhaps he had some supernatural help."

"Eternal life, immortality … I don't think so …" but suddenly I was thinking of Mrs Milverton and her Royal Jelly from African bees. "Sounds like an early urban legend but I can't take all this Black Magic stuff seriously."

"Practising witchcraft or worshipping Satan in this country with consenting adults is not a crime.

"How many people in this country believe in God? About 50 per cent? Then about the same number must believe in the Devil. Satan appears in Judaism, Christian and Muslim religions. He is the one constant they all believe in. Evil is very real. More evil is carried out in the name of religion than anything else. Most of our wars were brought about by religion. That's why I chose to give it all up and become an atheist until someone proves me wrong." Sebastian smiled. "However I do have some nutty contacts among the mumbo jumbo brigade and I will check out the names you have given me to see what I can find out."

"There, I told you he would be a useful contact," Peter slurred.

"I cannot drink any more. I must go home but I will see you tomorrow with the picture," I said to Peter.

"I need to communicate with the spirits some more. I am in the right place," Peter said.

I left them in the chapel still drinking.

So the next day I ventured to the huge ugly glass skyscraper where Peter worked.

The building itself was as sleazy as the newspapers that were published there. Security was tight. I sat in the reception watched over by a massive portrait of Marquis Thorn.

I began reading the latest edition of their flagship newspaper while I waited.

I skimmed through it for anything to catch my eye. Then I found something. It interested me for three reasons: it was a story local to me, it had a Peter Wilde by-line and the couple in the story had been mentioned to me by Estelle.

It was about Rick and Zoe Leppard, husband and wife animal-loving veterinary celebrities who sometimes appeared on television in animal medical programmes. The story was about Haven, the state-of-the-art animal hospital they were having built in Surrey.

When completed, this hospital would have treatment facilities and medical technology far in advance of the average NHS hospital, it was claimed. This included MRI scanners, high technology operating theatres and custom-made artificial limbs for animals that had lost legs. They used titanium rods and prosthetics to replace the amputated legs and feet of not just cats and dogs but horses, pigs and cows as well. Haven was a health spa for the pampered pets of the rich and included animal psychiatry, organ transplants, diet programmes for obese animals and advice on tummy tucks and cosmetic surgery. There was even a dentistry section that provided false teeth or complete dentures.

It was surreal. I wondered if they did breast implants for animals as well.

"When Haven is complete, we will be able to offer a surgical and medical service for our non-human patients that is as good as or better than anything available to people," Rick Leppard was quoted as saying.

If I needed an operation, I would take myself off there rather than my nearest NHS hospital, I decided.

Then Peter came to fetch me. He had to sign me in and I wore a visitor badge.

He took me through to vast open plan offices and row upon row of computers.

"I remembered that name for a fear of computers. It is a real mouthful – Logizomechanophobia. Many old timers had a real phobia about computers and thought they could kill them. But then they became unemployable. I have never liked computers but realised that I had to embrace new technology if I was to continue working as a journalist," Peter laughed. "You wouldn't be able to walk inside this building if you had Logizomechanophobia."

There were some journalists bashing away at their computers and shouting on telephones but most of the workstations were unmanned as it was lunchtime. He led me to a meeting room in a corner. Once inside, he closed the door and silence descended.

"We can talk in private here," Peter said.

"I would like to see where you work," I commented.

"You can't at the moment. I have some IT guy looking at my computer."

"Have you broken it again?"

"No but there are always glitches that need sorting out. I have never seen such an odd IT guy."

"What do you mean?"

"Well normally they are young nerds but this one is much too old to be of the computer generation. In fact he looked too old to be working."

"Get used to it. Because of the pension crisis and changes in the law on compulsory retirement we will see many more oldies in the workplace."

"Hey, I of all people am not ageist. But this guy was creepy and his breath nearly knocked me out."

"Halitosis?"

"I don't know what it was but his breath stunk as if he was if he was decaying inside."

"While I was waiting, I read your story on the Leppards and their vet hospital," I said. "I am glad they are still letting you go out and get stories."

"That is not the story I would have liked to have written. I got leaned on to write them up. In truth I did not like them or what they were doing," Wilde explained.

"But you are an animal lover. I thought you would have approved of their new hospital," I said.

"There was something very false about that pair but I was not allowed to be critical. I am suspicious of the motives of people who will pay a lot of money for their pets to look pretty. Guess what company is building the hospital for them?"

I hesitated for a moment and then it came to me: "QPL?"

"Got it in one. A massive conglomerate that hides its light under a bushel. Its CEO is even more mysterious. I did manage to find a video of Hoad laying the foundations of the new QPL building, however. Watch."

Peter switched on a remote control and a television screen in the wall came to fuzzy life.

A gathering of people stood on a white concrete floor watching a tall man standing by a cement mixer. It was hard to see above the heads of the crowds but his distinctive, pure white hair made him stand out.

He spoke to the crowd:

"I am proud to welcome you here at the laying of the foundations of QPL's new headquarters. Here we will be able to centralise all the various subsidiary companies and research facilities that QPL has acquired over more than 150 years. This building will be a monument to all that this group has achieved. It is being constructed with our own Anubis Concrete.

"The building will be a tribute to our in-house building materials and an advert for the strength and possibilities of Anubis Concrete, which will revolutionise the building industry."

He paused to lower his head.

"While here, we should remember the man who was the architect of all this, my predecessor Nick Mercer. We don't know where you are today, Nick, but when we walk over the floor of this building we will feel your presence beneath us, inspiring us to greater things. We have named the building Mercer Tower in recognition of your vision."

100

I looked at Peter. "Did you get the feeling that Nick Mercer really is buried in the foundations? He was almost boasting about it."

Peter smiled and switched off the screen. "Nothing would surprise me but you would need some hard evidence before you could get the foundations dug up to look for it. Have you been following the court case against Danny Stein that is going on at the moment? Stein is a major crime boss with links to some respectable UK companies. Guess the name of the biggest company that he is in cahoots with? It is QPL of course but this has not come out at the trial because the police seem to have messed up the evidence."

"Oh yes I can believe that – evidence messed up to keep QPL out of it."

"Anyway have you got the photo?"

I took out the photo of Felix Hoad from my bag. I hated looking at it. The man still seemed to be sneering at me.

Peter snatched it up. "He looks like Jesus with white hair. I have never seen such white hair on someone so young." He walked to the door. "Come with me. My computer should be free by now."

He took me to his cluttered cubical. There were piles of papers all over his desk.

"So you never embraced the idea of the paperless office," I said sarcastically.

Peter ignored me and opened the printer/scanner and placed the photograph face down on the Perspex top.

"Well at least the IT man has gone although I am sure he has left his stink behind. He could at least have left it switched on for me," Peter complained as he peered into the blank screen.

He switched on his computer and the scanner at the same time. The scanner began to growl and vibrate as if the photo freaked it out as well. There was a flash and the computer hissed and spat out a bright spark. Then the whole thing blew up in his face.

I was thrown back by the loud and fiery explosion and covered my face as burning bits of plastic and wiring showered down around me.

People began screaming, shouting and running.

A siren sounded and then a recorded announcement sounded over the Tannoy: "There is an emergency. Please evacuate the building in an orderly fashion. Go immediately to the designated exits. Use the stairs, not the lifts."

Then the sprinklers came on and rained water down on me and the smouldering remains of Peter and his computer.

I jumped up and went to Peter who lay back in his chair, his face unrecognisable. It had become charred black and red mush and flames burned on the hair on top of his head. A jagged shard from the shattered computer screen was embedded in his skull. I shook his shoulder to see if he was alive but he slumped over sideways and fell to the floor.

Water from the sprinklers doused the flames.

I wasn't sure whether to cry or be sick. How cruel for Peter Wilde to die like that just when he had discovered a new enthusiasm for his work.

Both computer and scanner had been reduced to piles of debris and angry spitting broken wires that sizzled as the sprinkler water landed on them. Felix Hoad's photo was just ashes.

Logizomechanophobia had turned out to be very real for Peter. His computer had been the death of him.

A security guard grabbed me and barked out an order: "You must leave the building at once. There may be other explosions. Do not use the lifts."

I joined the fleeing throng that fled down the stairs and congregated outside the building.

I spoke to one of the fire marshals who was busy counting heads on the lawn outside. "Look, I don't work here. I am just a visitor…"

"You stay. The police will want your details," he snapped at me.

There was a flurry among the crowd. A man I recognised straightaway from the many times he had been on the news as well as his portrait in the reception was being herded through the crowd.

He was in his fifties with gold-rimmed glasses and an immaculate pepper and salt beard.

An entourage of big, black-suited bouncers and corporate suck ups in striped blue shirts surrounded him and were keeping the panic-filled workers at bay.

Suddenly the man halted in his tracks and turned. His army of minders started flapping around him and tried to put him back on the path they wanted but he would not go. He was looking straight at me through those gold rimmed glasses. Then he began walking over to me.

Marquis Thorn stopped in front of me and spoke. "So, Ronan Bell. You came to visit my business and you brought death, chaos and destruction with you."

I could detect a strong hint of a South African accent. I recalled that he had been born in South Africa.

"I am amazed and flattered that you know who I am, Mr Thorn," I stuttered.

"Next time you come you must ask for me personally and I will see to it that you are well taken care of," he smiled, flashing teeth that also had gold in them.

"Oh I don't think I will be visiting again," I said.

"Then we must visit you."

I had a vision of him calling on me with his hunting rifle. "You would be welcome but I don't think you would like my humble home."

"Oh I wouldn't come myself. I would send someone or something." Thorn flashed another golden smile at me.

Had I just been threatened by one of the biggest media magnates in the country? Yes, I was sure I had.

Then a big man in a pilot's uniform complete with helmet and goggles pushed the crowd aside to confront us. "The helicopter is parked on the roof but we cannot get up there till we have the all clear," he also spoke with a distinct South African accent.

"Thank you, Andries," Thorn spoke to him. "I have to get away from here."

I guessed Andries was the pilot who flew Thorn over the herds of wildebeest so he could take pot shots at them with his rifle. The two of them turned away from me and hurried off.

Then I was visited by uniformed police who came and took a statement. When I told them that I was standing right next to the man who died when his computer exploded, they did not seem that interested.

"Has someone told his wife?" I asked. "She lives near me."

"Don't worry about that. It is being taken care of," the policeman closed his notebook. "You can go home now, Mr Bell. We have your details should we need to contact you again."

"Will there be a proper investigation into Peter Wilde's death?" I persisted.

"Oh yes the Health and Safety Officers will make a full investigation."

"Yes but what if it wasn't a Health and Safety issue. What if...?"

The police had gone onto the next person before I could voice my gnawing suspicion that perhaps it hadn't been an accident.

The next day I saw a very short news report about the incident on the back pages in the newspaper that Peter worked on. It read:

"Peter Wilde, 57, one of our senior journalists, died yesterday following a freak computer short circuit in our offices. The offices were evacuated for a short time while the accident was investigated but work resumed once it was established that there was no further danger. It is believed that highly volatile alcohol had been spilled onto the computer causing it to burst into flame when it was switched on. Mr Wilde had worked at the paper for several years through the different changes of ownership and leaves behind many old friends in the media. He lived in Surrey and is survived by his wife."

I threw the paper down in disgust. Another death dismissed and swept under the carpet! The bit about volatile alcohol sounded as if Peter was being blamed for his own death.

I had to speak to someone about this but whom to trust?

I first tried my new friend Father Sebastian Fullalove but all I got was his voicemail. Was he too hungover to talk I wondered or wrestling with another nun?

I left a muddled message on his voicemail: "Sebastian, it is Ronan Bell here. Peter has been killed now. I feel the threat from these people is more than hocus-pocus. We are dealing with ruthless murderers. The danger is real and I need some real protection. Call me..."

After pondering it for a while I then telephoned Detective Superintendent Ives.

I got through straight away. He sounded friendly but he didn't mince his words.

"Hallo Mr Bell. Are you ready to confess?"

"Look ... I saw someone else murdered yesterday and it is being hushed up as an accident. I am sure it was a murder."

"Oh yes. People have a habit of dying around you. Who was it?"

"Peter Wilde, a journalist, a friend and a neighbour. I am sure it was murder because I was threatened almost immediately afterwards by his boss, Marquis Thorn."

"Marquis Thorn. Your paranoiac fantasies go to the very top. Only the other day you told me it was Felix Hoad who was after you."

"The only reason I telephoned you was that after getting bullied and shouted at by that Craven cop from the Surrey police I felt you were a bit brighter and some of what I told you registered with you."

106

"Possibly but don't get your hopes up. Come up and see me and we can talk about this in more detail."

"Can I get to come to Scotland Yard now?"

"No, but close by. I want to talk to you outside a police station and I don't want that country bumpkin Craven involved." Ives directed me to a pub called 0The Feathers that was next door to the former Scotland Yard headquarters in Broadway.

I viewed the fact that he was willing to talk to me and on neutral ground as positive.

I met him at later in the afternoon when the pub was less crowded and we could talk in confidence.

We sat at a table at the quieter end of the pub and Ives launched straight into it.

"First I have checked out the death of Peter Wilde. As he was your friend you probably know he was an alcoholic who had numerous warnings on his personnel file for being drunk on the job. A younger man would have been sacked but they felt they owed him something for his length of service. He had been referred to a psychiatrist and to Alcoholics Anonymous for help, but his drinking had got so bad that he was now on pure, neat alcohol. He didn't care what he was drinking. He was on denatured alcohol."

"Denatured alcohol, what is that?" I asked.

"Like drinking methylated spirits. It is highly inflammable and highly volatile. He smuggled it into the office in Coke bottles, which they found, but with his shaky hands it is not surprising that he spilled a lot of it onto and into his computer."

"Look, that story is just not true. I know Peter drank a lot but I also know for a fact he only drank wine these days. Did you find out anything about the old IT man who had been working on his computer just before he switched it on?"

"There was no old IT man in the office that day. No one else saw him."

"It was lunch time. Many of them had left the office."

"Sorry but his computer workings were soaked in denatured alcohol. When he switched it on all it needed was one spark…"

"So you don't believe anything I have told you?"

"I wouldn't say that," Ives mused. "Samuels had a criminal record. There is no doubt that there were some very odd goings on at Grimoire Priory. Felix Hoad is a bit of a mystery man. He has got himself into a very powerful position as CEO of the QPL Group and no one knows much about him but he seems to have a hold over people who are powerful in their own right and do not work for QPL. I had my own reasons for wanting to meet you in this pub, Mr Bell. His influence could extend to some of my colleagues in the police force."

"That is frightening. I know that there were concerns about members of the police force belonging to the Freemasons some years ago but the Freemasons run charities and hospitals, don't they? Hardly evil."

"They are a secret society and a cult of sorts but I do not think the Freemasons have anything to do with this. Freemasons today are more like grown up boy scouts. However secret societies do exist and the more successful they are the more secret they are. But trust me, Mr Bell, I think that you could be in danger and it may be the men I assign to protect you who could become your biggest threat."

"That seems a bit over the top," I laughed. "Do you think there is something to all this Black Magic nonsense?"

"Well in our job we have to. That is not to say that we believe that there is anything to it, just that some people carry out criminal acts because *they* believe that there is something to it. The South African police have a dedicated occult crimes unit which we have consulted with on certain cases. While we do not have the equivalent in the UK there is a section in centralised police services that collects and cross references all cases that seem to have an occult angle.

"Practising witchcraft or worshipping Satan in this country is not a crime so I cannot arrest anyone for it."

"I can't believe in Devil worshippers in this day and age," I said.

Ives grabbed a nearby newspaper and turned the page to show me a picture of a man with black, hate-filled eyes under bushy black eyebrows. The headline above the photo read: Stein innocent!

"The evil I have to deal with every day is down to earth, flesh and blood, like this monster. This is Danny Stein. We have been after him for years and worked to build a cast iron case against him. He is a known gang boss, extortionist and mass murderer who is so confident now that he does not even attempt to conceal his crimes. After a lengthy and expensive trial, a jury has found him not guilty. It makes me despair. This case is personal to me as I was among the many who worked on it. Stein started out as a yob and petty criminal on a South London council estate and now he is a billionaire thanks totally to his crime business. My dream is to arrest the man myself and put him away. We are losing the battle against all that is sick and wrong with society." Ives tossed the paper aside, showing real emotion for the first time.

"In spite of all the evil that man has committed, people treat him like a folk hero. I suspect that many members of the jury were taken in by his loveable rogue image and found him not guilty in spite of all the evidence against him."

"I sympathise with your anger. I want closure on the death of Estelle and Peter. I feel that there is something huge, ugly and very bad behind all this," I said as I retrieved the newspaper, wanting to read more about Stein later.

"Oh yes and he is the new owner of Grimoire Priory. Buying it was the first thing he did after he was found not guilty."

"Danny Stein has brought Grimoire Priory? That building really is a focus for evil."

"One thing that could never be brought up at the trial was Stein's close ties to QPL. And why? Because the proof was amongst the cases of evidence 'lost' by the police. Go home, Mr Bell, and keep your head below the parapet. I will assign men to watch your house, men I think I can trust, but I cannot do it for too long. You won't see them but they will be there. I will continue to investigate and personally find out what I can about Felix Hoad and his friends. I will let you know the minute I discover anything I think you should know," Ives attempted to reassure me, "it is in God's hands now."

"I do not believe in God," I said.

"Neither do I, except in moments of extreme stress," Ives smiled.

It had been good to talk about my fears but I did not really feel comforted. I took Ives' advice and returned home.

Chapter Twelve
: Night Terrors

I was exhausted and although it was early, I collapsed into my bed. I had trouble sleeping that evening. Looking up Danny Stein on the internet before turning in hardly gave me peace of mind. That man lived his life completely without ethics or any moral compass. And yet some people regarded him as charming, a character. Even some celebrities loved to be seen with him. He attracted them like a magnet.

Why? A shudder ran through me.

It was good to be back in my bed, however. A full moon shone down through the skylight.

The room was muggy and I opened the skylight the smallest notch to let the air in.

I drifted off into a disturbed sleep. A growing unease caused my heart to race. I was in a cold sweat and I tried to open my eyes.

When I was able to look up, I saw a gallery of moving faces swimming in front of me in the pitch blackness. Their mouths were moving as if they were talking but I could hear nothing.

The faces dissolved as I became aware that I was not alone in my bed.

A woman lay next to me and snuggled against me, her hand on my chest. Her naked body felt warm next to mine.

The moonlight streaming from the skylight shone on her face.

It was Estelle and she lay there smiling at me. She was as she used to be, beautiful, not the old hag I had last seen.

"Estelle, you are dead!" I tried to pull myself up and away but I could not move.

She spoke in Estelle's voice: "Be calm, Ronan. I am here."

"You can't be. I went to your funeral. I saw you cremated. You were in the coffin."

"That was someone else. It was a mistake. I am here but out of your reach now, Ronan. You are now the one in danger. You must protect yourself. Death is not the worst thing that can befall a person. The cylinder from Pan must be protected from them at all costs. It must never be opened. You have no idea what you could unleash."

"I will guard it with my life."

"Remember me. Forget the bad times. Remember the good times and save my soul," Estelle murmured.

She gripped my wrist hard with her hand. She was changing. Suddenly her body sagged and sunk and blood poured from the cracks in her flesh and onto the bed sheets. Her skull had split and her face was flattened, her nose broken. Splintered bone tore through her arms and legs. Blood ran from her ears, eyes and mouth. It was the body of the woman who had fallen to her death to slam onto the concrete paving.

I screamed and tried to free my arm but she held on tight.

Suddenly Felix Hoad appeared at my bedside. He grinned down at me through clenched teeth. "Why, Mr Bell, you have become a nuisance. I will have to have you cast off into eternal damnation," he snarled.

He reached down for my throat. I tried to move but I was paralysed with fright. I screamed as loud as I could and Hoad's face disintegrated into black ashes that fluttered away.

I kept screaming until I woke myself up. I threw myself out of bed and switched on the light. I was alone and there was no blood in the bed.

It had been a dream but I could still feel Estelle's fingers squeezing round my wrist.

Blood dripped from my left hand and onto the carpet, from the cut where I had smashed Hoad's picture.

There was a noise downstairs. I am not a nervous person but for once I regretted having a house so isolated and far away from the nearest neighbours.

It sounded like a furious kind of scratching.

I went downstairs in darkness. It was coming from the front door.

I stood still, listening. Suddenly my outside lights came on in a blinding flash. I had sensor operated security lights in the garden and sometimes a roaming fox would be enough to activate them but I did not feel it was a fox this time.

After a moment they switched off and it was pitch dark again.

The noise was coming from the bottom of the door. I had bolted the cat flap and something was scratching at it in a frantic attempt to claw its way in.

114

I had to see what it was. I knelt down and drew back the bolt. The scratching stopped suddenly. I raised the cat flap and peered out. Nothing but black night.

"Hallo, is someone there?" I called.

I went to close the flap again. Something slashed at my wrist and I pulled my hand back in sudden pain. All I had seen was a blur.

I slammed the cat flap shut, pushed the bolt back home and sat down to inspect my wrist. There was a bloody scratch across the veins in my wrist. I felt faint for a moment and feared I would pass out.

I went into the kitchen and put TCP onto the wound and bandaged it as well as re-bandaging my hand.

There was a throbbing in my arm as if some nasty infection was crawling up it.

At least it was silent outside. I gulped down a glass of whisky in the hope that it would help me go back to sleep and climbed the stairs with shaky legs.

I collapsed on the bed and pulled the sheets around me. The moonlight created ghostly shadows all around my bedroom.

The whisky was working and I was relaxing but feeling strange at the same time.

I closed my eyes and welcomed the darkness.

There came a loud tapping and scraping on the glass of the skylight above me. I opened my eyes but for a moment all I could see was the bright full moon.

Then something leprously white scuttled and scampered from one side of the glass to the other and out of my sight.

My body was weak and trembling and I tried to rise but wobbled like a drunk. My vision was blurred.

Suddenly the white ghost was back on my skylight doing some horrid dance on its many legs as it tried to find a way in. It scuttled to and fro, faster and faster, growling and grumbling a chant in some guttural language that I could not understand.

I was unable to rise from the bed and run or defend myself. I was almost paralysed and could only stare upwards at the hideous thing that ran around my skylight working itself up into a rage as it attempted to get at me.

I reached out for my bedside lamp but my hand was shaking so much that I knocked the lamp to the floor.

The creature paused to glare down at me with a pair of reddish bloodshot eyes that glowed luminously in the dark and were full of hate. Its mouth opened on fang-like teeth in a grotesque grin. Slimy saliva oozed from that evil maw and drooled onto the glass.

Suddenly it was moving and dancing again, only stopping when it found the open window latch. It tried to get through the gap but it was too narrow for its sickly white body so then it began scratching at the latch.

I was terrified and wanted to leap out of bed and run out of the room but my body would not respond. I was weak and unable to move.

It spat and snarled as it rattled at the latch. The whole skylight shook and clattered.

Then it began jumping up and down on the window, hitting the glass with a shuddering thud each time.

The glass began to crack. Still it jumped on the cracks which slowly spread across the pane in all directions. My God, it was going to break through!

My body was frozen either with fear or some sort of sickness because I was trembling and nauseated.

A final desperate jump from the creature and the glass shattered. The thing dropped straight down into my bedroom in a shower of falling glass. The thing dropped silently out of sight at the bottom of my bed.

Silence descended and the room became freezing cold as the broken window let in the night air.

I grabbed the edge of the bed sheet and tried to sit up, peering into the darkness.

Slowly a black face with two upright pointed horns on top of its head rose from behind the end of the bed and glared at me through two red eyes with green in the bloodshot centres.

It snarled at me and made to leap onto the bed.

I raised the bed sheet in front of me, partially for protection and partially to hide the hideous thing from my sight.

It sprang at the sheet and began raking at it with its claws. The sheet started to tear and a claw slashed through, scratching my cheek.

It hurled itself at me and two fangs sunk into my neck.

Somehow, I got the strength to fight back. I threw myself forward out of the bed and brought the sheet down over the spitting, snarling horror. I knotted the sheet round its squirming body so it could not get out and then rolled onto the floor, still holding it.

I began whacking the floor with the screeching monster trapped inside the sheet. I hit the floor with it again and again. When I saw blood spreading on the white sheet, I knew that what I was fighting was flesh and bone and from this world – not something ethereal.

I continued to swirl it around and whack it against the floor until some horrible death rattle came from inside the wrapped sheet. The thing shuddered violently and then was still and silent. I dropped the gruesome bundle and collapsed. I was weak and exhausted.

After a while I recovered and grabbed a corner of the bloody sheet and unrolled out the small body inside.

I needed a better view. I went to the light switch and turned it on, looking back at the corpse.

It was Mr Gilgeaous. His white fur was matted and wet, slicking it down so it didn't look like fur. Blood ran from his mouth and his once green eyes were bloodshot – he looked like he'd been eaten up from the inside by some sort of poison. What had looked like horns in the dark were his two black pointed ears that jutted up from the top of his head.

I staggered and fell back on the bed, my brain swimming. Whatever was in Mr Gilgeaous' blood had made him go psychotic, then it would have entered my bloodstream as he bit and scratched me.

For a moment I wondered if the cat had died of rabies, in which case it had given it to me and I would die as well. But there was no foam at its mouth. No, it had been poisoned with some deadly drug.

"So Mr Gilgeaous, you found your way back home," I spoke to the small cadaver.

Marquis Thorn had said he would send something to visit me. Was this his handiwork? A cat that never liked me driven murderously insane by hallucinogenic drugs. I suppose that if Mr Gilgeaous had torn my throat out, he could have killed me but the police would not have treated it as murder.

For a second, I thought of reporting this to the police or Ives directly but what could I say? I was attacked by a cat. Hardly a major crime.

118

And what about the men Ives had said would watch over me? I now had the feeling that he had said that just to fob me off.

I suddenly felt very violated and very angry. They would not get away with this. I went crazy and though I could hardly stand up I wanted revenge.

I got to my feet, swaying all over the place, gathered up the dead cat in the sheet and staggered downstairs. I knew what I had to do even though it was the middle of the night. Danny Stein had bought Grimoire Priory, the big secluded mansion that was at the heart of all this evil and I would drive down to see if he had taken up residence with any other of the Felix Hoad gang. If he had I would confront him. And if Marquis Thorn was there, I just wanted to punch him in the face and knock those gold teeth out!

Hardly sane thinking I know but I had just been frightened half to death and some of the drugs that had killed the cat were in my bloodstream.

I looked round for a weapon. All the antiques in my place and nothing I could use as a weapon... Then I found a sterling silver letter opened designed to look like a Persian dagger. That would do.

So I drove to Grimoire Priory in my van. Fortunately it was in the middle of the night and roads were deserted otherwise I might have hit someone. My driving was erratic to say the least. If I had been sane, I would never have driven there, into the Lion's Den.

I made it and pulled up outside the iron railings. I found that the gates were locked but I wasn't going to use the speaker in the brick column to announce my visit. I wanted to surprise them.

I kept a torch in the van and put it in my pocket. I was going to need it tonight.

Holding Mr Gilgeaous in one hand, still wrapped in a bloody sheet, I climbed onto the roof of my van and from there I mounted the top of the railings, a dangerous business as they were spiked on top.

From there I jumped down to the ground, a jump I would never have attempted if I had not been out of my mind.

I stood up in the grounds of Grimoire Priory and started to fight my way through the branches and brambles that seemed to reach out for me as I made for the house.

It was pitch dark but I ploughed ahead to where I sensed the building would be.

I stopped suddenly and waited quietly for a moment. There was a rustling in the bushes behind me. I had the strong feeling that I was being followed. Perhaps they had guard dogs?

I reached in my jacket pocket for the comforting feel of the silver dagger but left it there.

There were more noises but softer and more furtive than any guard dog would make.

Whatever lurked in the deep dark woods was smaller than dogs and there was more than one of them. The branches swayed and trembled as small things scuttled in and around them.

There were barely heard whispers as if the things were talking to each other. They were closing in on me.

I started running ahead, faster than ever, oblivious to the thorns that scratched at me as I tried to find my way out.

Suddenly I was out of the bramble and in the open grounds before Grimoire Priory. I looked behind me. I sensed rather than heard a deep sigh and glimpsed a black shadow retreat into the trees and disappear into the woods.

I approached the far from welcoming Grimoire Priory. The building with its turrets and unlit windows—even the murky stonewalled pond before it – looked more menacing at night.

I ignored the front door and circled the building looking for a way in. In the end I settled for an unsubtle approach and smashed a window with a rock. I reached in, unfastened the window, climbed over the windowsill and dropped into clammy darkness.

I was inside.

I pulled out my torch and switched it on. I was in a small room with lots of old paintings hung on the wall. They looked like pictures of Victorian hardcore pornography. Most were naked obviously but the hairstyles gave the age of the paintings away which were more than a century out of fashion. The women wore severe buns while the men sported long side whiskers and moustaches that drooped down to their chins.

The paintings portrayed more than just crude sex. There was cruelty and graphic, bloody murder. It was the gallery from Hell.

"Disgusting," I said aloud. I was glad to find a door out of the room.

Once through the door I found myself in a long corridor and I moved along it towards large double doors at the end. There was a chink of light under the doors.

If there were people there, I would confront them.

I pushed open the double doors and bright light flooded out, making me blink and wince. It was coming from a crystal chandelier that hung from the high ceiling.

I was in a huge hall with a blazing walk-in fireplace in one wall and a huge dining table down the centre set with plates, cutlery and wine bottles and glasses. The centrepiece of the table was the biggest silver platter I had ever seen covered with a giant, curved, ornate silver lid, big enough to cover a whole full-grown pig.

Where were the diners? I looked around. The hall appeared empty apart from a man and woman dressed like a butler and a maid. There was something very odd about them. They stood still and stiff like a pair of guards on duty, holding empty trays and they did not register my entrance. They were about thirty, good looking but expressionless. The woman had on a very short black skirt with a frilly petticoat beneath that pushed the skirt upwards so I could see that she was not wearing any underwear. The man was no better. He had on very tight, shiny black trousers with open flies to let his genitalia hang out.

They seemed to be waiting for someone to tell them what to do. I cleared my throat but before I could speak the silver platter on the table moved and the cover above it clattered.

I was startled. Was the main course still alive?

"What is under there?" I asked the servants but they continued to stare into space without reaction.

I reached out to lift the lid.

"Take your hand away, Mr Bell, or I will pin it to the table!" The familiar voice that sounded behind me was that of Mrs Harriet Milverton. I turned round to face her. She had removed one of the long steel bobby pins from the bun in her hair and held it like a dagger, ready to strike.

I gingerly pulled my hand back from the serving dish.

"Hello again, Mrs Milverton. I have brought you a gift," I said as I tossed the bloody corpse of Mr Gilgeaous on the table.

"Unhygienic." Mrs Milverton twisted her face up at the dead cat, making her look even uglier than she already was. Then she stuck the pin back in her bun.

"I've had enough of the murders, attempts on my life and all the cover ups. I have come here to have it out," I swayed before her. "What happened to your guests?" I gestured at the empty chairs.

"They will be here. We are awaiting the host," she grinned, showing yellow teeth.

"And what is with those two?" I gestured to the butler and maid with the embarrassing dress sense.

"He is Pooh and she is Piglet. Those are their slave names. They have no agenda of their own except total obedience and surrender. They would have ignored you as they have not been instructed to serve you."

The double doors burst open and slammed against the wall. A man entered, a big, broad man with a tightly trimmed black beard and moustache around his thick sensual lips and big sad brown eyes. He trundled around to the far side of the table and placed a box of doughnuts on the table.

"I guess you have just carried out a kill," Mrs Milverton said to him.

"Indeed. You know me. I always need a sugar rush afterwards." He started devouring the first of the doughnuts. His voice was rich and fruity, like a classically trained actor. He waved at Pooh the butler who poured him wine into a ceramic chalice to wash it down. "Who is this?" he asked Mrs Milverton as he examined me.

124

"Ronan Bell," she answered.

"I have heard much about you Mr Bell." He regarded me with his large sad brown eyes as he continued to munch at the doughnut. "Abel Vasko, assistant managing director, QPL, at your service."

The doors opened again on another man, much older and thinner this time. His hair lay on his skull like damp quills and his skin was grey, slimy, wrinkled and unhealthy looking. He rushed in with a mobile phone to his ear, a tinny ringing sound could be heard emanating from it.

The old man spoke to me. "I am Ocious Squibb, spelt with two bs, director, QPL. The two bs are important to me. I get angry when my name is misspelt. And you are the Ronan Bell who has been causing us some annoyance I presume?"

"Mr Squibb is our most prolific assassin," Mrs Milverton told me with some pride.

I looked at the scrawny old man with disbelief. "You?" I asked.

"You think that all killers are muscle bound thugs? I am an intellectual assassin. I get many ideas from Shakespeare: blowing of poison into an ear, drowning in a vat of wine and so on. However I have also moved with the times. Much like the assignment I am working on now. I just have to complete this job before we start," he apologised.

Then his phone was answered and he sat down.

"Mr Fabian?" he spoke into the phone with a thin, reedy voice. "This is the British Gas engineer here. We have sorted out all your heating and hot water now. We just need you to turn on the boiler to test it. Try it for me and let me know if it comes on."

125

He waited in silence, tapping his teeth with a fingernail.

There was a loud explosion heard over the phone. Then it went dead.

The old man smiled, a cold, heartless smile, and threw his mobile phone across the room and into the fireplace where it burned up among the coal and logs.

"A disposable phone that cannot be traced back to anyone," he said as he rose from the chair and made towards me.

"I don't suppose that you checked to see if the man's wife and children were at home before you blew his house up?" Vasko asked Squibb.

"Why should I? I just carried out my contract."

"That is the difference between us," Vasko said as he gobbled down a second doughnut. "I would have. I have killed many over the years and decades gone by but they were all men. Never women or children. And I hardly ever used a gun. I hate the things."

"What just happened here? Did you kill someone by telephone?" I asked, numbly, knowing the truth.

"Yes, it would have blown his whole house up. I always say that there is never any reason to meet up with a target to dispatch them." He chuckled and drew close to me. "In fact I am an exponent of the contactless kill."

And as he chuckled his foul breath hit me. I grimaced and turned away. His breath was bad enough to cause fresh meat to putrefy. Suddenly I remembered Peter Wilde telling me about the ancient IT guy with halitosis who had worked on his computer.

"It was you – you caused Peter Wilde's computer to explode in his face," I accused him.

"Guilty as charged. Getting away with murder is so easy when you are not there yourself," Ocious Squibb said with pride. As he smiled his teeth clicked and clacked in his mouth, his ill-fitting dentures moving independently of his shrunken gums.

"Peter Wilde was my friend. I will make sure that you answer for that, you nasty old man!"

"You wouldn't believe how many people have threatened me over the years and, guess what, I have survived them all," Squibb smiled. "You should take the blame for Wilde's death yourself. After all it was you that provoked him into sticking his nose into things that were none of his business."

A new voice spoke from the doorway: "I am still angry about the way you despatched Wilde. You could have got rid of him without costing my newspaper half a day's work and many water-logged computers." I turned to see Marquis Thorn swagger in.

"It had to be a suspicion free accident," Squibb shrugged.

Thorn was followed close behind by Andries, his helicopter pilot. Now he was not wearing his pilot's uniform I had a better view of him. He was very big and walked with his legs wide apart. His arms were also held out at his side with a clenched fist at either end. He had the stance of a weightlifter or body builder. His unusually thin lips looked as if they had been sliced out of his face and gave him a permanent sneer. Andries sat down at the table.

"It was overkill," Andries backed up his boss, speaking in that same South African accent.

"Death always has consequences," Squibb dismissed their criticisms but froze as he caught sight of

127

the remains of Mr Gilgeaous. The change in him was instantaneous. He staggered back in horror and seemed to go even greyer, if that were possible. He tottered back to the other side of the table and sank into a chair, turning it round so he did not have to look at the table.

I think I was starting to understand why Squibb preferred to kill from a distance.

Thorn nodded in my direction: "We meet again, Mr Bell. Can we expect some more murder and mayhem?" He then glanced at Piglet the maid who instantly brought him a chalice of wine.

"I didn't know that the help was being invited to this dinner party," Mrs Milverton directed a sneer at Andries.

"Andries is more than my pilot," Thorn defended him. "He is a bloodied member of the inner circle."

"My name, Andries, is Dutch for warrior and I live up to my name. Don't make an enemy of me, you ugly old hag," Andries scowled at her.

Of the two I was more frightened of Mrs Milverton.

In spite of my drugged up state I was forcing myself to remember all these names as I planned to tell Ives the full story the next day and also to get him to investigate any fatal gas explosions.

Then someone else entered and the atmosphere in the room became more threatening.

I looked round to see a smartly dressed man with soulless, black eyes that were too close together, under bushy black eyebrows.

His face was fixed in an expression of pure hate and it was a face you would never forget.

Danny Stein.

128

Ives would certainly want to know when I told him that Stein was at the party.

Those black unblinking eyes settled on me.

"I see we have a gatecrasher," Stein spoke in a deep, rasping voice. "Would you like me to get rid of him?" He flexed his fingers till the bones cracked, as if he was preparing for a fight.

"Hold off for the moment," Vasko spoke to him with a smile. "We do not want to have to get you off another murder so soon. This is the Ronan Bell you have heard us talk about."

A nervous Pooh brought Stein a large whisky.

Stein brought his face within inches of mine. "I find you irritating, Mr Bell," he said. "And that is enough motive for me to kill you."

He stared at me for what seemed forever. "My late wife always said she found me irritating as well," I stuttered. "I can't help it."

"I might let you live if you can be of use to me. I have just bought this place as I had to have somewhere fitting to live for someone of my status. A load of junk came with the property and while I would like to chuck it all out some of it may be valuable antiques. I understand you are an expert in valuing and restoring old stuff. You must go through it all for me, saving what is worth saving and ditching the crap."

The last thing I had expected from Danny Stein was an offer of a job. "I would be happy to," I murmured nervously.

"I have a lot of close celebrity friends. Real Hollywood stars. I want to invite them here for dinner parties and impress them."

"I can go through it all and restore what needs to be restored," I said.

"Make sure you do. It is not good to cross Danny Stein. That ends badly," he threatened.

He watched me silently as I sweated and squirmed. It was a great relief when he looked away and moved off.

He was about to sit down when he realised that he was about to sit next to Ocious Squibb. He grimaced and moved to another chair. "I can't sit next to that Pen and Ink," he said.

I wondered if Squibb knew enough Cockney rhyming slang to know that Pen and Ink meant Stink. Squibb smiled coldly, causing his dentures to click and clack.

"For goodness sake it is like Spanish castanets. Dentists don't fit plates anymore. Get yourself some modern implants!" Stein growled.

They were all sitting down so I sunk down into the nearest chair.

I was wondering how many more dinner guests there were to come when the next one burst through the doors.

He was big and black and wore a vicar's dog collar and a heavy gold crucifix on a chain around his neck. I felt he was vaguely familiar.

"Now the Shaman has arrived we can have prayers before dinner," Mrs Milverton said with some contempt.

"Please, just Archbishop Augustus Ighodaro will do," the black man spoke in a deep, booming voice. He looked at Mrs Milverton with distaste.

Yes, I did remember him. Augustus Ighodaro came to the UK as an illegal immigrant from an African country ruled by a despot. He had been a police chief there and it was said he arrested and condemned many of his own country men and women to death just for speaking out again the tyrant. Of course, as always happens with tyrants, the ruler eventually turned on him and he had to flee for his life.

Once in the UK he made a great play of repentance and found a new profession in the church. He gained a name for himself as a Bishop who worked in council estates and inner cities to rehabilitate drug addicted young criminals. He was portrayed as the saviour of the disaffected. And then suddenly he was appointed an Archbishop at one of our historic cathedrals. He had been tipped as a possible future Archbishop of Canterbury.

Ighodaro looked at me. "We have an outsider, I see. I hope you can join us in worship, Mr Ronan Bell. I prayed for your wife. May God protect you tonight, my son." He chuckled, a deep, mirthless sound.

Then the covered silver platter on the table jolted again as though something stirred beneath the lid.

"What have you got under there?" I asked no one in particular.

"That is a speciality of the house," came a new voice from the doorway. A man and woman entered the room with linked arms. He wore a white coat while she had on an expensive looking mink coat.

It was the woman who had spoken and she waved a finger at me: "Not yet. It will not be served until we are all here."

"I hope it is swan again." Squibb leered. "I do so love committing treason with a knife and fork in my hand."

I recognised the couple from Peter's newspaper story.

They were Rick and Zoe Leppard, the animal loving vets who were opening Haven, the controversial state-of-the-art animal hospital.

Rick looked down at the corpse of Mr Gilgeaous.

"Looks like you had quite a fight," he said. "All that GBH was unnecessary. It was only a matter of time before his heart would have burst after we infected him."

"I thought you were animal lovers!" I said.

"Don't believe everything you read. I love occasions like this when I can drop the animal loving pretence and wear my furs," Zoe Leppard pulled the mink coat around her. "We use our furred and feathered friends in our quest for higher power. The old ones who we follow were constantly using Mother Nature for research, hence the creation of the black sparrows. Now we can combine the old wisdom with the latest technology to create creatures to serve us and our causes".

"What did you do to Mr Gilgeaous?" I asked.

"What a ridiculous name. Your late wife asked us to take care of him and we did. We had help in turning that ugly cat into a killer. Mrs Milverton has been a treasure when it comes to old drug and herb research and she assisted in helping us drive kitty crazy," Rick Leppard seemed happy to explain. "We gave your cat just a drop of this." He produced a phial of clear liquid from his inside pocket. "It is a blend of old mind-altering opiates such as Laudanum and classic witches' weeds like Datura, mixed with modern synthesised hallucinogenic drugs. A drop on his tongue, paws and teeth was enough to make him go completely psycho

132

and also infect you when he bit and scratched you, but not enough to kill you. However this phial contains enough of the stuff to kill not just you but a whole herd of cows. We have nick named it Harriet's Hellfire." Rick Leppard returned the phial to his pocket. "The great thing about Harriet's Hellfire is that it can drive you mad or kill you, depending on the dose, but it quickly dissipates from the body and does not show up in an autopsy. It is the perfect murder weapon."

"I know hundreds of ways to kill without it looking like murder," Mrs Milverton waved a hand. "Let us get back to tonight. If dinner guests continue to arrive we should soon have 13 for a proper coven."

"It only works if all are true believers," Squibb said. "Pooh and Piglet only believe what we tell them to believe so they don't count and Mr Bell is certainly a non-believer. So we are far from the magic number."

"C'est la vie," Mrs Milverton slipped into a bit of uncharacteristic French. "But tonight is going to be really unusual I promise you." She gave a jagged smile that chilled me to the bone.

The door opened behind me and everyone looked up. It went very still and quiet for a moment. I looked round.

Detective Superintendent Ives stood in the open double doors.

"Nobody move. This is a police raid!" he barked.

Relief swept over me but it did not last.

"Hallo, hallo," Danny Stein rasped. "It's the fuzz."

And then everyone relaxed and laughed.

"My dear Mr Bell," Ives smiled and looked at me. "I see you have met everyone and made yourself at home." He walked round the table to Danny Stein and gave him a warm hug. "So difficult keeping up the pretence of hating you all the time, you old psycho," he said to Stein.

"All coppers are bastards but you are an exception," Stein retorted.

They parted and Ives sank into a chair.

"You were part of this all along?" I was flabbergasted. "Of course - it was you who sabotaged Stein's evidence from the inside to make sure he got off."

"That and I helped bribe and terrify jurors," Ives shrugged. "I got myself assigned to Estelle's case just to meet you and find out how much you knew. I wouldn't normally involve myself with the suicide of a washed-up old bitch."

"Go to Hell," was all I could think to say.

"I hope so," was his answer.

"Is that dead thing still on the table?" Squibb spoke from behind his hands at the end of the table.

"Not any longer," Mrs Milverton picked up what was left of Mr Gilgeaous and tossed it into the fireplace. The fire roared and burned bright blue for a moment as it consumed the £2,000 corpse. Then the fire died as the dead cat extinguished the flames and the temperature dropped almost instantly. However it continued to smoulder.

It seemed to create a lot of smoke. Suddenly it was billowing out of the hearth and filling the room, choking white smoke that made me cough and my eyes water.

"A side effect of Harriet's Hellfire," Rick Leppard explained. "It is very combustible."

And then it was hard to see anyone as we were all enveloped in the swirling smoke.

134

"What the fuck is going on? Open a window someone," Danny Stein complained.

No one answered and the silence became heavy and oppressive. Acrid smoke continued to billow out of the fireplace until that was all I could see.

I turned suddenly as I had sensed movement in the blinding fog.

The cut on my hand started to bleed again, blood dripping to the floor. I tried to stem the flow with a handkerchief.

The plates and chalices on the table began to shake and clatter. The table was moving, a gentle tremor to start with but getting more violent. The giant silver server vibrated. My chair jolted suddenly and I gripped it hard. Other chairs around the table also shuddered and shook to the alarm of those who sat in them.

The clouds of smoke were forming into a shape in front of me.

Gradually I made out the outline of a tall, spindly, crouching male figure with an abnormally large head. It wavered and shimmered indistinctly before me. The overlarge head trembled as if it was too heavy for the long scrawny neck. It raised a ghostly arm and the table stopped shaking. A silence descended as we all stared at the apparition.

Then a voice came from it. A voice like no other – golden, mellow and hypnotic. And it spoke to me.

"How dare you sit uninvited with my disciples, Ronan Bell Esquire?"

"It is him. It is Quincy Pitt. Praise be," Zoe Leppard spoke in hushed tones, unseen in the fog.

The ghostly figure wavered in the white mist as if it was trying to tune in to them.

135

I felt I was facing Lucifer himself. I pulled the sterling silver dagger from my pocket and threw it at the spectre.

It spat and hissed at me and then began to dissolve as the smoke dissipated and was sucked away up the chimney. It was as if a giant vacuum cleaner had been switched on.

The air cleared and I could see the people round the table again. Standing before me was not the stooped, ancient and spindly Quincy Pitt but the man I recognised as Felix Hoad. He was tall, straight and strong, immaculately dressed, with ruffs at his collar and sleeves. His face was surrounded by long white hair; even his eyebrows and lashes were snow white. He regarded me with contempt.

"Just some simple magic of mine. An illusion of the master to prepare you for the real thing," Hoad spoke to the gathering in a silky voice. "You are not ready for the master yet but soon it will be time for his ascension."

He held my silver dagger, caught in one hand, and threw it back at me. The dagger stuck deep into the wooden tabletop before me where it quivered.

"You can't harm me, pathetic maggot," Hoad spat at me with disgust. "I am invincible."

I found some courage. "What is this? Some sort of last supper for you and your disciples?" I asked.

"It will be a last supper for someone," Hoad chuckled as he walked round the table.

As he passed me, he looked at my cut and bleeding hand and said: "That will teach you to treat my picture with more respect.

"You have met everyone. Today they are all rich and powerful but when they first met me they were

136

losers; ruthless, determined, angry losers. Once they accepted me and my beliefs and ambitions, I was able to transform their pathetic lives."

He touched Archbishop Augustus Ighodaro on the shoulder and the man flinched as if he were to be struck.

"He was an illegal immigrant in a detention centre about to be deported back to the dictator who would kill him when I saved him. In return he dedicated his life to me."

Then his hand moved to Danny Stein who for the first time looked really uncomfortable.

"A drug dealer and petty criminal heading back to jail when I met him. Look at what I have made him. Even the Krays would fear him now," Hoad gloated.

Next, he touched Marquis Thorn. "A small-time newspaper proprietor in South Africa when first we met. Now he ranks as one of the biggest media barons in the world."

Then he put a hand on both of the Leppards. "They were running a sleazy veterinarian practice in the middle of nowhere when I came across them. A place of shit, straw and disease. Now they are famous television stars and we are building them an animal hospital that is the envy of the National Health Service. They are continuing many of the experiments on living creatures carried out by the old alchemists. We look to them to redesign and create new life to surpass our black sparrows. The ultimate aim is to be able to artificially produce the homunculus, tiny people endowed with magical insight and power. Our friend Rodney Scobey had carried out much research into the creation of his own homunculus but we do not know how far he got because he refused to share his results with the rest of us. He was not a team player. His secrecy probably cost him his life.

"Tell me, Mr Bell, how was your walk through the woods to here?" Hoad suddenly asked.

"Why do you ask?" I was surprised by his question.

"Well whatever Scobey was working on escaped and tore him to pieces. They are now lurking in the deep dark woods around this house. It is hard to see them let alone catch them but I think they are more than lab rats," Hoad chuckled. "You never know who or what you might meet out there."

Of course, whatever they were, they would not go far, I thought, because Grimoire Priory was a magnet for everything foul and unclean.

Hoad moved on. His hands rested on Ocious Squibb and Abel Vasko at the same time.

"These two are different because both were successful directors of the QPL group when I first encountered them. Both are proficient killers but with very different styles. The QPL group offers a Blue-Chip assassination service. We orchestrate everything. The death we provide is rarely seen to be murder unless there is someone convenient to frame and we make sure that those who have hired us are well alibied and above suspicion. Squibb and Vasko formerly worked under Nick Mercer who was CEO at QPL. Mercer had mentored me to take over from him so when he disappeared so suddenly, I was ready to step into his shoes."

Then he grabbed Ives by his ear. "This one was a humble police constable with a penchant for bribery, corruption and the torture of suspects until I gave him focus and pushed him up the ranks. He is now our inside man at the highest level of law enforcement."

Hoad then came over to Harriet Milverton. "Of course I cannot forget my dear Harriet who has introduced me to so much and made all this possible. None of this would have happened without her. My dear, sweet Mambo." Hoad leaned over and kissed her on the lips.

"Her lips may be dry and shrivelled but she can give oral sex like no one else," Hoad smirked.

I felt sick.

"One last introduction. Our main course – our star prize." Hoad reached for the huge silver platter and lifted the lid.

A naked red-haired girl crouched on the platter, her eyes glazed and glittering. She rocked gently, murmuring to herself. Her body was dusted with freckles and she appeared to be in her late twenties. She blinked at her surroundings but seemed to be in a world of her own.

"Who is she?" I asked.

"She is Tipota. That is the name she has given herself – Tipota, which is Greek for Nothing. She is a homeless street urchin without traceable identity. I have used her for sex already but I did it without damaging her. She is a Nobody which is the name I prefer to call her. It is important that she is not damaged too much for tonight's winner who will be able to do with her whatever they want," Hoad leered.

She was a beautiful lost soul and my heart went out to her. "None of those depraved scum bags will have her. I will save her," I promised myself, not sure how I could keep such a promise.

The girl turned on the platter and looked up at me as if she had heard what I had thought.

"Let us all sit down and relax and drink to the next election. Let's hope for a change of party so I can get more of my followers into the government." Hoad dropped into the biggest chair at the end. Like the other men he took off his jacket and hung it over the back of the chair.

I noticed Vasko furtively remove the jacket and hand it to Pooh – who almost dropped it as it was weighed down heavily on one side from something concealed within. Pooh took it away.

I sank into a chair and was given the same ceramic chalice as everyone else. Piglet filled it with wine.

I looked at it suspiciously.

"My wife Estelle. Was she part of all this?" I asked the room.

"We are the modern Hellfire Club. Estelle joined us with enthusiasm at the beginning but she had no stamina," Hoad answered. "When we got down to the real, bloody business, she reverted to being a provincial housewife with no stomach for our ungodly work.

"I was happy for Harriet to give you her address as you were starting to be a nuisance as you searched for her. I hoped that would end it but as it turned out you just became even more of a nuisance with all your questions and bringing in other people on your quest. It is a pity because Estelle was delightful and gave me much pleasure in the early days before she, belatedly, developed a conscience."

"You are not touching your wine, Mr Bell," Ives said.

140

"You people have already poisoned me once tonight. I don't think so," I said.

"Swap with me," Rick Leppard gave me his chalice and took mine. He sipped from what had been my chalice. "See, no poison."

"A toast to The Greater Bad," Hoad raised his chalice and the others followed and gulped it down.

My toast was different. "To retribution," I said and began drinking.

The red wine felt warm and peppery as it flowed down my throat.

"This is not the best wine in the cellar. I still have Rodney Scobey's vintage wine collection. Mrs Milverton, you know where the best wine is kept. Go and fetch us some," Stein asked her.

"I am not your housekeeper," Mrs Milverton stood up. "However I want to drink the best tonight." She left the room.

Almost immediately Andries stood up and followed her out of the room.

"It is always the strongest looking ones who have the weakest bladders," Thorn smiled.

The alcohol was strong and in my drugged condition it went to my head. Everything had slowed to slow motion and there were cotton wool clouds in my head. I tried to pull myself together as I needed to have my wits about me. "So what are you? Devil worshippers?" I asked.

"We are sybarites, worshippers of the sensual vices. And of course they worship me as their deity," Hoad smirked.

"And who do you worship as your deity?" I asked.

141

"I expect you think it is Lucifer, the prince of darkness, but no. It is Quincy Pitt."

"Some long dead Victorian. Why?"

"He is my mentor from beyond the grave and the founder of our empire. Tall and imposing, a man everyone worshipped. He founded QPL and we are all carrying on with his good, or should I say bad, work. He has a sixth finger on his right hand, a powerful symbol of his power. He lived long and some say he was immortal. He foresaw the sun setting on the British Empire and America becoming the most powerful country in the world. He took his teachings to the New World and some say he never came back. It is reported that he died in America at the end of the 1800s when he was set upon by an angry mob from the Religious Right of the day. They chased him into a Florida swamp which sucked him under. They never found a body and never will," Hoad chuckled.

"Surely you can't believe that this man is still alive?" I asked.

But before he could answer Rick Leppard spoke: "Oh dear. Have we all drunk our wine?"

They all looked at their empty chalices and nodded.

"Then I have to report a mishap." He pulled the phial out of his pocket again. Only this time it was not full of Harriet's Hellfire. It was empty!

"I appear to have spilled the whole lot into someone's drink. There was enough in there to kill ten people. I wonder who drank it," he laughed.

Andries came back into the room and looked around. "What have I missed?" he asked.

"One of us is about to drop dead," Hoad told him. "I wonder who?"

142

And then they were all looking at me.
"Oh Christ," was all I could think of to say.

"It works very quick. Any moment now," Zoe Leppard watched me closely.

"Pity. I had something much slower in mind for you, Mr Bell." Hoad regarded me with amusement. Then he looked around. "Where is Harriet? She is taking a long time to get that wine."

Abel Vasko spoke: "That woman has too much power. She rules through you. We should get rid of her."

Hoad looked taken aback. "I had no idea you thought about Harriet like that. Do you dare to question my choice of deputies?" He stood and looked as if he was going too continue berating Vasko, but nothing but a strangled cough escaped his lips. He twitched and trembled all over his body. "No, you wouldn't dare…" Hoad gasped and then shuddered. "What have you done?" He fell and doubled up on the floor, bending in half at his stomach which seemed to be wracked with violent cramps.

"Harriet!" Hoad cried. "Come quick. Bring the antidote!"

He reached up for the back of his chair but then realised that his jacket was not there. "My jacket, where is it?" Hoad gasped.

He crawled away from the table on his hands and knees and away from them as if he were looking for a dark corner to curl and die in.

"Too late for any antidote or flushing of your system. You have consumed much too much," Ocious Squibb looked down at him without pity. Squibb did not seem squeamish about watching someone being poisoned. It was blood he seemed to have a phobia about.

"I locked Mrs Milverton in the wine cellar as instructed," Andries said.

"We had to get her out of the way. We knew she would come to your defence. I hope she is not contaminating the wine. I am not releasing that old witch," Danny Stein said.

"Why have you done this? I am your God. I gave you everything," Hoad gurgled as he squirmed on the floor.

His eyes had become deep red and blood flowed from the sockets and down his cheeks. Squibb looked away, confirming my suspicion.

"We all wanted to be free of you and your power over us," Marquis Thorn spoke to the dying man.

"I am going to become the next CEO following your sad death," Vasko told him.

"Not if I have anything to do with it," Squibb protested.

"Pitt, Pitt do not forsake me!" It was Hoad's last cry as his red eyes suddenly flickered out and the life light behind them was extinguished. He slumped into a heap on the floor.

"Is he really dead? That seemed too easy." Zoe Leppard peered down at the body.

"Let me check." Her husband walked across the room and knelt down beside Hoad, feeling his pulse. After a moment, he stood up. "Trust me. I can put your minds at rest. The beast is dead. Give it a few hours and then they can carry out as many post-mortems as they like but the only possible verdict will be natural causes. Do you want to say a few words, Archbishop?"

"Fuck off, Felix. There is a special place for him in Hell, I am sure," Archbishop Ighodaro sneered at the corpse.

Rick returned to the table and they all sat down.

"We should dump his body away from here. I do not want to be implicated," Danny Stein said.

"We can always blame our unwanted guest," Ives was smiling at me. "We have CCTV footage of him breaking in here. He is on record as threatening Felix Hoad." He turned to me. "You are the perfect patsy. You of course cannot leave here, ever. You will be blamed for his murder and you will commit suicide immediately afterwards."

I backed away but Ocious Squibb blocked my retreat. "Death is your only escape, Mr Bell," Squibb grimaced, his foul breath washing over my senses.

"You devise how best you want to kill Mr Bell but I would like to lay claim to Miss Nobody here," Archbishop Ighodaro said. "We don't have to worry about anything she saw here. She is too far gone to be a witness. However tomorrow, August 1, is Lammas Night. A time to give homage. My cathedral is closed for renovations. What better time for me to drag in my own faithful congregation from the council estate and offer her up as a sacrifice within the Holy Cathedral."

146

"It is a great idea. If she was slaughtered as part of a Black Mass it would defile and desanctify the historic cathedral forever." Thorn smiled.

"I won't let you do it. I am taking her home," I protested, sounding braver than I felt.

"Not so pure after all, are we, Mr Bell? You want your own pretty little slave to play with," Ocious Squibb leered at me. "Sorry, she is for sacrificing tomorrow and you are next for the chop tonight."

"I will hold Black Mass at 8pm. Danny, can you provide a bouncer to man the doors and keep any intruders out? The password is Black Sparrow," Ighodaro announced. "It will be Miss Nobody's last day on earth and a Lammas Day to remember."

"Sure. Brogan will be the ideal doorman. Thick as shit but a trusted lieutenant and no one gets past him when he is on guard duty. I'll send him down tomorrow," Stein promised.

There came a loud shrieking and crashing from below. They all stood up and started out.

"You two, guard the body!" Stein barked at Piglet and Pooh.

Then everyone else rushed out. Still feeling doped out of my head I tugged my silver dagger free of the table and followed them. If I had been clear headed, I would have realised that it was the perfect opportunity to grab the girl and run for it.

We scurried down stone steps to find an old oak door with iron hinges and an iron lock dangling from the smashed door.

"Mrs Milverton. She has broken free!" Zoe Leppard screamed.

147

"Where does that old crone get her strength?" Vasko chuckled in amusement.

There was no sign of the old woman. We returned to the banqueting hall. The girl - Nobody – still lay on the platter.

Then Zoe screamed again. "The body! It has gone!"

It was true. Hoad's corpse no longer lay where they had left it.

Piglet and Pooh lay stretched out on the floor with blood on their heads. Zoe Leppard examined them.

"They are still alive. They have been knocked unconscious," she pronounced.

"Who moved Hoad's body?" Vasko strode around the room. "Someone must have dragged it away while we were gone."

"It couldn't have been Mrs Milverton. She wouldn't have had time," Thorn mused. "It can't be far." Thorn marched through the double doors into the corridor.

With a deafening shriek, Felix Hoad leapt out of the darkness and on top of Thorn, his hands clasping Thorn's throat.

"Get him off me. He is still alive!" Thorn gurgled.

Hoad looked insane. His red eyes were enlarged and bulging from their sockets and foam flecked his lips.

Danny Stein came up behind and clubbed Hoad on the back of his head with a wooden chair.

"You should have let me kill him," Stein grumbled. "When I kill them they stay dead."

The blow knocked Hoad off Thorn and onto the floor for a moment but then Hoad sprang to his feet and leapt at Stein.

Andries, the not so gentle giant, grasped Hoad and began to pull him off Stein but Hoad lashed out and

148

flung Andries against the wall. Where did the man get his strength?

Vasko waded in and brought Hoad down with a rugby tackle. He then began punching his face.

Hoad pushed the heavy Vasko off him and sprang up once again. He stood there looking around at them all with blood running from his nose and mouth and searing hatred in his burning red eyes.

"So much for Harriet's Hellfire. She must have known our plan and changed the potion for something harmless," Zoe chimed in.

"You cannot kill me. I am immortal. How dare you defy me and turn against me? I will have vengeance. You will all suffer a long slow death at my hands for this," Hoad croaked.

"I am going for my gun. Let me see you survive a bullet." Stein started for the exit.

But Hoad turned and ran ahead of him, running along the corridor towards the door to the outside.

Hoad reached the doors and pulled them open.

"Stop him!" Squibb held back but shouted orders; the sight of blood had caused him to go sick and woozy again. "Don't let him get out amongst the trees. We could lose him!"

I had joined in the chase but to be honest I did not know whose side I was on – hunters or prey? If they all killed each other it would be justice.

Hoad turned in the open doorway and glared at them all, waving a clenched fist, his face twisted in rage. "I made you all and I will destroy you all. Everything you are you owe to me. You will pay in pain and blood for this treachery!" he hissed in a shower of blood-flecked spittle.

Archbishop Augustus Ighodaro reached him first and stood before Hoad, his head bowed.

"Augustus! I saved your life. Don't let them do this to me!" Hoad pleaded to the Archbishop.

In one vicious movement Ighodaro head butted him in the face. "Bless you my son," he chuckled. Hoad staggered back with more blood pouring from his mouth, nose and eyes.

Vasko and Ives pushed Ighodaro aside, crashing against Hoad and knocking him out into the grounds.

Hoad punched them away, turned and tried to run. They were outside the house now and in the wild, overgrown garden.

Rick Leppard had found a spade in the garden and advanced on Hoad with it raised above his head.

He reached the fleeing Hoad and swung the spade. It hit Hoad firmly on the back of the head with a resounding clunk.

Hoad was propelled forward, hitting the brick wall that surrounded the slime-filled pond with the non-working fountain in its centre.

Andries had found a garden fork and he jabbed it in Hoad's back.

With a great bellow Hoad plunged headfirst into the green water. He struggled and splashed, getting caught up in the foul-smelling vegetation.

"What if he cannot die? What have we done?" Zoe joined her husband.

"Everyone dies but we may just have made it harder in his case," Rick answered her.

"We should never have played around with regeneration." Zoe was sobbing.

"Which is why we did it. And we can undo it," her husband reassured her.

Rick hit Hoad with the spade again and pushed him down till only his head was visible above the sludge. Vasko and Thorn knelt at the pond side and pushed down on his head while Hoad gasped, cursed and spat out the stinking muck. Andries and Stein came over and helped push his head under.

In spite of them Hoad pushed back and his head bobbed above the slime, gasping for air, his face covered with algae.

Ives came charging into the fray with a broken tree branch and thrust it against the drowning man. Finally Hoad sank from view with a lot of gurgling and choking.

They held him down for a long time while the stagnant water bubbled and heaved. Hoad seemed to fight and struggle beneath the mire for a long time.

Then it was silent and the men pulled their hands out of the pond. Stirring up the pond released the acrid methane gasses that had built up beneath the surface and the rancid odour was all pervading.

My hand had finally stopped bleeding.

Stein stood up. "I think we can safely say he is brown bread now. We cannot leave his body there. It will float up to the surface eventually."

"Brown bread?" Zoe queried.

"Dead," Stein translated the cockney rhyming slang for her.

"Leave his body to the frogs, water slugs and the fish to have a feast," Zoe suggested.

"No that is not the QPL way. We leave no evidence. Let us hook it out," Vasko took charge.

151

Rick and Andries plunged the spade and fork deep into the murky depths and probed the slime for the body but after a while gave up.

"It seems to be very deep. I can't find the bottom of the pond," Rick said.

While I was not the centre of attention I crept backwards into the dark shadows and slipped unnoticed amongst the tall trees.

I ran for my life. They must have realised that I had escaped because I heard shouting behind me. They were giving chase.

Then I felt a new unease and the darkness in the woods seemed to form shapes around me. The woods were alive.

Chapter Fifteen
: The longest night

I was torn between my murderous pursuers and the unknown menace in the woods.

All that talk of a homunculus and the experiments into artificial life that had escaped into the woods served to terrify me.

The trees seemed to move with a life of their own and claw out for me with thorn covered branches.

I had one thing to get me through: the torch in my pocket. I took it out and flashed it around, pushing back the shadows.

Then I ran for my life. I couldn't find the wall and I wasn't sure if I was running in the right direction. Panic started to grab me. What if I couldn't get out?

I sensed and heard all sorts of small life forms stalking me through the woods. Was it my imagination? Was it harmless rabbits or mice? My imagination started to run wild, picturing the nameless horrors that could have been chasing me.

If I could only see them I was sure that the mutated monsters that I imagined could not be as bad as the reality.Then my torch beam lighted on the spiked railings. How on earth had I got over that without impaling myself? It was too high. I moved along it and the railings became a brick wall. Then I found a tree next to the wall, climbed it and crawled along a branch to the top of the wall. I dropped off it onto the pavement.

My van was close by. I ran for it.

It was still the middle of the night and impossible to see if anyone or anything was chasing me. I just opened the door, climbed in and drove away as fast as I could. I made it home without incident.

Once inside my house I returned to my bedroom and in spite of the cold wind blowing through my broken skylight I drifted off to an exhausted sleep with a gnarled old walking stick beside me.

I don't know what woke me first: the sound of my front doorbell or the feel of wet blood from my hand.

I was bleeding again.

I wasn't going to answer the door. I sat up and waited in the darkness.

The doorbell rang again, jarringly loud in the silence.

I waited, still and silent, hoping whoever it was would give up and go away.

My outside security lights came on suddenly, lighting up my garden with a blazing glare. I crept over to the bedroom window and peered out. The lights were too bright and shining in my eyes.

Then I saw him.

Felix Hoad was in my garden, standing very still, and staring up at me, grinning.

I only glimpsed him for a second because just as suddenly the lights switched off and black night descended again.

It could not have been Hoad, I decided. The monster was well and truly dead. I was still half asleep and had imagined it.

154

Then I heard the sound of a ladder being thrown against my house.

I grabbed the walking stick and crept to the bedroom door.

Someone was above me, running over my roof.

I slipped out into the landing. There was a built-in airing cupboard where I hung my towels and sheets. I slithered into it and closed the door, watching the dark hallway through the wooden slats.

There was a crash from my bedroom. Someone was inside the house and moving around my bedroom. I heard my bed being turned over and flung to the floor. Drawers in my dressing table were pulled open and thrown down.

Then silence. Suddenly a rasping, masculine voice called: "Where is it?"

A shadow fell across the wooden slats. Whoever it was stopped just outside the cupboard that concealed me. I gripped the gnarled walking stick.

The blood was pouring profusely from my wound now. So much that I feared the intruder could hear it dripping onto the floor.

"Where have you hidden it, maggot?" the rasping voice called out. The man's breathing was laboured and heavy.

I peered between the wooden slats.

A tall, white, ghostly shape shimmered in the darkness. It moved along the landing to the top of the staircase. Then it stopped and bent double.

There was a choking noise and the spectre seemed to vomit liquid which splashed onto the floor.

Then it rose and glided down the staircase. There was the sound of my front door opening.

155

It waited an eternity for any more noises but hearing nothing I got up the courage to leave the cupboard and walk to the top of the stairs.

A cold wind blew through my open front door.

There was a filthy smell. I peered down at the disgusting liquid that had been spewed up at the top of my stairs.

It was green, slimy and foul – stagnant pond water mixed with algae.

"It can't be-?" I gasped in disbelief.

Then a hand reached up and grabbed me.

With one hand I switched on the lights and swung down with the walking stick with the other hand - but I was not quick enough.

A white-faced Felix Hoad sprang at me and knocked the stick away. Then his hands were around my throat and pushing me down.

His eyes were red and boggling and green slime still dribbled from his mouth and down onto his white shirt. Hoad looked rabid. I couldn't breathe and collapsed back on to the floor with him above me.

"Where have you put it?" Hoad demanded in his distorted voice.

I tried to gurgle an answer but it was hard to speak while being strangled.

He struck my head hard against the floor and I fought to keep conscious.

I was vaguely aware of someone else running up the stairs.

Someone shouted something that seemed to be in Latin.

Hoad looked aside at the source of the Latin incantation. The speaker was Father Sebastian Fullalove and he carried a large bag on straps over his shoulder. He reached in the bag and pulled out a metal container. He unscrewed the lid and tossed the contents of the container into Hoad's face.

Hoad shrieked like a scalded cat as the clear liquid splashed his face and his skin smouldered and smoked.

Still shrieking, Hoad jumped back, pushed past Sebastian and stumbled down the stairs and out through the open door.

I lay there breathing heavily and looking up at the defrocked priest.

There came the sound of a car driving away outside, then silence.

"Whoa, what is happening here? I got your confused phone message and thought it sounded desperate enough for me to come straight over," Sebastian said. "Thank God I came armed."

"That was Felix Hoad," I said. "Was that holy water? I have often seen holy water being used to burn demons and vampires in movies but I didn't think it could really happen."

"No it was battery acid from my car stored in a cocktail shaker. Mr Hoad will be scarred for life. But he was killing you. I had to do it."

"But I thought you chanted something in Latin."

"I did but only for effect. It was Peni Tento non Penitenti - the slogan of the original Hellfire Club and it translates as: Better penis tense than penitence."

"What sort of priest are you? Who carries battery acid around as a possible weapon?" The blood flow from my left hand had dried up almost instantly. As I looked at my hand I said, "Hoad has gone. It's safe now."

"Let us sit down and talk about this over a drink," Sebastian suggested. So we did.

We sat downstairs with a large brandy each.

"I guess Hoad drove away in that Passat Estate car I saw parked outside your house when I arrived. I think there was a woman behind the wheel but I could not see well in the dark. Who was it?"

"Mrs Harriet Milverton if I am not mistaken. Think yourself lucky not to have met her," I said. "Felix Hoad has an amazing capacity to survive whatever is done to him. I swear I saw him poisoned with blood streaming from his eyes, then I saw him drown in a pond of slimy water earlier this night. I don't believe in all this mumbo jumbo but I don't know why he is so hard to kill. I can't go to the police now. I don't trust any of them. But we must stop this girl they call Nobody being sacrificed in some Lammas Night ritual in the cathedral tomorrow evening."

"There must be some police we can trust," Sebastian frowned.

"Ives is a member of their coven and Craven is no better I am sure – if nothing else, the man is an idiot. No police. We must rescue this girl ourselves but what do you do to break up a Black Mass?"

"What do you think I am – an exorcist? Let's catch up on some sleep, then in the morning, after a coffee, we will be able to think and plan how to gatecrash their party," Sebastian suggested.

He was horrified that I could only offer black coffee. "If I am going to stay here to help you my first job will be to buy some milk."

So I let him sleep on my couch while I shivered in my draughty bedroom in preparation for the next day

158

when just the two of us would head to the cathedral and do battle with its occupants, human or otherwise.

Chapter Sixteen
: Requiem Massacre

The next day, the first of August, should have been
warm and sunny but it turned out to be a gloomy and
oppressive day, a hint of things to come.

It was midday before we awoke. We had missed a
night's sleep after all.

I turned on all the radio, television and checked the
internet for any reports of the death of the CEO of QPL
but there was nothing. Either Felix Hoad was still alive
somehow or, more likely, the QPL Group was remaining
characteristically mysterious in the face of the media.

Over brunch I told Sebastian everything. While the
drugs had gone from my system, I was still suffering
from shock and I gabbled out my story. Sebastian was
great at getting me to pause and explain things in a
calmer fashion. He was a natural counsellor.

"So that pious protestant Archbishop Augustus
Ighodaro has used his front as a saviour of petty
criminals and drug addicts on council estates to develop
his own Devil worshipping congregation."

"So how do we stop them? Do you have some real
holy water this time?" I asked.

"Please…" Sebastian mocked me. "I brought some
other protection last night but I was only going to use it

160

as a very last resort." He pulled a gun from his pocket and laid it on the table.

"It is a bit big isn't it?" I asked as I stared at the old-fashioned looking pistol with a handle and a wooden stock.

"This is a valuable antique, a German Mauser pistol manufactured in the 1930s. It was smuggled back as a souvenir by one of my parishioners who had been a soldier in World War Two. He confessed to stealing it from the dead to me and I said I would absolve him if he gave me the gun. It is loaded but it has not been fired or cleaned in well over 70 years so pulling the trigger might result in blowing your hand or face off. That is why I said I would only use it as a last resort."

"I have my silver dagger. Doesn't silver have some supernatural-?" I started.

"No, only in vampire or werewolf movies," Sebastian held up a hand before I could finish. "But bring it anyway. It is a weapon. I am really looking forward to gate crashing a genuine Black Mass. One of the priests I trained and worked with told me how he had infiltrated a Black Mass but found it disappointing. The worshippers were just oversexed neurotics who liked prancing around dressed in nothing but a mask he said."

"I think I know why Hoad came to my house. He kept asking 'where is it?' There was a metal cylinder with a leather strap inside the statue of Pan. I kept it and have hidden it in my loft. I am sure that was what he was after. It is important enough to them to kill for it," I told him.

"I will have a look at that cylinder but not today. First we have to save the life of a damaged young woman."

"Are there any special prayers I should say?" I asked.

"You are an atheist, aren't you?"

"Yes."

"So am I but if some words or images give you extra confidence then use them. Goodness knows what we will be up against. We will need all the help we can get. Just don't expect me to bless you."

"Will you give me the last rites if I am killed?"

"Fuck off."

"That is comforting."

"Will they be wearing robes with hoods and carrying flaming torches?"

"I don't think so."

"Damn, why is this not like the movies? I have a couple of anoraks we can wear. They have hoods that can be pulled over our heads so we are not recognised in the dark. I'll bring some battery powered torches."

"Go for it. Fully charge the mobile phones ready for an emergency call to 999."

"Do you realise that the number of our emergency services is 666 upside down?"

"We could call the Devil but they will have done that before us. Look, we rescue the damsel in distress and get out of there as quickly as possible. Then we phone the police anonymously, from a phone box."

"Should I be scared?"

"Just remember whatever you see will be a meaningless ritual and it will have no power to harm you unless you let it. We will take my car. Your van is too obvious."

So we kitted out and drove off to the cathedral city. It took a couple of hours.

Just before we arrived, Sebastian pointed out the new town full of soulless, characterless brick housing barracks and high-rise flats.

"Welcome to New Cannon Town, Hell on Earth, the estate built on the outskirts of the historic cathedral city to keep the disenfranchised at bay. It is here that Ighodaro finds and converts his apostles. You don't want your car to break down in New Cannon Town. They would have your car and wallet stripped in seconds.

"If only Ighodaro had been genuine. New Cannon Town is a ghetto we have created for those on benefits and to keep the poor well away from the middle classes who at the end of the day are little different from them. These estates are full of those addicted to cheap but strong beer and cider and heroine while the middle classes who look down their noses at them nurse their own upmarket addictions of vintage wine, port and brandy as well as cocaine, gluttony, gambling and snobbery. People are trapped in the downward spiral of despair that many of these estates such as New Cannon Town have become. They need to be rescued and shown the way to a better life."

"Now you are sounding like a proper preacher," I said.

"Well perhaps when this is all over, I may do something about it." Sebastian sounded thoughtful.

He sped through New Cannon Town, only slowing down when it was behind us and the cobbled streets and dreaming spires of the old city came into view.

We drove up to the cathedral, ancient, majestic and surrounded by gardens, stone crucifixes and graveyards. Lights shone through the stained-glass windows but the whole area was cordoned off and deserted. There were large signs with the message: "Danger. Do not enter. Renovation in progress."

Large iron gates were padlocked and chained together but if you pushed against the gates you could open enough of a gap to squeeze through. Once again, I was breaking into property, this time accompanied by Sebastian. We pulled our hoods up and crept towards the huge wooden double doors at the entrance to the cathedral.

Stone statues of praying angels looked down upon us and seemed to be warning us away.

A large man with tattoos on his face guarded the doors.

"That must be Brogan, the bouncer," I whispered. "It is nearly eight. Mass time draws near. Let us hope they haven't changed the password. Look confident."

We got to the doors where Brogan glared at us through angry, cruel eyes.

"Black Sparrow," I said.

He hesitated, those cruel eyes peering at us.

"How are you, Brogan?" I asked.

That was enough for him. With a loud grunt he pushed the doors apart and gestured us through.

Once inside, the doors boomed shut behind us. The interior was gloomy. It seemed the electricity was off and the only light came from the large wax candles that burned and flickered in gold candlesticks throughout the massive cathedral.

An organ was playing and a choir sang. The music was somehow out of tune but following a weird discordant arrangement of its own while the choir sang some repetitive chant.

164

We moved forward for a better look.

A number of people sat in the pews, men and women, young and old, scruffily dressed and united by a lost, vacant look on their faces.

Mrs Harriet Milverton sat at the organ striking the keys with gusto.

The choir was made up of teenage boys dressed in robes. They all seemed to suffer from varying degrees of acne and stained, broken teeth. They twitched and swayed alarmingly as they wailed out their fractured hymns. An older choirmaster with long, wild hair performed a staggering dance before them and conducted them with flailing arms.

We found an empty pew and sat down; our heads bowed.

Suddenly the music and wailing ceased and an expectant silence descended.

Then Ighodaro walked in and approached the altar, supporting himself on a Bishop's staff with a crook at the top.

"Welcome to this special Mass to celebrate Lammas Night," he spoke to the congregation in his booming voice. "Bring out the offering!"

Two men brought out the girl they called Nobody. She looked disorientated and frightened, held without struggling between the two men. They had wrapped her in purple robes.

"The poor child," Sebastian whispered in my ear. "We must save her."

"That's why we're here but let's wait for the right opportunity," I whispered back.

"We offer up this youthful creature to the one and only true master of us all," Ighodaro boomed. "Let us rejoice while she is prepared."

The choir began screeching again while the girl was carried to the altar by the two men and laid out on top of it.

In one quick movement the men whipped the purple robe out from under her and Nobody was naked again.

Ighodaro raised a hand and the nerve jarring wailing stopped.

"Is she a virgin?" the long-haired choirmaster asked. "It has to be the blood of a virgin to satisfy Astaroth."

"Don't interrupt my service with ridiculous questions," Ighodaro barked and struck out with his staff, hitting the choirmaster so hard in the chest that he fell over on his back.

The chastened choirmaster climbed back to his feet, rubbing his sore chest while two 'altar boys' (they looked about 20) carried out red wine with a chalice and wafers on a silver tray and stood either side of the Archbishop.

"Now for the Eucharist. Please come up in an orderly queue to receive communion. Take the body of our true Lord and eat and feed upon him. Drink also the blood of our true Lord and eternal life will be yours."

First the choir shuffled up to sip from the chalice and take a wafer on their furry tongues. For most of them a simple sip of wine was not enough, however, and they took great gulps from the chalice. In anticipation of this, the altar boys had brought numerous opened wine bottles to keep refilling the chalice.

"Don't go up," I hissed at Sebastian. "He might recognise me."

We kept our heads lowered in prayer while the rest of the congregation stood up and shuffled up to the altar. The altar boys were taking their own swigs of the wine straight from the bottle. The two men who kept the helpless Nobody pinned down on the altar took it in turns to go up and receive the body and blood of the Anti-Christ.

Mrs Milverton watched like a vulture from her perch at the organ. She did not take communion. Ighodaro chuckled loudly as he carried out the ceremony, but he did not take the wine himself.

When the taking of communion was completed Ighodaro stopped and raised a hand while his gaze roamed over the audience. He pointed at Sebastian and me with his Archbishop's staff.

"Who are you two who try to hide your faces and don't take communion?" he bellowed.

Sebastian threw caution to the wind, stood up and threw back his hood while I still huddled in the pew.

Ighodaro paused for a moment and then as recognition dawned said: "I know you, fallen Romanist. Father Sebastian Fullalove, disowned by the Catholic Church as a heretic. Damn rosary rattlers."

"I have no doubt that your own protestant church would disown you as well if they knew who you really worshipped," Sebastian came back at him.

"Someone bring them to me! Don't let them get away," Ighodaro spoke to the general congregation. "Who says we have to limit ourselves to just one sacrifice?"

Mrs Milverton came over and stood beside him.

"I thought you had all fallen out after you took Hoad's body," I said to her.

Mrs Milverton smiled and said: "We don't trust each other. We are all criminals after all. But in the end, we all want the same things and it pulls us back together."

My left hand was suddenly warm and wet. I looked down to see blood dripping from it to the floor.

"Hoad is here," I whispered to Sebastian.

"What? Don't be ridiculous…"

But his words were cut off as just then the double doors were thrown back to crash against the wall. Brogan came into view, walking slowly and strangely up the aisle. His shirt and jacket had gone. A blood red cross had been carved on his chest. The cut started at his belly and finished almost under his chin while the horizontal cut went from nipple to nipple.

He was trying to talk but only blood bubbled from his mouth.

He lurched forward, holding onto a pew to stop himself falling and the wound in his chest widened and suddenly his intestines uncoiled from the gaping split, splashing onto the ground. His guts continued to tumble out until he finally flopped to the ground into his own entrails.

If this had been a normal congregation this is when I would have expected the hysterical screaming to start. Instead there was laughter, some of it loud and raucous, and some of it just sly sniggers. I was rooted to the spot in horror, but at least Sebastian and I seemed to be forgotten about.

Then someone else entered through the door. Felix Hoad stood there and looked around him. In one hand he held a bloody butcher's cleaver. His once coldly handsome face had been transformed by the acid into something twisted and scarred. It was the face from a white stone statue that had been chiselled out of shape.

"Eat, drink and be merry for tomorrow I live. You held a sacrificial Mass and you didn't invite me! You are all traitors!" Hoad's shout trailed off into a maniacal laugh. Then he waved across at Harriet Milverton with the cleaver: "Thank you for retrieving my jacket, my ever-faithful Mambo."

"Get him!" Ighodaro climbed up to the pulpit and cried out to his befuddled audience. "The intruder has been sent to disrupt our Mass. Your Lord commands that you destroy him." He waved the Bishop's crook at the approaching Hoad.

Hoad looked around at the gathering and bellowed at them: "Will no one rid me of this troublesome priest?"

The crazed congregation seemed to hesitate, unsure which way to jump.

As Hoad came nearer, Ighodaro cried out: "Get him away from me!"

Then the Archbishop leapt from the pulpit and down to the altar where he grabbed the naked Nobody by the arm. He yanked the girl up and dragged her with him as he ran to a side door.

I could just make out a spiral stone staircase the other side of the door. Ighodaro ran to it, pulling the girl along behind him. He paused in the doorway to look at the man who had returned from the dead.

Hoad went to give chase but a red-eyed worshipper was crazy enough to try and stop him. Hoad swung the cleaver once and the man fells back with a torrent of blood gushing from his throat.

169

"This is where I join the party," Sebastian said as he leapt into the aisle with the Mauser in his hand, aimed at Hoad.

For a second Hoad paused, staring at Sebastian and his ancient pistol with sparkly, insane eyes. I was remembering what Sebastian had said about the gun and hoping he didn't have to fire it.

With a deafening shriek Mrs Milverton threw herself at Sebastian, knocking the gun out of his hand and kicking it forcefully all the way to the other side of the cathedral. She had one of her steel hair pins and rammed it in the side of Sebastian's neck.

He crashed down stiffly, suddenly frozen, as if he had been paralysed. He lay there stiff and twitching, his eyes moving from side to side and the needle jutting from his neck. It seemed that Mrs Milverton knew acupuncture and had rendered Sebastian helpless by stabbing him in just the right nerve.

She stood up, looking down at the helpless Sebastian for a moment, before looking around for any other foes in the congregation. I ducked down and hid.

Then one of the choirboys went berserk. His eyes had turned red and he howled, spraying those around him with a shower of discoloured spittle. He began attacking the other choirboys but they jumped on him and began hitting him.

The man in the pew in front of me began to shudder and shake. Then he turned and looked down at me. His eyes were red and watery. Suddenly he choked up black vomit. I backed away to stop it splashing over me.

Then a fight broke out across the aisle. Someone else was clambering up into the pulpit, gibbering and crying. Another worshipper was laughing, loud and crazy. A red-eyed woman sat on the floor tearing the pages from a hymn book and eating them.

A woman screamed as she was chased by a knife wielding choirboy intent on slashing her to death. A man sat cross legged on the floor, stabbed himself in the stomach, and drew the knife up into his chest. He laughed as he viewed his own internal organs through his bloodshot eyes.

Suddenly they all turned on each other and chaos reigned. People were running, dancing, singing and trying to murder each other as they were infected. Their bodies juddered and quivered and their eyes bulged red.

"Dance, my children," Hoad raised his arms as if he was conducting them. "Dance and prance till your feet are bloody stumps."

"You have drunk of my nectar. Let it transform you." Mrs Milverton danced herself, spinning around in circles, but uninfected and in control. She watched the mayhem with obvious pleasure and laughed out loud. "Welcome to a foretaste of the Hell that awaits you."

A man clawed at me with blood running from his eyes. I backed away, jumping across to the next pew to escape him.

I realised what had happened. All the wine had been doctored with Harriet's Hellfire and all who had drunk it were being driven mad by Datura, the witch's weed, and the other poisons it contained.

Ighodaro witnessed it all in shocked disbelief. He had obviously not known the wine was doctored. He turned away and pulled Nobody with him as he fled out of sight up the spiral stone staircase.

Hoad saw him go and immediately gave chase.

171

I tried to get to Sebastian who still lay paralysed on the floor. I was hoping that if I extracted the hair pin he would recover and be able to move again.

Before I could reach him, an obese woman came crashing down on me, pinning me underneath her, while she groped for my groin with her sausage-like fingers. Her red eyes burned with lust. She had long dangly earrings that swung over my face as she brought her jowly face closer to mine. She pursed her bloated drool covered lips to kiss me.

I somehow managed to find the strength to roll over and push her off me. She scrabbled on the floor, trying to get up.

A straggly haired, unwashed looking man was standing on top of the altar chanting loudly at us all. It was all too much for a brutish thug who climbed up onto the altar and sprang at him, his hands closing around his throat in an effort to silence the chants. They were trying to strangle each other when they both toppled off the top of the altar and fell to the floor.

A thin, naked, blood covered man lurched at me. I punched him hard and he fell back. I pulled out my silver dagger. I was ready to use it and kill if necessary, to save my life.

Someone was bashing at the organ creating an ear drum blasting din.

Some of the riffraff were staggering through the open doors and outside. This was a good thing. I hoped. While the riot was confined to the cathedral, which was cordoned off and away from other buildings, it could pass unnoticed. But once the crazy rabble spread into the streets the police would be called.

Above all the noise I heard the screaming of a young girl. It was Nobody, I knew, and it came from above.

I instantly made her my first priority. She was at the mercy of both Ighodaro and Hoad. I had to save her from the monsters.

People were reaching out for me and trying to pull me into their fights. I dodged the grasping hands, leapt over the injured that crawled over the floor, and ran towards the altar. Up on the dais I ran for the open doorway and the spiral stairway beyond.

I raced up the stone steps towards the screams of the girl.

Round and round, up and up the narrow spiral I went till I felt giddy. Then I reached a wooden door and pushed it open.

It was hard to see at first but the flickering flame on the end of the big candle that had been rammed down Archbishop Augustus Ighodaro's throat, together with the moonlight coming through the small, iron barred window, gave me enough light to get my glimpse of what I did not want to see.

The Archbishop's hands were outstretched either side of him and had been nailed to the floor through the palms. The candle had been forced down his throat, deep enough to choke him, but as it burned, the melting wax had run into his mouth, across his reddened face, and on the floor around his head. His eyes bulged almost out of their sockets.

But that was not the worst thing. His head that was now a candlestick was not attached to his body. It had been sliced cleanly off at the neck. Hoad's cleaver!

Across the room, the girl called Nobody was being raped by Felix Hoad. He cheered as he gyrated above her while she screamed, squirmed and tried to fight him off. She clawed at him with her nails.

"Stop at once or I will kill you!" I shouted and went for him with my silver dagger.

He leapt up from her in an instance and tucked his disgusting long white penis back in his pants.

"My knife is bigger than your knife," he gloated as he produced the butcher's cleaver.

We ran at each other, slashing out with our weapons.

I have no experience of knife fights. He swung down at me and I dodged aside but not before the cleaver had cut into my upper right arm.

I staggered back, worried about how deep the cut was. Then he kicked out at me. His foot caught me square in the stomach, knocking me back through the open door.

He kicked out a second time and this time I flew back the way I had come and began tumbling down the long, hard, stone staircase. I lost my dagger along the way and tried to reach out to slow my fall but I bounced off walls and steps all the way down.

He kicked the severed head of Archbishop Augustus Ighodaro after me.

It bounced down the stairs with the candle still rammed down its throat.

I rolled out of the staircase and back onto the raised dais that supported the altar.

I lay on my back in agony. I tried to rise but sharp pain stabbed me all over. I couldn't move and a fear that maybe I'd broken my spine and been paralysed gripped me. A fear which was quickly replaced by a more urgent

174

one: I could hear Hoad walking calmly down the steps towards me.

Hoad kicked the head to one side and stood over me, smiling, and waving the cleaver in his hand.

"I have begun my personal journey of vengeance. Each and every one of those who took part in that futile attempt to kill me in Grimoire Priory will experience their own slow destruction by my hands," Hoad warned me. "I will send them out of this world only when they have completely given up their pathetic lives to me. Beg me for the mercy I will never give you. You know you want to."

He raised the cleaver, ready to strike.

"I can chop small pieces off you all night without killing you," Hoad boasted as he went to swing the cleaver.

Suddenly he stopped and looked up. The girl called Nobody had come down the stairs and entered the cathedral. She had put on the robes of an altar boy to cover her body. Her eyes were not red so she had not been infected but they were harder and more focussed than I had seen them before.

"Well, well, little Miss Nobody has come to watch." Hoad sneered.

She raised her hand to show that she was holding the German Mauser that she had picked up from the floor.

"Stop calling me Nobody. I am Tipota," she said calmly as she pointed the old pistol at Hoad's face.

"Miss Nobody has a toy. Put it down before you hurt yourself, little girl," Hoad mocked.

"My name is Tipota," she insisted as she pulled the trigger.

The shot echoed in the high ceiling of the cathedral. A puff of smoke came from the muzzle but the gun did not blow up.

A gasp of surprise came from Hoad who staggered. Blood trickled from the deep, dark hole that had been blasted in his forehead. He toppled backwards, crashed to the floor and was still.

There was the briefest moment of stillness and silence and shock.

"No!" Mrs Milverton screamed and ran over to his fallen body.

Tipota yelped suddenly and dropped the gun, shaking her hand like she'd been burned. As it hit the floor it fell apart. It had only been good for one shot but that had been enough.

With a supreme effort I grabbed a pew and pulled my painful body up from the floor. I was not going to be paralysed but how about Sebastian? I lurched over to the helpless Sebastian and collapsed down beside him. I pulled the needle from his neck.

Sebastian screamed but unfroze and moved instantly. Holding his neck he clambered to his feet.

The shrieking, writhing congregation scrambled away.

"Come, we must get out of here!" Sebastian gathered me and the girl up. Then the three of us followed the crazy, weaving crowd that were already fleeing to the exit.

I felt as if every muscle in my body was torn but I forced myself to run.

We ran through the graveyard to the padlocked iron gates and squeezed back out through the gap.

The girl viewed us with obvious suspicion.

"We are not your enemies. You are among friends now," I tried to assure Tipota as I guided her along.

"Next time you tell me that Hoad is near I will believe you," Sebastian said to me.

"There won't be a next time. He has a bullet through the brain," I said. "This time, he has to be dead."

"Not necessarily. People have parts of their brain removed in surgery all the time and they survive," Sebastian said. "Only recently a teenager was shot completely through his head and brain by a spear from a harpoon gun and he recovered."

"Don't say that. I could do with some words of comfort."

It was a long drive back and we were hungry and thirsty. There was no way we were going into a restaurant in our blood-stained clothes but we were lucky enough to find a drive through burger bar where we could buy three burgers and three teas to consume in the car. I was also able to buy some milk for my guests at a garage shop.

"We are going to have to cover our tracks and get rid of these clothes. The last time an Archbishop was murdered in a cathedral it was Thomas Becket. There will be a nationwide police investigation. How is your arm?" Sebastian asked.

"Still bleeding slightly."

"It will. You should go to a hospital but there will be questions. I can fix it in your house."

"Oh dear. You will have to do that. I may have needle and thread but no anaesthetic."

"Do you have whisky?"

"Yes."

"You have a workshop. Do you have a strong polymer-based adhesive?"

"Yes," I answered again, now puzzled.

"Then that will have to do for your pain and for the wound."

"Where am I going?" Tipota asked suddenly.

"To my home. You will be safe there. Then we can take you anywhere you want," I told the girl who suddenly seemed remarkably calm and clear headed. "If you hadn't killed him, I would be taking you to a police station to charge Felix Hoad with rape."

The journey did not take long at that time of night.

Once we arrived at my house Tipota asked if she could have a bath. While she was in the bathroom, I used rolled up emergency car windshield replacement plastic for a temporary repair of the broken skylight in my bedroom.

We three would spend the night at my house: Sebastian on my leather sofa, me on an inflatable mattress in my spare room and Tipota in the bedroom.

I had a wardrobe and chest of drawers full of clothes that had belonged to Estelle. I showed them to Tipota and told her to help herself to anything she wanted.

Then Sebastian and I sat down with whisky while he examined the cleaver wound in my upper arm.

"It will probably leave a scar," Sebastian warned.

"Well keep the stitches neat."

"I won't use a needle and thread. Where are your adhesives?"

"Are you mad? I thought you were joking," I protested.

"Don't worry. During my time in Belfast I had to help many shot and stabbed victims of the Troubles who could not draw attention to themselves by going to hospital. I became a bit of an expert in treating bullet and knife wounds."

So I helped him find a strong but solvent free adhesive and he glued my wound closed.

The whisky helped with the pain and afterwards we made the mistake of switching from grain to grape and opened a bottle of wine.

It was then that Tipota emerged wearing one of Estelle's red dresses, her hair brushed and combed and her face and body scrubbed clean.

"Wow," I said involuntarily. She was beautiful.

She sat down with us at the kitchen table.

"Have some wine and tell us about yourself and how you got mixed up in this business," Sebastian pushed a glass of wine across to her. "I am a priest used to hearing confessions. You can tell me anything."

"He is an ex-priest." I scowled at him and then smiled at her. "I can't imagine what you have been through but it is important that you know you can trust us and that you will only get the truth from us."

"My story isn't so different to many others'," she said. "Lousy parents, foster care, abuse. It got so bad I ran away and chose to live on the streets and become a Nothing. Tipota is the name I gave myself." She stared at her glass of wine, her eyes hard, angry. "They gathered me up from the gutter as fodder for their sick games. I knew I was going to die today and to begin with I didn't care. I was done. I just wanted to escape from it all. But then you came to my rescue and suddenly … I was fighting back."

"You may still have a way to go. What drugs were they keeping you on? You are bound to feel withdrawal symptoms soon."

"The craving is there and will always be there but drugs are a part of the past I want to leave behind. Today I said no more to myself."

"The road to Damascus," Sebastian muttered.

"I will do anything I can to help," I told her.

"Why? What's in it for you?" she asked.

I hesitated. I barely knew how to explain my desire to help so much to myself. Then I thought of Estelle, rotting in her apartment, alone. Maybe if I had done more, tried harder to find her… but this girl didn't need to be burdened with my guilt. "Because it is right," I said, simply.

We talked about her experiences but Tipota did not know anymore about QPL than I did. As far as she was concerned, she had been kidnapped by a cult of rich perverts who kept her drugged to use her as part of their sick games.

Sebastian was the first to fall asleep but as he had been doing all the driving it was not surprising. He collapsed on the sofa.

I took her to the bedroom and was about to leave when she grabbed my hand. "I do not want to sleep alone tonight. But I do not want sex. Can you lie with me without wanting sex?" she asked.

"Yes," I promised. My heart hurt for her. Had she ever known protection or compassion without something being expected in return? Had she ever known either full stop? At all costs, I wanted her to know I would care for her.

The next morning Sebastian saw me coming out of the bedroom and the unspoken question was in his eyes. I shook my head.

After a fried breakfast we sat in the front room drinking coffee, me with my usual black coffee and them with milky coffees and watched the news on television.

The death of Archbishop Augustus Ighodaro made the headlines followed by the riots in New Cannon Town in which many were injured and some killed.

"The Archbishop had made it his life's work to help the poor and disenfranchised," it was reported, "and now it seemed those he tried to help had turned on him and murdered him in a drug fuelled frenzy."

His corpse had been found headless. There was no sign of his head.

The reporters had got the story the wrong way round, however, saying the violent drug fuelled behaviour had started in New Cannon Town and spread to the cathedral leading to the death of the Archbishop and others in the cathedral.

There were pictures of burning buildings and cars, shop windows being smashed, people being attacked. Various experts blamed the riots on the economy, the isolation of a dysfunctional sector of the population in a dormitory town, a new, stronger class of drug, and cutbacks in benefits and social services. The warm August weather had also made people more volatile, one expert said.

Those who had taken part in the riots were found to be in a dazed state with little or no memory of what had happened the night before.

"Do you think they will leave us alone now?" I asked Sebastian.

"Absolutely not." Though I knew he was right, my heart sank.

"I will kill myself before I let myself be taken by them again." Tipota became agitated.

"We will make sure that doesn't happen," I said.

"I think we should attack first," Sebastian said.

"How?" I asked.

He paused and seemed to go into deep thought.

I looked at Tipota. "That has him stumped," I chuckled but she did not respond. She seemed to have drifted off into deep thought as well.

I looked back at Sebastian. His eyes had closed. Tipota slumped in the armchair and her head tipped forward.

"What is the matter with you two?" I shouted at them.

They didn't answer. Something was very wrong.

The front door opened and closed. The stocky Abel Vasko entered the room, ambled over to my sofa, and sank down in it, smiling at me.

"Breakfast smells nice. Do you have any left? I am quite hungry after the drive down here," he said.

"What's going on?" I was very rattled.

I looked at Sebastian and Tipota. They were not moving. They didn't even seem to be breathing.

"I gather from a surviving verger that she shot Hoad through the head."

"That's true. He is finally dead."

"The problem with that is once again there is no body. If I am to take over his job, I do need proof of death. My late parents would have been so proud to see my success today. They came to this country as starving refugees from Hungary in the 1950s, fleeing the Russian invasion. Now I am set to become CEO of a multi-national conglomerate."

"Mrs Milverton may have taken Hoad's body. She was weeping over it when we left. Why don't you go find her?"

"Yes. She took it last time," Vasko mused. "She may be having sex with it as we speak. I can imagine that old crone is into necrophilia in a big way."

"What has happened to Sebastian and Tipota? What did you do?"

"They are dying."

"What, how?"

"A little something I slipped in the milk earlier before you all woke up. Drinking you coffee black has saved your life. For now," Vasko said all this with a smile. "Don't worry it's not Harriet's Hellfire. They won't burn up inside or go mad. It's just something that slowly closes down their organs one at a time and then leaves no trace afterwards. A peaceful death really. I am not a sadist like many of my colleagues. With me it is just business."

"How can I save them?" I jumped up and went over to him.

Without leaving the sofa, Vasko kicked my legs out from under me and then stamped on my chest as I lay on the ground. I lay there gasping and in pain.

"Don't try and fight me. I can kill you in a second without leaving this sofa and then you could never help them. Just listen. I have the antidote to the poison they have taken. It has to be given almost immediately if it is to work. All I want from you in return is that which you took from inside the Pan statue."

He leered down at me but I didn't move or say anything. My mind was racing.

"Quick, quick, the window of opportunity is closing. The longer you delay in giving it to me the more likely it will be too late to save them."

184

"Give them the antidote now and I'll get it for you," I pleaded.

"The cylinder first," he held out his hand.

Seeing it as my only option, I got up and ran upstairs, then pulled down my loft ladder. I ran up the steps into the loft, grabbed the metal tube and rushed back down and threw it at him.

"Gently," he said, catching it. "It is very delicate. It contains an early Edison wax cylinder recording of the voice of Quincy Pitt, made about 1890. The voice of Pitt was said to be golden, mellow and hypnotic, with the power to command the strongest personality. It is his testament for today. We need an antique phonograph to play it but it will be heard one way or another."

"I don't care. Just give them the antidote!"

"Sorry, I lied. There is no antidote," he admitted, still smiling.

I looked helplessly at the still figures of Sebastian and Tipota.

I sprang at him but he struck my throat with the edge of his hand and sent me reeling back.

"I am an expert in killing, Mr Bell. I am responsible for one of the most successful business arms of QPL, our VIP assassination service. My personal favourite is the staged car accident. The police never investigate car accident deaths too closely. We are the Life Stealers.

"If it was up to me, I would let you all live as I cannot see how you are a threat to us. But I have my orders. You all know too much and I have been contracted to tidy up the loose ends."

"You evil bastard!" I made another attempt to strike him but he was too quick for me and floored me with a mighty blow. "I thought you never killed women!"

"She is not so much a woman as a nobody and an unhappy nobody at that. I have put her out of her misery." He lazily pulled a gun from his inside pocket. "You know, I really wish I didn't have to do this, if that helps." His eyes misted over, but his aim was unwavering. "I have trouble sleeping. I dream that I am trapped in a tunnel with no way out and surrounded by all the men I have killed. They are reaching out for me and shuffling towards me from all directions, dragging their broken and mangled bodies. Every time I kill someone new, another damaged man joins the shuffling crowd."

Vasko stood up, waving the metal cylinder, the gun still trained directly at my head. "Thank you for this. I will think of you when I am playing it. We will wait for the grand opening of Mercer Tower to listen to its secrets. For the moment I will place it in the safest place I know, inside the ancient altar that lies deep under the foundations of Mercer Tower. I keep all our secrets there in the old underground church. The stolen evidence files from Danny Stein's case are also kept there, a little life insurance for me and a hold over Ives and the others."

I knew he was telling me this because in his eyes, I was already dead. I started to panic.

"My neighbours will hear the shot and call the police!" I shouted at him as I staggered to my feet.

I started for the door but he was before me in a flash. I turned and made for the stairs.

"I don't think you have any close neighbours, Mr Bell. I always do a recce before a job. However if you say so…" Vasko pulled out a long silencer and began to screw it onto the muzzle of the gun. "Did you know that silencers are much harder to buy than guns? You may want a gun just for target shooting or some other

186

innocent reason but the only reason for a silencer is to carry out a quiet murder."

"I thought guns weren't your thing," I said as I backed up the staircase.

"They are not but that does not stop me being a crack shot. I am master of the clean kill. I know human anatomy better than a surgeon and I take just one shot, one bullet, no more, no less, to do the job." Vasko smiled. "As I said before I am not a sadist like many of my colleagues and it helps if the person I have to kill deserves it. Sadly, you are just collateral damage. Tell me, is your fridge well-stocked? I do like a snack after an execution." Vasko began moving up the stairs, still smiling and relaxed, the gun pointed in front of him. "Killing you is going to give me a real big appetite."

I turned to run but I had trapped myself upstairs. I went into my bedroom looking for a weapon. So much junk but nothing I could fight with.

He followed me into the bedroom. I pushed the wardrobe over in front of him to block his way and while he was trying to get round the wardrobe I leapt at the doorway. I ran back to the stairs but he was right behind me.

"Stop. End of the line," he said.

I turned and faced him at the top of the stairs. The gun was pointing at my face.

"If there were any other way…" Vasko shrugged and pulled the trigger.

The gun fire was muffled and smoke came from the end of the silencer. My head seemed to explode and redness splashed into my eyes. I was knocked back and tumbled down the stairs.

I was not ready to die. I tried to hold on to life as I rolled down the steps but there was nothing for me to grip onto and I floated away from my body. All my dead friends and family stood along the staircase: Peter, Estelle, parents and grandparents reaching out to catch me and stop my fall. I tried to grab their hands but I couldn't get close enough. All that was me spiralled away into darkness and a cold, empty infinity. I was alone. I was gone.

There was the singing of sweet angel voices in the darkness. I came round to a mixture of male and female voices singing a tuneful rendition of 'Nearer My God to Thee'. There was a distant light, a chink in the blackness.

Had I gone to another world?

Just for a moment I believed in heaven and believed that I was there.

"Turn that fucking row off... Oh, don't bother I'll do it myself," growled a familiar voice.

Then the sweet melody was silenced as the speaker kicked in the television which smashed with a puff of smoke. He came over and stared down at me.

I opened my eyes and looked up into Danny Stein's ugly sneer. Standing beside him was his friend Detective Superintendent Ives.

"Never liked Songs of Praise. Hope you weren't listening. Time to wake up," Stein snarled at me.

"What happened? I thought Vasko had killed me."

"Change of plan," Ives smirked. "Vasko told us how you refused to find the cylinder for him. Not even to save your friends, hm? Surprising. Plus we need you to take the fall for Hoad's death. Once we're certain he's dead, that is. You are a suspect in three other deaths so you are ideal. You fit the profile of a serial killer. They

189

are usually sad, wimpy, loner types like you. And guess what? I am leading the nationwide police hunt for you. You killed an Archbishop. That makes you really high profile."

Stein looked at my wounded scalp and commented: "Vasko knocked you out with a nice single shot. Not my way. I like to empty my gun into my victims."

I looked around me. I lay at the foot of the staircase. My body felt bruised. My head was bleeding. When I tried to reach for the top of my head, I discovered that my hands were tied behind my back with my own strong nylon rope. I struggled to my feet, watched by a smirking Stein who made no effort to help me. I looked in the hall mirror and saw a shallow bloody groove along the top of my skull that had parted my hair.

I had been unconscious for a very long time. It was getting dark outside.

I looked for signs of Sebastian or Tipota.

"My friends. Where are they?" I asked.

"Vasko always likes to clear up after himself. He's a true professional. He had got rid of their bodies before I arrived."

"Listen, I don't know what he told you but Vasko has the cylinder," I protested.

"Liar. He couldn't find it. We will have to torture its whereabouts out of you."

Why did Vasko lie to his partners in crime? He didn't trust them, hence the hidden evidence files, and perhaps he wanted that precious recording just for himself. None of them trusted each other. There was no honour among thieves.

Was I alone with Stein and Ives, I wondered? If so, I just had to escape from them. They were both far tougher and stronger than me and my hands were tied but I had to try something. I ran backwards to the front door, pulled it open with my tied hands and turned around. Marquis Thorn and Andries stood there, smiling at me.

There was a helicopter parked in my front yard!

"The girl and the priest, are they-?" I started.

"'Fraid so. Without a trace." Thorn spread his hands. "No one will miss the girl as she was off the grid anyway and the Roman Catholic Church will just issue a massive sigh of relief over the disappearance of Father Sebastian Fullalove."

"I offered to drop them into the sea from my helicopter but Vasko wanted to dispose of them personally." Andries attempted to smile with his slit of a mouth.

I wondered if their bodies had also ended up in the foundations of Mercer Tower.

"Well if you don't need me now-" I tried walking past them.

With a mighty blow Andries knocked me back into the house and against the wall.

"Look, we have been told to keep you alive but Vasko did not specify about what condition you need to be in." Stein glared at me. "I am in the mood to mete out some punishment."

"We came here to find the wax cylinder and I understand that is the only reason why we are keeping you alive," Thorn said. Then, turning to the others, "I think we should kill him anyway and take the house apart. We are bound to find it."

"If I am found murdered then the police will start to believe my stories," I said desperately.

"I can make the evidence say whatever I want. I have done it before," Ives chuckled.

"And I will write your story. Everyone will hear about the insane Ronan Bell and his murderous rampage. The British public will see you as a modern day Jack the Ripper. I will make you a star." Thorn flashed his gold teeth at me.

"Fuck it, I agree with you," Stein said to Thorn. "I'm a man who gives orders, not takes orders. Let's finish him off."

They all looked at me with death in their eyes.

Suddenly my left hand felt wet. I was bleeding again. I turned and held my cut hand up and let them see the dripping blood.

"He's here," I said.

"Who?" Thorn and Stein asked together.

"Felix Hoad."

"Don't be ridiculous," Thorn snapped, though he sounded unsure. "He's dead. The man was shot through his brain."

"I did think I heard a car outside," Stein frowned. "It drove away very quickly."

"I'll have a look around," Andries volunteered. He left the room and went outside, gun in hand.

The four of us waited in silence. Stein looked angry but nervous while Thorn tapped his teeth with his fingernails.

Then those damn sensor-operated security lights flashed on and flooded my yard with blinding light.

"Go see what that is," Thorn barked at Stein.

"Why don't you go? I don't work for you," Stein growled back.

There was a noise upstairs: the sound of someone or something dropping onto the floor above.

"Watch him." Stein gestured at me to Thorn and ran up the stairs.

Once he was out of sight a tense silence descended. Now it was just me, Ives and Thorn.

"What's going on?" Thorn shouted up the stairs.

Silence. I could hear my own heart beating.

There were footsteps, slow, measured footsteps, walking along the landing towards the head of the staircase.

We all looked up and gradually Stein came into view staggering towards the top of the stairs.

"I've got a fucking splitting headache," Stein croaked.

Then we saw the top of his head. The butcher's cleaver was deeply embedded in it, slicing his head almost in half, so that the blade reached the start of his nose. Stein's eyes were clouded over and blood ran down his face and dripped off his chin. Red tears ran down from his eyes.

His mouth opened and closed like a fish out of water. He spoke, blood gurgling from his mouth: "He is risen."

Stein reached the top step. He tried speaking again. It was a death rattle: "I'm brown bread."

Then his legs buckled.

Stein's body came rolling down the staircase. It tumbled to the bottom and lay still. We stared at it in a state of shock. Then Thorn snapped out of it.

"Andries!" Thorn yelled for his henchman, his voice quivering with terror.

"What the fuck. I wish I'd brought a gun." Ives reached into his inside pocket and produced a black police baton, the modern truncheon. "This will have to do." He extended it with a flick of his wrist.

We stared up at the staircase. Felix Hoad stood at the top looking down, his scarred faced twisted into a grimace, and the blackened bullet hole prominent in his forehead.

"How-?" Thorn started.

"Life's a bitch and then we don't die. Believe in me and everlasting life shall be yours," Hoad spoke in a cracked and croaking voice. Then he launched himself off the landing.

Thorn had pulled out his mobile phone and tried to make a call for help.

Felix Hoad came flying down the staircase, his feet hardly touching the steps, and flung himself on top of Thorn. Thorn gasped as Hoad's fingers closed round his throat and he toppled over backwards onto the floor with Hoad on top of him.

With his other hand Hoad grabbed Thorn's mobile phone and smashed it into pieces on the floor.

"Haven't you got into enough trouble with telephones, you stupid hacker? There is no escape for any of you. None of you can ever kill me. I have eternal life. I am immortal!" Hoad spat the words down into Thorn's purple face.

Ives hung back, indecisive and showing no sign of entering the fray. Then suddenly he snapped out of it and swung his baton down on Hoad's head. It had been a violent blow but it had no effect on Hoad.

This was my chance. I left the resurrected Hoad and the others to fight it out while I ran for the door.

194

I opened it quietly with my tied hands only to see Andries appearing from behind the helicopter and walking back to the house with a gun in his hand.

"Stop or I'll shoot you!" Andries bellowed, waving the gun at me.

I changed direction and ran to my adjoining workshop. I expected Andries to fire on me at any second but he seemed to have taken the order to keep me alive to heart. He started after me.

I had just reached the door to the workshop and was pulling it open when Felix Hoad burst through my front door and pounced upon Andries.

I left them fighting and rolling on the ground while I ran into my workshop and closed the door behind me. It was difficult with my hands tied behind my back but I managed to ram the bolt home. It was unlikely that I could hide here but this is where I kept all my tools and it was possible I could find something to cut through the rope as well as a suitable weapon to defend myself with.

It was quiet again. The fight with Andries seemed to be over but who had been the victor?

Someone thudded against the workshop door, straining it at its hinges.

Silence again.

A horrible rasping noise sounded from the other side of the door. I backed away into a corner of the workshop.

It took me a while to realise that the rasping noise was Hoad, trying to speak. I listened intently, trying to hear the words he formed.

"No one can stand against me, especially not a pathetic maggot like you," Hoad growled and snarled through the door. "You will all die acknowledging me as your master and I will be restored."

The breathing was unnaturally loud. Each gasp was a death rattle.

I went back to the door, fumbled for the light switch with my bound hands and turned on the light.

I lit up my workshop. It was here that I restored, polished and painted the junk that I breathed new life into and (sometimes) turned into valuable antiques.

It seemed that someone had also breathed new life into Felix Hoad.

He crashed against the door again and wood began shattering and splintering.

Where did he get the strength?

If only I could untie my hands. Then I could at least defend myself.

Hoad threw himself against the door with such force that it was ripped off its hinges. The shattered door crashed to the floor and Hoad stood in the doorway looking around him. He was a living nightmare; the flesh on his face crinkled and scarred and the hole in his forehead seemed to be pulsating and throbbing.

There was a single fly circling round Hoad's head, puzzled by the dead and rotting thing that still walked.

Hoad ran at me. I leapt up like a footballer and kicked him under the chin. It made him pause for a moment as his head toppled sideways and lay on one shoulder.

Hoad reached up and pulled his head back on straight with a horrible crunching noise.

His mouth opened so wide that his jaw dropped onto his chest and he shrieked at me, advancing on me, his hands raised and his fingers curved into hooks.

196

I backed away. Could nothing stop him?

I tried kicking him again but this time Hoad was expecting it. He dodged my foot and struck me hard with his fist.

I stumbled back. Hoad continued to come at me. Another blow from him sent me slamming against the wall. There was nowhere else to run.

Hoad sprang at me, grabbed me by the hair and pulled my face close to his.

He smelt of decay. I was staring into the face of a demon.

"Love me, worship me, die for me," Hoad spluttered green spittle into my face.

I tried to pull away but I did not have the strength. Exhausted I reached beside me for support.

I touched cold machinery. It was my sandblaster. It was only to be used when the operator was wearing protective clothing, a face mask and goggles, for it shot tiny particles of sand and grit out of it, like a cloud of tiny bullets to blast rust, grime and corrosion from iron, metal and stonework.

A burst of adrenalin gave me the sudden strength to fight back. I kicked him hard and away from me. He staggered as if he would fall but was back on his feet in a second.

I swung the sandblaster around so that the mouth of the flexible hose was pointed at Hoad as he sprang at me. Then I reached behind me with my bound hands and switched it on.

I lowered my eyes and curled up into a protective ball. There was a great whoosh sound as compressed air propelled a sandstorm directly at Hoad.

He let out a hideous shriek as he became engulfed in the whirlwind of sand and grit that threw him across the room and against the further wall. I glimpsed a writhing, dancing, screaming figure before Hoad disappeared from my view to be buried beneath a mound of sand.

The sandblaster emptied its contents and I switched it off. The mound of sand shifted, crumbled and spread and then lay still. Blood pockmarked the wall behind it.

I slid down to a sitting position, exhausted. I coughed and spluttered as dust filled the air.

Then Thorn, Ives and Andries came crashing in through the broken door. Thorn was holding the gun this time and Andries was holding the bloody cleaver he had obviously pulled from Stein's skull.

I had hoped that Hoad had killed them and I could get free. They had torn clothes and bruised faces but they were very much alive.

"If you want Hoad you will have to dig him out," I said, nodding at the pile of bloody sand.

"Is he really dead under all that?" Andries asked.

"He would have suffocated as the sand filled his lungs," I said, and hoped I sounded like I believed it. "I have killed him for you. The least you can do is untie me."

They ignored my plea.

"I don't believe it is finally over. The man is not human. He has survived death too many times. I need to really make sure this time," Thorn said. "Let's have a look."

Hoad's feet were sticking out from under the mountain of yellow sand. Andries grabbed them and tried to pull Hoad's body out from under it. However he only managed to free the legs before the weight of the sand was too much for him and he gave up.

"I have to know that he is not going to get up and chase after us again," Thorn grimaced. Then he pulled Andries to one side and said to him: "Chop his legs off!"

"Good idea, boss," Andries crouched down beside the buried body and raised the blood-stained cleaver.

He swung it down with a sickening crunch and began hacking through both legs at the upper thigh, slicing through trousers, flesh and bone. Blood spattered into his face as he chopped away.

Thorn watched him with a smile on his face. "A good day's work," he said. "Felix Hoad is finally laid to rest and Danny Stein is killed off in the process. That will teach Stein to buy Grimoire Priory before I had a chance. First thing I'm going to do when we get back is put in a fresh bid for that property. Grimoire Priory will be my country seat."

The pattern continues and it goes from one evil owner to the next evil owner, I thought.

Andries was finished with his amputations. He pulled the trousered legs away from the rest of Hoad's body then he stood up, wiping the blood from his face.

"Should he still be bleeding? Doesn't the blood congeal after death?" Andries asked.

"You should know. You've killed enough times in the past," Thorn said. "I have an idea."

He went to my landline phone and made a call, speaking softly so I could not hear.

When he replaced the receiver there was a satisfied smile on his face.

"I phoned the Leppards. QPL is spending a fortune on building their super animal hospital. We are going to see Haven first-hand before anyone else and put it to use," Thorn said.

"I didn't know it was finished," Ives commented.

"It isn't but the animal crematorium is working so we can get the remains of Felix Hoad completely incinerated to ensure he won't ever be coming back."

"What about him?" Andries nodded at me. There was nothing but cold malevolence in his expression.

"We take him with us. What better place to get him to talk than a hospital full of medical equipment that can become instruments of torture. We can make Mr Bell scream for mercy and tell us what we want to know. Could be fun," Thorn said as he regarded me without pity.

"I have told you I know nothing. Ask Vasko. He has the cylinder," I pleaded.

"Oh you will talk. Why … they even have instruments there for castrating rams and bulls." Ives leant over me and grimaced.

Chapter Nineteen
: Tripping with the Devil

"We can fly there but the helicopter might be a little overloaded with all of us and Hoad's dead body," Thorn said.

"Yes and we don't want Ronan Bell squirming about and trying to escape while we are in the air," Ives said. "Let us make use of Mr Bell's van. We'll lock him in the back and I'll drive him to Haven."

"Good idea. I'll come with you. That way there will be two of us to cope with any problems and Andries can fly to Haven and pick us up there," Thorn said. "We need to get a QPL clean up squad here to remove any evidence that we were here. Stein's body can stay here. Just another murder to be blamed on our Mr Bell."

"Come here," Andries pulled me up and dragged me out of the door.

"Can you at least untie my hands? I really need a pee now," I begged but my pleas were ignored.

I was dragged over to my own van and literally thrown in the back. Andries slammed the doors shut and locked me inside. There were no windows to the outside, only the small window that looked into the driver's seat up front. Otherwise it was just a tin box that kept me prisoner.

I don't know how long I lay there trying not to think about my bladder.

Then the door was opened and Ives and Thorn were looking down at me. Ives threw in something wrapped in blood-stained tarpaulin. I couldn't see what was inside but I could guess. If I had any doubts, my left hand began bleeding again. I backed away from it.

"Some company for you," Ives chuckled. "Your trip will be in the company of greatness. Rest in pieces."

They turned at the thock, thock sound of whirling propellers. The helicopter rose into the dark sky behind them.

"There goes Andries. Enjoy your trip, Mr Bell, because once we get to the hospital all you can look forward to is one long scream," Ives said as he slammed and locked the van doors, leaving me alone with the tarpaulin covered corpse.

I heard Ives and Thorn get in the front seats and then the van started moving. It jolted and bumped over the unmade country roads making my journey even more uncomfortable.

I looked to one side. The tarpaulin wrapped package was being jolted around as well. We turned a corner and it began slithering over towards me. I backed up against the van side and kicked at the tarpaulin, halting its slide.

Then we seemed to be driving along a main road and the driving was smoother, keeping the covered corpse dead still.

I lay back, my heart racing, and trying not to think about what new horrors awaited me.

I closed my eyes, trying to relax.

There was a rustling noise.

I opened my eyes and looked around. I could not be sure but it seemed that the wrapped corpse had shifted slightly.

I stared at it hard.

The van slowed. I could see what looked like movement in the tarpaulin.

Then the van engine noise changed as it went into a lower gear. We were going uphill.

The floor slanted downwards.

The tarpaulin was slipping down, slowly uncovering its contents.

I watched, frozen with fear.

The shrouded body began to rise from the waist. It moved slowly, jerkily, as if it was just discovering that it had no legs.

It sat upright.

The tarpaulin slithered off and revealed what was beneath.

It was a nightmare. Hoad's jaw and teeth were fixed in a permanent grimace with no skin or lips to cover them. The sandblaster had shredded the skin on his face and exposed the white skull beneath. The flesh of his nose had been torn away to expose the bones of his nostrils. One of the eyes had become a deep, dark, empty socket but the other eye had survived and boggled out of the other socket. The long white hair flopped like a wig on top of the skull.

Some skin and flesh had survived and clung to his face and hands but like his clothes it was torn and pitted. Wisps of white beard dangled from the skin that remained on his chin.

The head turned slowly on a creaking neck till the one bloodshot eye fixed on me. It was filled with malevolent hatred.

Then Hoad raised one arm and pointed at me with a finger that had become a white skinless bone held together by sinew.

His jaw clacked up and down as if he was trying to speak but he only emitted a rasping death rattle.

It was then that my bladder gave out.

Hoad found his voice. He spoke to me in a deep inhuman growl: "Witness the death of death, Mr Bell. I wish to share it with you and then you can experience torture and suffering for all eternity without release. You will know then that Hell is very real." Then he threw back his head so his jaw dropped wide open and he laughed. It was a ghastly cackle.

"God help me!" My atheism was pushed to one side in my terror.

Suddenly the brakes of the van were slammed on and we jolted to a halt.

Hoad crashed down on his back and lay still.

There were footsteps outside and then the van doors were pulled open.

Four people looked in at me. Ives and Thorn had been joined by Rick and Zoe Leppard.

"Welcome to critters' clinic." Rick Leppard smiled at me. "We will be taking over your care from now on."

"Hoad is still alive. He sat up!" I blurted out.

"Harriet Milverton will try and take the credit for his immortality but, in truth, we know now that it is down to us. We weren't sure what would happen but it worked: we have made him invincible. And we did it with science we developed here rather than her hocus-pocus. Through our many experiments we have isolated the gene to regenerate old and damaged organs. We are working to give all believers everlasting life. However we have to rid ourselves of Felix Hoad and he has been brought here so we can finish him off once for once and all with total incineration," Zoe Leppard said. "Get them out!"

Rick Leppard climbed inside the van and looked down at Hoad. "What a mess. There is no way that body can have any life left in it!"

"Trust me it does," I said. "Can you at least untie me?"

He ignored my desperate request, wrapped up Hoad's remains and kicked them out of the van. He jumped out and once again the doors were slammed and locked on me.

After a while they were opened again. Then I was grabbed by Ives and Thorn who pulled me outside. I was in the grounds of Haven. There was no sign of what was left of Felix Hoad. Zoe Leppard ripped my sleeve.

"So, you won't give up the cylinder. Trust me, after I give you this you will tell us every single dark secret you have," Zoe produced a hypodermic and proceeded to inject its contents into my arm. "This serum is experimental. It will be good to have a human guinea pig to try it on."

I felt the effects straight away and buckled at the knees but they held me up. It was as if I had drunk a galleon of whisky.

"The dirty animal has pissed himself. Come, I have a cage for dirty animals." Rick Leppard dragged me off.

Ives and Thorn backed off and gestured at the waiting helicopter in the Haven grounds. "We will get off now and leave them both to you. Let us know when Bell talks and you have completely disposed of Hoad's remains," Thorn said.

"Yes, and I will be keeping Vasko and Squibb in the loop." Rick Leppard gestured a goodbye to them and dragged me into the grand white building, assisted by his wife.

I was only vaguely aware of my new surroundings. My mind was going into melt down.

I felt so weak. I could not fight back.

They dropped me on the floor in the reception and I could only lie there while they bolted the front entrance.

Then the happy couple came back and stared down at me.

"Well we have had a shortage of human subjects for our experiments my darling but now our prayers have been answered," Zoe spoke to her husband.

Rick leant down over me and whispered in my ear. "We are the only three people in this place. There will be no one to rescue you or stop us. It will be such fun, for us anyway. And when it is over, we don't have to worry about disposing of your body. We have a lot of hungry animals that need feeding. You will never be found."

Zoe wheeled out a gurney and they lifted me onto it. Then they pushed me through double doors and down a long white corridor with doors on either side. The wheels of the trolley squeaked as we trundled deeper into the centre of Haven.

I wanted to roll off and run for it but my drugged body would not respond and my hands were still tied.

They pushed me into an operating theatre with bright lights where steel scalpels and clamps were laid out on metal trays.

However that was not to be my destination. They pushed me further and into another room that was more like a laboratory.

I heard a fierce growling.

There was a long, low, black mesh metal cage on a long table. They opened the grill door on one side and rolled me inside. I lay still and flat while they fastened the gate. I was imprisoned and the cage was too low for me to stand up.

The growling came again.

I turned over to see what was behind me and then fear washed over me.

207

A grill separated me from the huge black dog that slavered and watched me through reddened eyes at the other end of my cage.

"It is a feral rottweiler. Or, to give the dog its proper German name, a Rottweiler Metzgerhund." Rick's voice entered my swimming brain. "I have been given him to put him down. He kills sheep and he bit his owner's face off so the courts ordered him to be destroyed.

"You are kept apart by the metal grill that divides the cage. However the metal grill is electronically operated and can be raised as slow or fast as I like. Once I take it away, he will spring at you and this dog is a merciless killer. Also it has been a while since we fed him so he will be desperate for a bite." Rick chuckled and Zoe joined in.

"Let's cut to the chase. The cylinder that was inside the Pan statue – where is it?" Zoe screamed at me.

I tried to blurt out that I had given it to Vasko but I was losing my grip on reality. The horror of my situation was too much and everything was drifting away from me.

Then I couldn't see Rick and Zoe anymore. I was alone with the vicious, mad dog.

I lost track of time and my grip on reality. I was flying up in the sky within a flock of black sparrows. I soared higher and higher. My flight seemed to take forever. There was bright blue light above me and pitch blackness speckled with flickering flames below me.

A beautiful, blonde-haired angel with huge, white wings flew alongside me. She smiled at me and held out her hand. I reached out to take it.

The dog snapped its teeth behind me and drew me back to the present. I looked round and I was grateful for the grill that separated us. Its lips were drawn back in a snarl showing its long, pointed incisors. There was nothing but hate and a desire to kill in its eyes.

Then it sprang at me. I thought the grill would stop it but when the dog hit the iron bars it seemed to burst in mid-flight, raining clumps of its black fur upon me. I covered my face with my suddenly free hands.

I took my head out of my hands and saw Felix Hoad standing outside the cage, naked and looking down at me. He was alabaster white but without a wound or a scratch on him and he had an enormous erection.

"Come Ronan, my son. Let us talk." Hoad extended a hand and unlocked the cage.

Then I wasn't in the cage anymore.

I stood up beside him and asked: "Am I dreaming?" There was no rope around my wrists.

"What is a dream and what is reality? Here, I decide," Hoad answered. "Look, you are bleeding again." Hoad held up my dripping left hand. "Know that the blood is real and so am I."

I looked around me and I was back in the cathedral again, the house of worship that had turned into a house of death.

The pews were filled with the derelict apostles from New Cannon Town. They were watching and leering up at the altar.

"Why are they here?" I asked.

They all began clapping. They all stood up as one and began swaying from side to side.

"We all work well with an audience," Hoad said. He raised his hand and the clapping stopped.

Then I saw what they were leering at.

Tipota lay naked on top of the altar. Somehow, she was relaxed and smiling at me.

I looked around at the clattering of a keyboard. It was Peter Wilde. He sat at a desk at his computer and he smiled at me. "I am finally getting my big scoop, old son. Make sure my story is printed won't you."

"But you are dead," I said.

"No you misunderstood. It's not that I'm dead but on a deadline."

"But I saw you die."

"Don't let a little thing like death stop the truth getting out," Peter smiled.

"Come, Ronan. I want you." Tipota writhed and squirmed on top of the altar.

"She is yours, my son. I know you have desired her since you first saw her. All you have to do is tell me where the cylinder is and you can have her." Hoad oozed charm.

"Tell him!" the audience shouted up at me as one. Then they began chanting, a rhythmic hypnotic prayer in a language I could not understand.

"I don't have it!" I blurted out.

"Liar!" Hoad's face turned to granite.

"Stop!" A new voice. It was Estelle. I could hear her but I could not see her. "Promise me that you will never give it to them."

"I would but it is too late…" I started.

"You must retrieve it and make sure it never falls into their hands. Swear that you will get it back and destroy it." Estelle's voice rang in my head.

"I will do my best."

"Damn you!" The still naked Hoad was holding his butcher's cleaver and he marched towards me.

210

"It is Vasko. He has it. I gave it to him I swear," I yelled and fell backwards and raised my arm protectively.

Hoad screamed aloud and the audience joined in, shrieking and wailing in despair. They stood up and as one, as if they were in the Colosseum in ancient Rome, all gave me the thumbs down.

"Kill!" they demanded with one voice that became a roar.

Hoad swung the cleaver down at me.

My heart seemed to jolt with fear and then suddenly I was back in the dirty, smelly cage again, my hands bound behind my back and the rottweiler snapping and snarling at the steel mesh door that separated us.

I thought it must have been a delirious dream but then I saw that my left hand was bleeding from the old wound that refused to heal.

"Ah, you are back with us," said Rick Sheppard who was smiling down at me with his wife by his side. "It seems that we have got all we can out of you. We now believe that you gave it to Vasko. You are incapable of lying under the influence of our special concoctions."

"What filthy poison did you inject me with?"

"It doesn't matter now." Zoe grinned. "Can I push the button?" she asked.

"Oh alright," Rick answered.

She reached down and pressed a button that was on top of a metal box beside the door that kept me and the rottweiler apart.

There was a soft whirring sound and the gate between us began to vibrate.

"Gradually the door will rise and open up and then you and the dog can be united. There will be nothing

211

between you," Rick chuckled. "Our poor puppy is very hungry, very angry and very insane."

"I want to watch." Zoe clapped her hands together and there was excitement in her eyes.

"No time, my dear," Rick told her. "We must get back to Felix."

"Felix Hoad? Haven't you cremated him?" I had to ask in my terror.

"Haven't you learned yet that you can't trust anyone who works for QPL?" Rick laughed.

"What does that mean? Is Felix Hoad is still alive?"

"Alive and no longer legless. We promised to regenerate him, he made us offers we just could not refuse. He will take me with him as he seeks the ultimate power. I will be on his right hand."

"Can he walk again?" I asked them as I watched the steel door rise from the floor and open up a crack.

"I am bored of talking to you. We must go and leave the dog to his dinner," Rick said.

"Bye, bye," Zoe waved at me.

Then they both turned and were gone.

Very slowly, imperturbably, the shutter was opening and now the dog had noticed and was trying to force his nose through the widening gap.

"Come back. There is more I can tell you!" I shouted at the top of my lungs but I will never know if the Leppards heard me or not. If they did, they ignored me.

The dog worried at the rising gate, snarling and drooling on the floor. I could hardly dodge out of his way. I could only lie flat, unable to move. There was not even a weapon I could use. I was not going to be able to fight off those vicious fangs with my bare hands.

212

Suddenly I could hear a woman's voice and she was singing softy, gently, a lullaby: "Hush, little baby, don't say a word, Mama's gonna buy you a mockingbird. And if that mockingbird don't sing, Mama's gonna buy you a diamond ring…"

The dog paused and turned its head as if it was listening. The lullaby seemed to calm him.

"And if that diamond ring turns brass, Mama's gonna buy you a looking glass. And if that looking glass gets broke, Mama's gonna buy you a billy goat…"

A great red dollop of raw meat was tossed into the cage from above and landed in front of the beast.

It tore into the meat and began devouring it as more chunks of meat fell from above.

I twisted my body to look up.

There was Father Sebastian Fullalove with his hands full of meat and Tipota standing beside him singing to the animal. Both were grinning.

"Are you real?" I gasped. "Are you ghosts?"

"We are both alive and kicking, old chap," said Sebastian as he opened the cage. "Glad you shouted. It helped us find you. Let's get you out of this room quickly and quietly because by releasing you we are also releasing your Hell Hound chum."

"I hope he finds his way back to Baskerville Hall," I attempted a little humour.

Tipota carried on singing as the three of us did a silent run out of the laboratory and shut the door behind us before the rottweiler knew what had happened.

Tipota kissed me but then recoiled back. "You smell bad," she said.

"I'm not surprised. I need a shower, a change of clothes, and a good meal and will someone please untie me? But tell me what happened to you. I am so glad to see you. I thought Vasko had killed you both."

"So did we," Sebastian told me as he freed my hands. "But it seems that he slipped us a Mickey Finn in the milk, not a deadly poison."

"What's a Mickey Finn?" Tipota was puzzled.

"Sorry, my dear. I forget how young you are. It's dope that knocks you out but doesn't kill you. It just gives you a bad headache."

"That's for sure," Tipota concurred.

Sebastian explained: "Once we came round Vasko dropped us in the middle of nowhere telling us that he did not see the point of killing us as we were no threat to him and were not worth killing. I thought it was strange at the time but I was not going to argue."

"Vasko kept his rule about never killing women," I said. "Who can figure that man? An evil megalomaniac with a conscience?"

"We decided to make our way back to your house to see what had happened to you and pick up my car," Sebastian continued his story. "Apart from Danny Stein and his splitting head, the place was deserted but there were bloodstains and signs of a fight as well as helicopter tracks on your front yard. Then I had the idea of doing a last number redial on your telephone and, guess what, the last number dialled had been the Haven hospital for our furry friends. So we drove here and arrived just in time to save you from being torn to pieces by man's best friend."

"Do you know the way out of here?" I asked. "I was drugged up to the eyeballs when they brought me in."

"Finding our way in was one thing. Finding our way out is another. This place is very confusing. That

214

seems to be a deliberate QPL design – buildings to get lost and trapped in," Sebastian said.

"Buildings to go mad in," Tipota added.

We seemed lost in a maze of white corridors.

There was the whinnying of horses, startled horses, in the distance.

"Let's see what is going on," Sebastian ran towards the noise.

I would rather have run away but Tipota and I followed his lead.

The noise was coming from behind a wooden door at the end of one of the long corridors.

We reached it and could hear the snorting and stamping of a horse coming from the other side.

Sebastian pulled the wooden door open.

The three of us fell back as a beautiful white horse galloped out and straight at us. Its eyes were bulging and it was running for its life, obviously scared.

We hung back and watched it gallop away down the corridor and out of sight.

"The only White Horse I like comes in a bottle," said Sebastian as he entered through the door.

"White Horse is a brand of whisky," I explained to a puzzled looking Tipota.

Sebastian spoke in a hushed voice: "I looked, and behold a pale horse: and his name that sat on him was Death, and Hell followed with him – an appropriate quote from the Book of Revelation. These must be the stables. Be careful. There may be other horses on the loose."

It smelled and looked like stables. However the horse stalls seemed to be empty.

I took the lead, feeling bolder now. I was about to make a quip about shutting the stable door after the horse had bolted but then I found something. There was a mound of hay in my way. I tried to kick it aside but my foot struck something solid.

I crouched down and pushed the straw aside.

Tipota screamed behind me. A bloody, puffy face stared back at me through a burst eyeball from the hay.

The three of us cleared away the rest of the hay to reveal the battered body of Zoe Leppard. The imprints of animal hooves were stamped all over her.

"Zoe Leppard has been trampled to death," Sebastian stated the obvious.

There came an angry cry from behind us. We turned to find Rick Leppard bearing down on us with a strange sort of gun in his hand.

"Get away from her!"

He pointed the odd gun at us. It was too big to be a pistol but too small to be a rifle. He kept it pointed at us while he looked down at Zoe's mangled remains.

"His gun doesn't shoot bullets, just a blade that stuns animals prior to slaughter," Sebastian muttered.

"I am sorry about your wife but it was not us," I started. "The horses must have bolted and trampled over her."

Suddenly Rick Leppard was laughing. "Good - the bitch is dead. Now I don't have to share the business with her and I can trade her in for a younger model."

"Don't you people have a caring bone in your body?" I was shocked.

"No, and that is why I am going to kill the three of you without a care in the world. By the way this is an old-fashioned captive bolt, not a modern stun gun. It penetrates the brain and kills instantly. The old ways are the best." Rick Leppard raised the weapon.

We ran. Sebastian, Tipota and I fled to the far end of the stables and out through the door at the end.

Rick Leppard yelled and gave chase.

We had hoped that the door would lead to the outside but it just opened on another long corridor. Haven hospital was a maze! We ran along the corridor to steel electronic double doors at the end. I pressed the panel beside the doors and they whirred open on a flight of steps that lead down into darkness.

We could hear Rick Leppard racing along the corridor behind us so we had no choice but to run down the steps into blackness.

Suddenly there was a beam of light and Sebastian stood behind it. "Good job I brought this," he said, indicating the torch in his hand.

He tried to find an inside panel so he could shut Leppard out but there was nothing. "Damn, you can only open and close these doors from the outside. Come, we have to run," Sebastian said.

The torchlight was not enough to show us the extent of the giant room we were in but I could sense that it was huge, an underground warehouse, filled with crates and tables and cages of all shapes and sizes.

As we ran further into the dark warehouse, the air seemed to get fouler.

"What is that stink?" Tipota asked.

"The odour of evil," Sebastian answered.

"Shush, Leppard will hear us," I cautioned. "Let's find another way out."

Sebastian kept the torch beam low as we crept through the huge hall.

As well as the really bad smell I was aware of strange noises all around us. Whimpers and growls with scratchings, shufflings and rasping.

"I don't like it here," Tipota said.

None of us did.

A loud screech sounded to our left. Sebastian swung the torch round and directed its beam at the source.

There was a cage with something inside it. It looked like an extra-large rat but it had very human looking hands so it could have been a mole. It was struggling to move as it was pinned to the floor with long needles. The creature screeched again, showing its long, pointed fangs.

"How cruel," Tipota said, "Take the light off it. I can't bear to look."

Sebastian moved the torchlight to the next cage. A bird with its wings spread but dragging on the floor walked in circles inside the cage. It had a curved beak and eyes that were blind.

Sebastian pulled the torchlight away and on to the next cage.

Something furry, possibly a dog, lay there breathing heavily, its stomach sliced and held open so its intestines were on show. A tube was inserted into its side and greenish fluid was flowing out of its body and into a plastic bag attached to the side of the cage.

The next cage seemed to be empty but when the light struck it something sprang out of the shadows, gripped the bars with long claws and stared back at us. It was about four-foot-tall and stood upright on two legs. It was naked, covered in bristly ginger hair but it had huge, feminine eyes, female genitalia and full pouting lips. It stared straight at me, blinking through those wide, long, ginger-lashed eyes that had naked lust in them.

It opened its mouth and a snake like forked tongue reached out for me.

"Get away!" I recoiled from the cage.

The creature hissed and spat green spittle at me, just missing me.

"This is an abomination," Sebastian spoke in a hushed voice. "This is vivisection of the worst kind, carried out in the name of their Satanic religion."

I recoiled in horror from the next cage that held a dog that was covered in diseased sores that oozed white poison.

"Keep back. It may be contagious," I warned.

The next cage contained something even more monstrous. It was a large ginger cat whose teeth and claws had been extracted and replaced with sharp-edged steel.

I thought then that nothing could shock me anymore but I was wrong.

Tipota screamed as the torchlight shone on the face of Archbishop Augustus Ighodaro in the next cage. His decapitated head dangled above the ground, hanging up amidst a web of wires and tubes. As we watched it opened its eyes and seemed to look at us. I had to believe that it was dead and that the opening of the eyes was just some sort of involuntary reflex, however I was haunted by a sense of awareness and terror in those eyes.

It quivered in the centre of the web as though it recognised us.

"The depravity of these people is without limits," I choked.

"This one looks normal." Tipota was looking at a white rabbit in the next cage. Then the rabbit bared its teeth at her and roared a vicious, unrabbit-like growl. Tipota jumped away, revulsed. "Perhaps not."

There were rows and rows of cages and they all seemed to contain some new horror. Some were recognisable as dogs, cats, rabbits, monkeys, baboons, hamsters, rats and guinea pigs but others had been carved and twisted into hideous mutations.

Something glowed bright yellow from a huge glass tank. As we got closer, we could see it was a large aquarium filled with cloudy, murky liquid where disgusting things that were neither fish nor fowl swam and breathed under the surface.

The yellow glow came from a massive, luminous jelly fish that floated on top of the liquid, quivering and pulsating. It was at least six feet across with two blinking eyes atop its almost transparent body.

I came closer and stared into the filthy liquid.

"Don't get too close," Sebastian warned. "Who knows what's in there."

I could just make out two blurry, chalky white human forms at the bottom of the tank.

"I think there are dead bodies in there," I said.

"Human bodies?" Sebastian asked.

Suddenly one of the bodies began floating to the surface.

"Whoa I think they might be alive," I gasped.

The head and shoulders of a beautiful woman emerged from the filth. She was naked and completely hairless. She was bald headed and without eyebrows but she was perfectly formed. She smiled and reached out for me with her right hand.

"Dead or undead?" Sebastian asked.

"Keep away!" Tipota screamed.

But I was enchanted by her and reaching out for her hand. "Let me get you out of there…" I muttered.

The woman in the tank spread her fingers as she grasped for me but then something strange happened. As she spread her fingers, they went from five to six.

I thought of Quincy Pitt and the six fingers on his right hand. Was there a connection?

Then the second body stirred in the murky slime.

The liquid swirled as the other body suddenly rose to the surface. The head and shoulders of a fully grown man emerged. Like the woman the man was completely hairless and perfectly formed.

He lifted his right arm out of the water and reached across his companion towards me. He gave me a friendly grin.

He spread his fingers as he grasped for me and just as suddenly, he went from five to six fingers.

They had to be the spawn of Quincy Pitt, I thought.

"Come away. They are not human," Sebastian shouted. "They look pretty but I sense they are deadly."

I turned away and heard the man and woman make gurgling sounds deep in their throats as if they were calling to me.

I did not listen but moved deeper into the zoo of horrors.

In another cage something scaly with an almost human face and a forked tongue slithered along the ground on its belly.

Then we found something even more disturbing. A black cat in a cage. But this was more than just a black cat. It stood upright on its hind legs and as we

221

approached the cage it turned and looked at us with eyes that seemed to suggest great intelligence and awareness. I almost expected it to speak.

A dog in the adjoining cage was barking at it but the cat regarded the dog with a barely concealed contempt.

"Wow, supercat," Sebastian gasped.

"I would like to let it out. I feel that this one is not dangerous," Tipota fumbled with the door lock on the cage but was defeated by it.

"The cage cannot be opened by us. It is some sort of electronic lock," I said. Then to the cat I said: "Sorry supercat."

I swear it seemed to understand.

Then we came to a much bigger cage. It imprisoned a full sized gorilla. Much of its fur had been shaved off and there had been an operation on its head that left part of its brain exposed. It was squeaking. I moved up to its cage for a closer look.

Then I swear it spoke to me. Just the one word: "Dada".

I fell back. "My God what are they doing to these poor creatures?"

"God has nothing to do with it. This is the work of those who worship the Prince of Darkness," Sebastian said.

"Their television programme was such a lie. No animal lovers could do this," Tipota was sickened.

"If we get out of here my first action will be to phone the police and the RSPCA. These poor living things must be put out of their misery," I vowed.

"Well we first have to get out of here. We seem to be going around in circles. There is nothing but rows on rows of cages," Sebastian complained.

We came to a much bigger cage. Sebastian raised the torch for a better look.

Something huge, hairy and black scuttled around the cage on its eight legs. It was a dog but they had given it four extra legs so it ran around the cage like a spider.

"Just when I thought it couldn't get any worse," Sebastian swung the torch beam away as the spider dog scuttled up to us, snapping and growling.

Someone shouted at us: "Leaves my babies alone! I will kill you all!" Sebastian swung the torch beam to the sound of the voice. The torch beam fell on the sweating face of Rick Leppard who was running at us with the captive bolt raised above his head.

The three of us dodged back as he fired the bolt. A long blade shot out and embedded itself into one of the wooden cages.

"You aren't getting out of here alive, you bastards," Leppard said between gritted teeth as he pulled the blade out of the wood.

Suddenly all the lights came on and the enormous warehouse was lit up.

Leppard looked up at a glass office that was a floor above. Whoever was in there would be able to look down over the warehouse.

"Who's there? Who turned on the lights?" he called up to the office.

A man came into view inside the office and looked down at us. It was Ocious Squibb.

He was holding a microphone in his gnarled and knotted hands.

"No one gets out of here alive," he said, his voice echoing around the hall from various loudspeakers.

"What are you doing here, you old relic? What is your game?" Leppard shouted up to him. "Where is Felix? He has made me his number two so you have to obey me."

"He told you what you wanted to hear to get you to patch him up. But now he has abandoned you to me. The Haven hospital has become a liability and I have been charged with closing it down. Harriet Milverton is driving him back to Mercer Tower as we speak. Oh yes, Vasko was his number two but now Vasko has stolen the recorded voice of Quincy Pitt for himself, Felix has made me his aide de camp." Squibb gave a dry chuckle.

Squibb looked down at the control panels. "Now I just have to tie up the loose ends. I can operate everything from here."

We could see him reach down and press a button.

The large steel double doors at the entrance slammed shut.

"Is there any other way out?" I asked Leppard. Suddenly we were on the same side.

"No and those doors are locked. We can't even get up to the office."

It was true. The glass office jutted out of the side of the hall and there were no stairs up to it. We were sealed in.

"As you know, Leppard, there is a lever up here that opens every single cage down there, releasing whatever is inside," Squibb continued. "I am going to operate it but I have set it on a five-minute delay. You know how I work. I don't like to watch the consequences of my actions and I want to be well clear before all these abused beasts escape and attack the nearest humans they can find. There are masses of them so you will be

224

overwhelmed very quickly. I would sing that song 'Who let the dogs out' for you but sadly I am tone deaf." Squibb chuckled without mirth.

"Don't, I beg of you…" Leppard shouted up at him.

Squibb ignored him and pressed down a lever with a heavy *clunk*.

"You have five minutes before all hell breaks loose. Enjoy…" were Squibb's last words before he turned away and was gone.

I looked around at the others for ideas. They all looked terrified and didn't seem about to come up with any escape plans so I took the initiative.

I pushed one of the tables across the warehouse and right against the wall underneath the glass office. We cleared the top of the table and lifted a second table on top.

"Come on. Climb up."

Before we could start climbing, there was a whirring and clunking sound as if the electronic locks on the cages were being opened. Our five minutes were up.

"Oh God they will be free and they will be lusting for blood. Get back. I'm getting out of here, not you!" Leppard screamed and gestured to us with the captive bolt.

We retreated and he sprang up on the first table and then hauled himself up on top of the second table so he was level with the glass office.

He put the captive bolt against the glass and fired it. The impact was terrific and the glass cracked and formed stars but did not break. It had to be Safety Glass.

We could hear the cage doors swinging open behind us and the animals squealing and growling as they sensed freedom and started clawing and clambering out of their prisons and slithering, limping and charging towards us.

The gorilla was out and went on a rampage, lashing out at the cages and smashing them. Brain damaged he might be but that didn't effect his enormous strength. He roared and kicked at the aquarium. There came a smashing of glass and sloshing of water as he kicked it over. Tank man and tank woman slithered around in the spilled liquid trying to find their feet.

The giant, luminous jelly fish was more mobile and slithered across the floor leaving a trail of yellow slime behind it.

Leppard started to panic and shot the bolt at the glass a second time. It jarred against the already cracked glass but threw him back with the recoil.

With a loud cry he fell backwards from the top table and thudded down on the warehouse floor still holding the animal killer.

"Quick!" I shouted. This was our only chance. I jumped onto the first table, pulling Tipota and Sebastian up after me.

We clambered up to the top table and I pounded on the cracked glass with my fists but it had no effect on the tough safety glass.

"Stand aside," Sebastian said and pulled a length of black painted wood out of his inside pocket. It was obviously cut from the branch of a tree and it ended with a shorter but much thicker knotty branch.

He held it like a hammer and swung it at the cracked window. He swung the Shillelagh at the window a second time. This time the cracks spread wider but the glass held firm.

226

There was a loud growling and roaring below us. Leppard had his back to the tables and was swinging the captive bolt wildly as the tortured beasts moved in on him from every angle.

The ginger cat with steel teeth and claws spring up at him and chomped at his face with those sharp metal fangs. Leppard screamed and fired the captive bolt at the cat. As it fell back, I could see that it had taken a huge bloody bite out of Leppard's cheek.

Suddenly the brain-damaged gorilla was before him and knocked the captive bolt from his hands. This time I definitely heard the gorilla say, "Dada."

"You are my children!" Leppard pleaded with the grotesque beasts. Then he screamed up at us: "Help me, please!"

Barking loudly, spider dog launched itself at Leppard. It landed on him with all its eight legs and brought him down.

His scream became a screech as spider dog pinned him down. Then other mutated monsters pounced and were upon him, biting, clawing and tearing.

The many tormented living things he had created converged on him. Birds that swooped down on him and went for his face. They were all getting their revenge and devouring him.

The giant jelly fish reached the fray and began slithering up the mountain of furry bodies.

"No, no!" Leppard's cries became a long scream. The giant jellyfish reached him and rose over his face. The luminous, transparent, yellow body enveloped his screaming head and silenced his cries.

All the while, Sebastian had been hammering desperately at the glass, and just as Leppard's cries were

227

silenced, the glass shattered with an almighty clamour, shards flying in all directions.

Sebastian then knocked out more of the broken window to make a hole big enough for us to get through and the three of us jumped off the table top and through the broken window into the office.

I looked behind me. I could not see Leppard now. He was buried beneath a heaving bloody carpet of living creatures with the jelly fish on top, quivering and pulsating.

I saw the man-like and woman-like creatures crouching on their hands and knees, still trying to stand. I wondered what would become of them.

One animal did not join in the attack. It was the black supercat who proved to be particularly agile. It broke away and began clambering up the tables towards us. Other animals tried to follow.

As soon as the cat had leapt through the broken glass, I kicked the tables away. They crashed to the floor and for a moment we felt safe from the murderous menagerie below.

The cat paused, standing upright, and looked at us, seemingly deep in thought.

"Hallo, puss." Tipota bent down to talk to it. I was afraid that it would suddenly lash out at her with its claws.

However, still upright, it turned and ran off through the open door and out of sight.

"Curiouser and curiouser," Sebastian scratched his head.

No longer running for our lives, we had pause to calm down and look around us.

There were electronic control panels all around us. The Sheppards could look down on their evil zoo and play with the temperature, lighting and door release systems from up here.

Sebastian began pulling open drawers and filing cabinets.

"Information is power. Let's see if we can find any more about who or what we are up against," he said. When he found a locked drawer, he just used the same crude club to smash it open.

"It's something I keep to remind me of Ireland," Sebastian said in response to my curious stares at the item he held which had saved us. "It's a Shillelagh. Very simple to make and when lacquered and hardened it makes a most formidable weapon. A cosh to smash the toughest skull."

He continued rummaging, then stopped and pulled out a bunch of keys plus electronic entry cards. They were attached to a business card for Mercer Tower with "John 844" written on it in black felt tip pen.

"I think I have found pay dirt," he announced.

"Is that a code of some sort?" I asked.

"Hmm…" Sebastian looked thoughtful.

"I see it as a sign. We've been shown a way into Mercer Tower. We have to go there and take back the wax recording. Vasko told me where he was going to conceal it - he was hiding it in an altar in an old underground church there, along with a lot of other incriminating evidence. I feel that Estelle will only be able to rest in peace when we have recovered that ancient recording," I said.

"Are you having doubts about your atheism?" Sebastian asked me.

"Are you?" I retorted.

"The important thing is not what you believe yourself but knowing what your adversaries believe."

"Let's go there and just hope we don't bump into Old Nick himself," Tipota tried to lighten the mood. "After what we have been through and survived, I don't think things could get any worse."

230

Chapter Twenty-One
: The Unspeakable

We left the hellhole that was Haven, clambered into my van that was still waiting outside and found, by some miracle, that the keys had been left in the ignition. Clearly the Leppards hadn't thought it important to take them out. I drove away as quickly as I could.

I stopped at the first telephone box I could find to anonymously tip off the police and the RSPCA. "The reputations of more celebrities are going to bite the dust," I said with some satisfaction after I had made the calls.

My next stop was a local High Street and a Travelodge hotel. I bought a change of clothes and rented a room so we could all have a shower. Then we found a local restaurant and got some food and drink in us.

"An army marches on its stomach," I reminded them.

Before we returned to the van Sebastian disappeared into a local bookshop and returned with the bulge of a book in his pocket.

I didn't ask what he had bought. I had a feeling that I knew. Then I drove us to Mercer Tower.

It was dark when I arrived at the building site by the black and glittering River Thames. The headlights picked up the corrugated fencing that surrounded the building. Notices warned that it was still under construction, patrolled by security guards, protected by alarms and watched over by CCTV.

A shudder ran through my body as I looked up at Mercer Tower's 40 floors. It was still incomplete and scaffolding encased the top of the building. It was a cold, sinister, menacing building. It jutted up into the night sky and merged with the blackness.

"Come, let's find a way in." Sebastian rattled his bunch of keys and entry cards.

I really didn't want to go. I had a horrible premonition that once I was inside, I would never leave that diabolical building.

There were security guards everywhere, marching in pairs. They moved in unison, robotic and mechanical, with faces set hard.

We got out of the van and explored the corrugated iron wall that surrounded the base of the building until we came to a padlocked doorway.

A pair of guards approached us in formation and stared at us with soulless, chilling eyes from behind visors. They were broad and burly and dressed in all black uniforms.

They didn't need to speak to impress upon us the danger we faced. We were forced to back away from the building. We stumbled back into darkness until we found a light.

The light came from a roadside cafe in a van. There was the smell of frying bacon from the open aperture in the side of the van and a sign above that read: Bert's Bacon Butteries.

"Welcome friends," a middle-aged, jolly looking man grinned at us from the counter. "Do you want something to eat or are you up to something that I can help you with?" When we didn't respond he continued, ""Being here I have to provide more than Bacon. So if you are not allowed to eat pork then I can do you chicken or beef butteries. Have no fear. I am no friend of QPL."

Still we hesitated to answer. Could we trust a stranger?

"You are working late," I said.

"I am always here because they hate it. They tried to get me moved but I am not on QPL land. This is common ground and I have a legal right to stay here and annoy them for as long as that building stands. This is my pitch. Bert's the name."

"What have you got against QPL?" I asked.

"I used to live in Blacksparrow Lane with my family. Then QPL compulsory purchased my house. My wife died not long after and then my kids scarpered. I have grandchildren I have never seen. I blame it all on QPL," Bert said.

"We're hungry but we have no time," I said peering inside his van. I was surprised to see candles and torches for sale. "Why are you selling those?"

"They laid new electricity cables for the QPL building and it uses masses of power. Some believe that it sucks extra electricity from the surviving end of Blacksparrow Lane. The Blacksparrow Lane houses were built at a time when electricity was a new gimmick. Some of the old houses still have the gas mantels for gaslight. The underground electricity cables in what is left of the original Blacksparrow Lane are old and worn out but the Electricity Company will only dig up part of the road and replace the cables when one of them wears out and the road is plunged into darkness. Believe me, people don't like being in the dark round here. Power cuts are more frequent than you might think. When the lights go out I make more money from my candles and torches than I do from my grub," Bert grinned.

Sebastian already had a torch but I bought one each for Tipota and me.

"We need to get inside, Bert, but the guards are a problem," Sebastian told him.

"No problem." Bert closed the hatch and got behind the wheel of his van.

He started it up and drove it into the corrugated iron wall that surrounded the building. He hit it with a resounding bang and then backed away.

The guards came out of everywhere but still in two by two formation and ran at him.

"I will bring that whole damned building down!" Bert shouted out of the window and then drove away into the night. All the guards followed him.

Bert had given us our one brief opportunity. We rushed back to the padlocked doorway.

Sebastian pulled out the keys and began trying them one at a time in the padlock. Part of me wished that we couldn't find a key to fit and that we would have to give up and go back home.

"Got it," Sebastian whispered as one key clicked in the lock.

He opened the creaking metal door very slowly and pushed it back quickly when a uniformed security guard with a dog on a leash strode by. We waited, Sebastian peering through the crack in the door, then when the guard was out of sight, he opened the door again.

"Quick!"

The three of us rushed through. Once inside, he pushed the door shut behind us. There was a building site before us but the whole skyscraper was close to completion. We ran over the muddy ground to a concrete slope that led to the underground car park beneath the building.

We ran through the car park, dodging behind pillars but there were no other guards to be seen. We came to a central base of the building that had row upon row of lift doors all around it. We went round pressing all the lift buttons but nothing happened.

"I don't think they're functioning yet," I stated the obvious.

"I don't fancy going up in one of those builder's cages that run up the outside of buildings," Sebastian grimaced.

Then as we circled the lower central core of Mercer Tower, we came across lift doors that were different to all the others.

The doors were pitch black and there were no call buttons outside, just a key entry pad with all the letters of the alphabet plus the numbers one to ten on it.

"What about the code that is written on the card?" I asked. "That might work."

Sebastian punched it in on the pad: John 844.

The doors opened. Inside, the lift was all pitch black, shiny metal like the doors. At least it was lit by a light in the ceiling.

We stepped in and looked for another pad but there was nothing.

The doors slammed shut, trapping us inside, and very slowly we began to descend.

"Hey, I wanted to go up," Tipota protested.

"I'm afraid this lift is taking us where it wants us to go," I said.

Sebastian pulled out of his pocket the black book he had purchased earlier. It was the Holy Bible. He opened it up and began to read.

"As I suspected. The code John 844 stands for the testament of St. John, Chapter Eight, Verse 44. Let me read it to you: Ye are the father of the devil and the lusts of your father ye will do. He was a murderer from the beginning and abode not in the truth because there is no truth in him. When he speaketh a lie he speaketh of his own; for he is a liar and he is the father of it."

"The Father of Lies," I said in a hushed voice.

We seemed to go down for a long time but then the lift stopped.

"Prepare for anything," Sebastian warned.

Then the doors opened.

At first, we looked into dark shadows and then our eyes got used to the darkness and temporary overhead lighting came on. Had they been turned on by some sort of sensor or had someone seen us and switched on the lights? Were we alone down there?

I could not see anyone else, just a stone path in front of us. We left the lift and walked along it, very cautiously.

It led to a hole in the ground. We peered inside. A stone spiral staircase spiralled downwards into blackness.

"I'll lead the way," Sebastian switched on his torch and began to climb down.

We descended and the lower we went the more fetid the air seemed to get. It smelled rancid and the fumes seemed to get into my brain and make me giddy.

I had to grab hold of the slimy wall for fear of falling down those steps. I could image myself tumbling down them deeper and deeper into the blackness with nothing to stop my fall.

Then we reached the bottom and stepped out into a huge, dark cavern. Sebastian shone his torch around.

The walls were covered with obscene, lifelike paintings of torture, orgies, screaming madness and human sacrifice.

"I think we have found our underground church," Sebastian whispered. He aimed his torch at the altar. It was covered with a purple cloth and a silver chalice filled with black coals lay on top. Fixed to the altar was an upside-down crucifix.

"If Vasko is to be believed, the wax recording they are all after is under the altar," I said and made for it on legs that were very unsteady.

The filthy air was getting to us. We all walked like drunks.

"What is that smell?" I asked. It was like bad eggs.

"It is sulphur," Sebastian answered.

I halted in my tracks. The black shadows in front of me seemed to have taken on a life of their own.

The shadows gathered together, solidified into a black hump, rose up from the ground and towered over me.

I froze, too scared to move.

"Though I walk through the valley of death, I will fear no evil…" Sebastian praying behind me.

The black hump quivered and then slowly dissolved. I started forward again.

A red glow came from the silver chalice on top of the altar. The black coals in the chalice were suddenly burning and glowing and giving off acrid black smoke.

The red light from the coals lit up what was hanging on the wall above the crucifix and staring down at us.

It was a framed portrait of a tall old man, if it was a man, seated in a high winged, black leather chair. The embers in the chalice flickered and glowed, giving the impression that the portrait was alive and moving. The eyes shone with evil life.

The man that glared down at us was from a different century and as we stared, aghast, at the evil creature before us, it became clear who it was.

"Look - the right hand. It has an extra finger. It's Quincy Pitt!" Sebastian cried.

The air was thick with loathsome fumes and I felt physically sick.

As I looked at the picture it seemed to take on a three-dimensional quality. The face became greyer with jutting cheek bones and there was a green glow in the eyes.

"Don't look at him!" Sebastian shouted at us.

"I can't help it!" Tipota sobbed.

She was not the only one. I was transfixed. Those malevolent green eyes in the mummified face bored into my brain. I couldn't tear my own eyes away.

Quincy Pitt was moving. He pushed himself up from the chair and seemed to continue to rise forever. Was he seven foot tall?

The shrivelled mouth opened and gasped like a hiss of steam. The huge skull nodded as if it were too heavy for the scrawny neck. Pitt raised his right arm and pointed at me with its sixth finger.

238

I tried to scream. I tried to run away. I couldn't. Terror froze me to the spot. Was it a ghost? Was it alive?

"Look at me!" it commanded in a golden, mellow, hypnotic voice.

"What do you want?" I gasped.

"I know you, Ronan Bell Esquire." Green spittle dribbled from his lips as Pitt spoke to me. "In time you will know me. Serve me. Worship me. Know that you are mine."

"Never," I managed to croak.

There were half-heard whispers all around me and solid black shadows that swirled and danced in the darkness.

Pitt raised his arms either side in an offered embrace. His image wavered as if it were trying to become solid. I felt that once he had hold of me, he would materialise and become real.

"Come! Surrender!" Green spittle showered from that ancient maw as Pitt called to me.

I found myself walking towards him. Slowly, hypnotically, like a robot.

Pitt's eyes became bigger and bigger till they became one blinding green light.

Suddenly I was pushed aside and thrown to the ground.

"The Lord is my shepherd. I shall not want..." Sebastian stood before the monster holding up the Holy Bible in one hand.

Quincy Pitt screeched and his imaged blurred.

Sebastian turned to me and shone his torch back to the entrance to the spiral staircase. "Take Tipota and run for your lives. Go now!" Sebastian yelled.

"But what about you?"

"I will fight the battle down here. Only I can. Take what is underneath the altar. You have other battles to fight," Sebastian said.

I reached beneath the altar and found a steel box. I picked it up, tucked it under my arm, grabbed Tipota with my other hand and ran for the steps.

"Don't go, Mr Bell, when so much is within your grasp," the voice of Quincy Pitt echoed in my head but I ignored it. "You will never escape."

I looked back to see Sebastian squaring up to the projection of Quincy Pitt. He was on his own now – or was he? There were a lot of dark shadows swirling around him.

I turned back to the entrance to the spiral staircase and pulled Tipota towards it. The torchlight was no more but the glowing embers gave me just enough light to see by.

"Stop! You will not leave here. Give me the box!"

It was a female voice.

Mrs Harriet Milverton stepped out of the shadows. She held her hand out, reaching for the metal box.

I dragged Tipota to one side and continued my run for the steps.

Mrs Milverton screamed and launched herself at me. I fell over backwards, losing grip of both the box and Tipota.

She was incredibly strong for an old woman. Damn that Royal Jelly!

"You have desecrated our holy altar and defiled our work," Mrs Milverton screamed in my face. "Die like all unbelievers."

I couldn't move. She had me pinned to the ground.

She reached up into her hair bun and extracted one of her steel bobby pins. She stabbed down at me with it, aiming for my eye. I twisted aside and the pin scratched the floor next to my head.

I tried to fight back but she was stronger than me.

She stared down at me with eyes full of hatred and rage and raised her deadly needle again.

Suddenly Tipota was behind her and trying to pull her off me.

"Get off me, you feeble kitty cat!" Mrs Milverton screeched at Tipota.

Tipota extracted another of Mrs Milverton's steel bobby pins from her hair bun. Next thing I knew Tipota had rammed the steel pin into the side of Mrs Milverton's neck.

"This kitty has claws," Tipota hissed at her.

Mrs Milverton's screams echoes around the huge cavern. She let go of me and reached up for her neck but Tipota just plunged the needle in deeper.

The underground church vibrated with her terrible wailing. Some of her blood splashed on me. Mrs Milverton recoiled back clutching at her neck and face. It seemed that Tipota had hit a nerve, as Tthe side of Mrs Milverton's face that had been stabbed drooped and sagged and folds of skin dropped over one eye. One side of her mouth twisted downwards in a permanent sneer.

Her screams choked into silence as half her face became paralysed.

I pushed her off me while Tipota let go of the acupuncture needle. Mrs Milverton quivered and twitched. She had fallen on her back, her hands covering her face, and was writhing on the ground, pounding it with her heels.

"Die, you evil old witch!" Tipota screamed down at her.

Then, as if I did not have enough to contend with, I felt warm wet blood flowing from my cut left hand.

"Oh no. Felix Hoad is here somewhere," I moaned.

"I don't see him." Tipota looked around in the darkness.

The thought of Hoad lurking in the blackness terrified me more than ever.

A deep chuckle echoed around us. It was Hoad. We didn't see him but we heard his voice although we couldn't tell where it was coming from. It was just a voice from the dark. "Stop them. They must not get away. You incompetent old crone, how could you let that pair of losers overcome you?" he screamed. "You have failed me! I need another Mambo."

Mrs Milverton was struggling up into a sitting position with her back against the wall. She plucked the needle from her neck but her agony showed in her distorted face.

She began chanting in an angry voice. I have no idea what language she was jabbering in but it became louder and louder.

I had the feeling that she was casting some sort of spell or placing a curse and I wanted to be as far away from her and the unkillable Felix Hoad as possible.

I pulled Tipota away, grabbed the metal box again, and then I could see no more as I was running up the dark spiral staircase with Tipota by my side.

Going up the spiral staircase took much longer than coming down and I was constantly afraid that we were being chased by something nasty from the crypt we had left behind. Suddenly there was light ahead. We came out onto the stone path that we had first entered by. I was desperately glad to be leaving that poisonous air. We ran along it till we came to the jet-black lift doors. I tapped in the code on the keypad, The key pad was outside and I could remember the code: John 844. I tapped it in. Tthe doors opened and we stepped inside. Once the doors closed the lift rose upwards. Once again, the lift was taking us where it wanted to take us.

This was as good a time as any to look inside the box. I opened it up. There was no sign of the wax cylinder from Pan. There were just masses of documents, flash drives, CDs, cassette tapes, paper files, blood stained chalices and other items sealed in plastic bags and photos. I pulled a photo out and showed it to Tipota. It showed Danny Stein and Detective Superintendent Ives shaking hands at the entrance to a casino.

"I am guessing this contains the evidence files that went missing during Danny Stein's trial and got him off. I bet that not only will this incriminate Ives but the whole QPL Group. Vasko must have kept it hidden for his own protection ... I wonder why he told me where it was."

"Because it didn't matter as you were supposed to die," Tipota came up with the most logical explanation.

I shut the lid. It would take hours to go through everything in the box.

Up and up we went, faster and faster, until I was afraid that the lift would smash through the roof of the building.

Then it jolted to a halt, so suddenly that Tipota and I were thrown off our feet.

The doors opened. We stepped out and the doors hissed shut behind us. This was as far as the lift went. I could hear it going down again. We were on the top floor; it was freezing cold up here. The floor was still being built so the wind gushed through glassless windows. There was no heating or lighting but we were so high up that the moon, glimpsed through the unfinished windows, seemed closer and lit our way.

"We have to get out of here but I am not going in that lift again," I said to Tipota.

"The only other way out is the stairs. How many floors did you say there were...?" She looked scared.

The lift came back and the doors opened again. Out stepped Detective Superintendent Ives. He was accompanied by a heavy-set man with a boxer's face, dressed as a QPL security guard.

"Fuck, you have the box!" He pulled out his modern police baton and with a flick of his wrist extended it to its full length. "Give it to me!"

"Run!"

Suddenly Tipota and myself were running for our lives again, with that damn box clutched under my arm.

"Get them. They must not get away!" Ives shouted as he chased after us, followed by the security guard who was clumping after him in heavy black leather boots.

I was going to hang onto that box whatever happened. I had a feeling it would prove my innocence and the guilt of many others.

We turned a corner and ran down the corridor to the door at the end. I pushed the door open and almost started through. A howling wind pushed me back. I clung to the sides and looked straight down to the dark and glittering River Thames hundreds of feet below.

The door opened onto nothing. There was a staircase being built below but it had not reached this floor yet.

Scaffolding encased this top portion of the building which was still under construction.

"Get back quick!" I shouted.

Tipota and I ran back and found another corridor that branched off the main one. We ran down it into darkness as we could hear Ives bellowing and howling after us.

I knew he would do anything to get that evidence box and Tipota and I would be killed before we could talk.

I took us down another corridor, hoping to lose Ives, but I could still hear him ranting and screaming behind us. He smashed his baton against the walls as he gave chase.

Tipota and I halted suddenly as the corridor came to an end. We were on a sort of landing. Below us was just a long drop. Ahead and above was a flight of steps leading up to a pair of double doors.

"The only way is up," I tried to sound cheerful as I pulled her up the steps to the double doors.

I pushed them open and we ran through. We were on the top of the world.

Chapter Twenty-Two
: Hell on High

We were on the roof of Mercer Tower. An inky sky engulfed us and a freezing wind rattled through the scaffolding. A few grey clouds hovered above us; they seemed close enough to reach up and touch. Floodlights fixed to the scaffolding lit up the wide expanse of rooftop. There was nowhere else to run. We could not go any higher and the only way off was to leap into space and certain death.

I looked back and saw a red-faced Ives on the landing, starting up the stairs after us. The uniformed guard was close behind, grinding his teeth in a murderous rage.

We were trapped.

I slammed the twin steel doors shut and looked for a way to fasten them. A length of steel pipe lay nearby. I picked it up and slipped the pipe through the two loop handles on the doors, fastening them closed.

I had been just in time. Ives crashed against the doors on the other side and cursed when he found he couldn't get through.

The steel doors bulged outwards as he and the guard charged against them again but they held firm.

"Unless there is another way up, I think we are safe for now." I backed away holding Tipota's hand.

There were a few more thumps and snarls at the steel doors but then it went quiet.

I stood there on the roof, buffeted by the freezing wind and holding Tipota close.

"He can't get at us. If we hold out long enough, we can get help," I tried to reassure her.

She did not seem worried. She had retreated into a world of her own and was singing softly under her breath. Poor damaged and abused child. This was her defence mechanism but I shouldn't knock it. Her singing had calmed the vicious dog that had been set to tear me apart in Haven.

"Ronan old chap listen to me," Ives was talking through the door, suddenly smooth and urbane. "This is a new building with the very latest in high security technology. Did you and your gang think that you were just going to break in here undetected? You can't escape but there is no need for anyone to get hurt. All I want is that box and you and the girl can go free."

"I'm not an idiot. Your homicidal friends have tried to kill me many times and you are not going to stop now. We just have to wait it out till daylight and then attract attention to get some help. I suggest you use the breathing space to skip the country and escape prosecution. We are going nowhere," I shouted back.

Ives snarled again and then things went quiet.

I examined our roof top trap to see if there was any other access. The wind was rattling around the scaffolding enmeshed roof. I walked to one side and peered over the edge.

Vertigo turned my legs to jelly.

The River Thames glittered an endless giddy drop away and a carpet of tiny winking lights was spread out

247

for miles around. There was at least 12 feet of space between the glassless windows on the top floor and the edge of the roof. There was no way anyone could get up from there.

I dragged myself away from the edge and, stepping over the scaffolding and girders, made my way back to Tipota and the box of files.

"It is so cold," Tipota complained.

"Just hold on till morning." I gave her my jacket to put on.

We both sat down and waited.

There was a noise above our heads and a disturbance in the night sky. *Thock, thock, thock...*

A howling wind snatched my breath away.

The helicopter came swooping out of the clouds at me. I lay flat down and pulled Tipota down beside me.

It hovered above us like a bird of prey, its whirling propellers an invisible blur.

I looked up with streaming eyes and saw Andries at the controls in the cockpit. Marquis Thorn's private helicopter!

Marquis Thorn himself stuck his head out of the cabin and shouted down to us: "It is over for you. There is nowhere left to run. Give it up!"

"If you think Hell is so great why don't you just go there!" I shouted back.

"I will force you off the roof!" Thorn promised as he pulled his head back inside.

The helicopter began to descend on top of us. We would be crushed.

There was a deafening clang as one of the helicopter skids bounced off the criss cross of scaffolding that caged the roof.

248

The helicopter reared back, manoeuvred around the roof, and tried to land somewhere else.

Once again it crashed against the scaffolding. The helicopter was forced to retreat. It rose up into the sky while Andries glared down at us. There just wasn't enough of a clear flat area for him to land the whirly bird, especially in that buffeting wind.

"Ha, they can't get at us!" I gave Tipota a comforting hug.

There was a puff of smoke from the cabin of the helicopter and something struck the scaffolding at my side. It was a bullet!

I looked up again and saw Marquis Thorn standing in the helicopter cabin, taking aim at us with his hunting rifle.

Thorn fired again and I could hear the bullet hit the ground near us. The gun spurted more smoke and bullets and cement chips bounced off the ground around us. Thorn ranted and cursed above us. We were open targets on the roof.

They couldn't land and the movement of the helicopter made precise aiming impossible but if he shot at us enough times, he was going to get lucky.

Our only hope was that Ives had given up trying to get through the door. We had to try and escape the way we came. I pulled Tipota to her feet and we ran for the doors.

Just for a second, I thought I heard the galloping of animal hooves the other side of the doors but I dismissed it in my head as just too ridiculous.

Had that white horse followed us here?

Then, as if I did not have enough to worry about, my left hand began to bleed.

I reached the double doors, pulled the bar from the handles and yanked the doors open.

The firing from the helicopter ceased.

Felix Hoad stood in the open doors; a living nightmare captured in the floodlights.

He grinned at us with a jaw that was fixed in a permanent grimace and a face that was more skull than skin. His one surviving eye boggled at us while the other eye had become a deep, dark, empty socket.

The bullet hole in his forehead looked deep and black. His long white hair flopped like a wig on top of his skull and white wisps of hair remained around what was left of his mouth and chin.

But that was not the worst thing. Felix Hoad wore a long coat but we could see the new legs he stood on. They were the legs of a goat; hairy, with wide thighs and cloven hooves at the end.

"Behold my cloven hoofs. Now I can really kick up a storm!" Hoad laughed and did a little dance on his new legs. His hooves made a loud clattering on the floor.

I quickly slammed the double door shut again, grabbed for the length of steel and shoved it back through the looped handles.

Something thumped against the steel doors and left a large dent. There was a second thump and the doors buckled, the bar through the handles beginning to bend. Hoad was kicking the doors down.

I pulled Tipota away and, still holding the box, we backed across the roof. But where could we run to? Still the helicopter hovered above, watching and waiting like a mechanical vulture.

I picked up another iron bar to give myself a weapon but as the doors were kicked again and began to crumple a sense of doom overcame me.

The iron bar through the handles snapped in half and flew in two directions. The doors crashed open and Felix Hoad stepped through and onto the roof.

"Why won't you die?" I asked.

"Haven't you heard the expression 'Never Say Die'?" Hoad chuckled.

"I prefer 'Always Say Die'," I said. "Now you really are half man, half beast."

He did another little dance to show off his new legs.

"My new prosthetic legs are modelled around titanium rods. A present from the Leppards who thought it bought them forgiveness for betraying me. Of course they didn't do human legs but then these are much more my style. I have become the new Pan! These are so much stronger and tougher than my old legs that were beyond saving anyway. Indeed I first tried these out on Zoe Leppard herself," Hoad boasted.

"It was you? You kicked Zoe Leppard to death?" as evil as she was, I was still horrified as I remembered the woman's trampled body with hoof prints all over it.

"Titanium is one of the hardest materials known to man. My legs have become deadly weapons. I am unstoppable." Hoad's exposed jaw clacked up and down as he spoke, the remining wisps of his white beard flying in the wind. "What do you think of my wonderful new building? Mercer Tower has been constructed as a temple to Astorath, the Crown Price of the Netherworld."

"I thought it was Quincy Pitt you worshipped?"

"Quincy Pitt was his prophet on earth and even after his so-called death he is still a channel between Astorath and this world."

"You are completely insane," I retorted.

"Like you, I was an unbeliever. I embraced the bad life because that is who I am. Then Mrs Milverton introduced me to the old religion and became my mentor. She gave my black desires a purpose and a focus. Now the pupil has surpassed the teacher and I am finished with her."

"Here, this is what you want. Take it and leave us alone." I threw the metal box at his feet.

"I was always going to get it." Hoad ignored the box and skipped over it, jumping about ten feet into the air to demonstrate the strength of his new legs. "But my first order of business is to inflict agony and death on you two."

The helicopter circled above with Thorn and Andries looking down on us.

The wind whirled around us in a freezing fury while Hoad closed in on us. There was only so far we could back away. Before too long we would come to the edge and one long drop.

I held the iron bar out in front of me while Hoad trotted towards us, making a clumping sound with his hooves on the concrete roof. I held Tipota by my side as we backed closer to the edge.

Suddenly we could go no more. Infinity dropped away behind us.

As I stopped Hoad chuckled and galloped at us.

I lashed out with the iron bar.

He warded my blow off with his arm and aimed a kick at me with one cloven hoof.

The kick caught me in my upper thigh and I fell back, full length, on the roof. My leg had exploded with pain.

Tipota launched herself at him, avoiding those hooves and going for his neck.

Hoad plucked her off him and raised her, kicking and screaming, above his head in his two hands.

He ran at the edge of the roof.

"No!" I screamed and hurled the iron bar at him. It bounced off Hoad without slowing him down.

He just laughed and then tossed her off the roof.

Tipota screamed once and then fell out of sight. She was gone.

My heart was broken and I was in a state of shock. I staggered up and lurched at him, trying to go for his face. I had a vague idea of gouging out his one good eye to leave him blind.

However those hooves were too fast for me. They landed in my stomach and kicked me across the roof top where I lay wheezing for my breath.

Hoad did not pursue me but walked to the edge of the roof and looked over.

There was no respite for me. A bullet reverberated off the scaffolding close by. Marquis Thorn had decided to resume taking pot shots at me.

I picked up a brick from the roof, pulled myself up and threw the brick at the helicopter; a futile gesture.

"Back off." Hoad waved the hovering helicopter away. "He is mine to obliterate."

The brick did not get anywhere near enough to hit the helicopter but fell over the edge where I heard it strike the scaffolding below.

"Hey, be careful. That nearly hit me," came Tipota's voice.

My heart leapt into my throat. Had all I had endured driven me insane at last? I went to the edge of the roof and peered over.

Tipota was clinging to part of the scaffolding that encased the top half of the building.

She was about ten feet below me and out of my reach but I gauged it was possible for her to climb back up. She had obviously grabbed onto the scaffolding as she fell and it had saved her life.

She was what Hoad had been looking down at.

"Hold on tight. You can make it back up. You just have to try," I called down to her.

I just hoped she didn't look down at the long giddy drop below her.

There was another shot from the helicopter and concrete chips sprayed round my feet.

I looked up to see Marquis Thorn scowling down at me, his smoking rifle in his hand.

I dodged back trying to get out of his range.

It was then that Hoad began kicking down at the scaffolding that surrounded the top of the building. It shook and quivered. He was trying to demolish it with his titanium hooves and send Tipota hurtling to her death.

The helicopter swooped down and hovered alongside. Now Thorn had a clear shot at me.

Hoad kicked out again and the whole jigsaw of scaffolding shook violently. Tipota hung on desperately as a length of iron tube broke away and plunged downwards.

"No one can defeat me. I am invincible. Worship me or die!" Hoad danced and pranced on the roof edge, waving his arms and shouting at the heavens. "Take these two pathetic souls, oh mighty Astorath!"

Then it happened.

I thought I had seen a black cloud moving much too fast towards us. I was not sure what I was looking at. A huge black blizzard circled the roof top, getting larger and darker as it blotted out the moon. I looked up and the blackness became a blur as it whirled around the roof.

Then it seemed to focus on a target and swarmed towards the helicopter. It struck the side of the helicopter and rattled against the Perspex.

"Dive, dive, get out of it!" I heard Thorn shout at Andries.

I glimpsed Andries wrenching at the controls before the helicopter swooped down to hover below us.

The black swarm did not follow but continued to swoop down on the roof.

I lay down on the edge of the roof and reached down, holding out my hand.

"Climb up and grab my hand!" I called to Tipota.

Hoad kicked at the scaffolding again. Tipota screamed but hung on as the whole structure rattled and shook. A section of the scaffolding lurched and broke away. I felt that it was about to collapse like a house of cards.

Andries and Thorn looked up at us from the helicopter cabin. Thorn cocked his rifle and in spite of the howling wind I am sure I heard the click of it cocking.

I also heard another noise.

It was the squawking of birds.

255

Felix Hoad suddenly staggered back, screaming with surprise and rage. I stared upwards in disbelief. I knew what the black cloud was.

Felix Hoad was being attacked by a vast flock of sparrows. Black sparrows.

Hoad bellowed and tried to wave the black sparrows away from his one good eye but there were too many of them. He tried to run but they swarmed over him, pecking, flapping their black wings and screeching in fury.

The flock moved as one, as if it were controlled by a single force. I thought again of Mrs Milverton and the curse she seemed to chant. Had she summoned them? I also remembered how she said that these uncommon sparrows had sharper beaks and claws than the common sparrow.

I watched the prancing Felix Hoad as the birds covered him. Howling, his whole face buried beneath pecking beaks and flapping feathers, Hoad stumbled towards the edge of the roof.

"Get off me, you filthy creatures!" Hoad yelled as he tottered on the edge of space, scrabbling at the air.

One cloven hoof came down on nothing. He tried to throw himself back but the weight of those titanium legs pulled him down.

He toppled forward and hurtled downwards, headfirst. He struck a protruding length of scaffolding and it seemed to knock a piece out of him before tossing him away from the side of the building.

In the helicopter cabin Marquis Thorn suddenly saw what was going to happen and screamed at Andries: "Fly away now. Get us out of here!"

It was too late.

Felix Hoad fell headlong into the whirling blades of the helicopter hovering directly underneath him.

There were ghastly tearing and wailing sounds as the spinning blades sliced him into mincemeat. Bits of flesh and bone were sprayed everywhere, splattering me and Tipota.

The top of his body was sliced and diced but the goat's legs got caught up in the propellers. The helicopter choked and stuttered as the legs tangled round the main rotor arm and jammed the propellers. They could not cut through the titanium rods. They ground to a halt.

The blades stopped spinning, sending the helicopter cabin below into a giddy spin.

Now it was the turn of Thorn and Andries to scream as they were tossed around inside the furiously revolving cockpit.

I watched the helicopter drop away from me in wild lurches, the engine spluttering and chugging.

With the blades jammed to a standstill and the cabin spinning wildly on its axis Thorn and Andries were flung around inside the hellish merry-go-round that the helicopter had become. It zigzagged downwards screeching like a wounded beast.

Finally it plunged into the Thames far below. There was a torrent of water followed by a fiery explosion that flung flaming metal in all directions. The wreck of the helicopter sunk slowly into the burning oil slick on top of the river.

In the road below Bert had shaken off the pursuing guards and returned his van back to its site. He heard the noise of the falling helicopter and saw the explosion.

He leapt from the van to run up a side road to the edge of the Thames to see what had happened. He watched the remains of the helicopter sink beneath the flaming water with much gurgling and hissing.

There was debris all around him in the road, some of it on fire. The air smelled of smoke, blood and burning meat. Glittering shreds of flesh flecked the pavement and dangled from the streetlight. Bert's attention was caught by something white and round that rolled and clattered in the road. He approached it and looked down at it with wide eyed disbelief.

It was a skull. It seemed to have a life of its own. It rolled around the ground in all directions. Its unhinged jaw clacked up and down. Then it rolled still and seemed to look up at him with its one remaining eye and a black bullet hole in its forehead.

It was just a skull and could not possibly be alive but the way it moved sent shivers all over Bert's body.

Then he saw the remains of the pure white hair on the head and chin.

"My name is Pringle, Bert Pringle. Remember my name, Felix Hoad, and take it to Hell with you!" he shouted and stamped down on the skull with his boot.

The skull cracked and shattered into a shower of bone splinters beneath his boot.

Bert paused to wipe the goo off the sole of his boot and then began to dance and sing.

"Zip-a-dee-doo-dah, zip-a-dee-ay. My, oh my, what a wonderful day..."

Our pursuers may have been dead but Tipota was still in peril and I had to wonder if that flock of vicious black sparrows would come after us next. After all, Mrs

Milverton wanted us dead as well. But when I looked up there was no sign of the diabolical birds.

Tipota did not have to be told what to do. She clambered up the shaky scaffolding as fast as she could.

Finally she was close enough that we could grasp each other by the hand. With a last tremendous effort I pulled her up onto the roof and safety.

"Let's get off of here!"

We hurried as fast as we could with our injuries, back to the open doors. We ran through them and down the stairs to the landing and then stopped.

Detective Superintendent Ives stood before us surrounded by a small army of uniformed policemen. He scowled at us, his face set like granite and his hands clasped behind his back.

"I can't fight anymore," I collapsed into a sitting position. "Just arrest me."

A man who looked familiar and wore a different kind of police uniform came to the front. He spoke to me: "I am the chief commissioner. I have taken charge of your case. You can relax. The truth is out and justice will be done."

Relief washed over me, making me feel faint. "There is a box full of evidence on the roof!" I blurted out. "It will prove my innocence and let you know that Ives here is up to his neck in all the corruption and murder that has been going on."

Detective Inspector Craven suddenly appeared from the back of the crowd and spoke to me: "Don't worry, old son. I had Ives pegged as a bad 'un and I've been telling the Met that you were just an innocent victim all along which is how they brought me into the case. We country mice can still teach these city coppers a thing or two."

I am not sure that I believed that Craven had been on my side all along but I wasn't going to argue with him.

"Show him." Craven tapped the strangely silent Ives on the shoulder.

Ives twisted round so I could see that his hands were handcuffed behind his back.

"Once we gather all the evidence, Ives is going down for a long time. We will have to review all his old cases now we know how crooked he is. Some wrongly convicted victims will be freed and the guilty will be jailed."

No wonder Ives did not look happy. A former Detective Superintendent in jail? Well, he wanted Hell. He had found it.

"Can we go home now?" Tipota asked.

I noted that she called my house 'home' and I felt all warm inside.

I tried to stand but my legs wouldn't hold me. I was exhausted. They carried me out of Mercer Tower in a semi-conscious state.

Chapter Twenty-Three
: Reunion

Going back to Sebastian Fullalove's home brought mixed feelings. I had been through so much since I was last here.

There was no sign of Sebastian when the police had entered Mercer Tower and rescued us. He had just disappeared. I thought he was dead.

I knew he had survived because I phoned him many times afterwards but he had been reluctant to meet or talk.

Finally he agreed to Tipota and me coming to visit him. I left the van and took the Overground to Wapping as I suspected there might be alcohol involved.

I rang the bell. A uniformed butler opened the door and let us in. He gestured us to a table. We sat down.

A maid with a short black skirt and a short, ruffled petticoat brought over two glasses of red wine and placed them before us.

It was Pooh and Piglet.

"Hello again," I said with some surprise.

"I can't drink this," Tipota told Piglet. "Can I have tea?"

Piglet smiled, nodded and disappeared into the kitchen.

"Welcome, survivors," Sebastian said as he came through the doors.

I had a shock. His once black hair had gone grey at the temples.

"At last," I said. "I was worried about you."

"Oh, I'm fine. You just managed to scare the shit out of me. I am glad to see you but I needed some time alone to get my head together after my experiences in the bowels of Mercer Tower." He sat down and joined us at the table.

Piglet returned with glass of red wine for him and a cup of tea for Tipota. Piglet stood to one side of Sebastian while Pooh came and stood on the other side.

"What is with those two? Do they work for you now?" I had to ask.

"They had nowhere to go after Grimoire Priory found itself without an owner again and they so needed someone to belong to," Sebastian shrugged. "It will be interesting to see who buys Grimoire Priory next and see if your theory about it attracting evil people continues. By faking an interest in the property, I've managed to get the estate agents handling its sale to agree to letting me know if they receive an offer for it and from whom. I did get the guided tour from the estate agents and that was when I found these two lost souls. They were hiding. I think they were terrified. I can turn no one away that needs my help as you know."

He wrapped an arm around each of them and pinched both their bottoms.

"They are low maintenance. All they want is food, drink, accommodation and to be able to live in complete servitude."

"Where do they sleep? Do you have another bedroom for them?" I asked naively.

"I have a big bed," Sebastian smirked.

I found it hard to understand how someone as hedonistic as Sebastian Fullalove could ever have been a priest.

"Talk to me you two." I looked between Piglet and Pooh. "Are you happy?"

They answered in unison: "Our joy is to serve and give pleasure. We have no agenda of our own except to be the property of another."

I shrugged. To each his own.

"Leave us, my pets," Sebastian clapped his hands and his servants departed, leaving us to talk.

"It is good for the three of us to be together again. We have been through so much and overcome vastly superior odds. We are the three musketeers." We chinked two glasses and one cup together in a toast. "How is everybody?" Sebastian asked.

"Well my physical wounds have healed but left me with scars – the bullet wound Vasko left across my scalp, the cleaver slice in my upper arm, and the cut in my left hand. At least that doesn't bleed anymore. The mental scars, now – that is a different story…" I started.

"We have all been changed by what we have been through," said Sebastian.

He produced that day's newspaper.

"Story in here about the QPL Group and how Abel Vasko has been appointed its new Chief Executive Officer following the disappearance of its previous CEO Felix Hoad. There is a history of QPL's CEOs going missing," Sebastian chuckled.

263

"I suspect that Ocious Squibb is working on the next disappearance. I think he wanted that job for himself and he certainly knows how to get rid of people," I said.

I looked at the story. There was a picture of Abel Vasko.

"Is it my imagination or has he put on weight since we last saw him?" I asked.

"He is not the only one." Sebastian winked at Tipota who had put on a healthy amount of weight and was looking all the better for it.

"We are having a baby," I answered for her. "We want to get married to make a proper family for the baby. Can you marry us?"

"Congratulations! But I'm afraid I have been stripped of my rank and excommunicated. Any marriage services I carry out will not be legally recognised. However there are ways round it. We will organise something."

"Are you ready to talk now? We left you alone in the crypt facing up to who knows what. What happened next?" I glanced warily at his grey hair again. I had to know.

"There are things I can't talk about yet because I don't understand them. One day I will, I promise. Tell me about what happened to you two."

Talking about it really helped me process it, so I told him every detail of our battle to the death and the rantings of Felix Hoad up high on top of Mercer Tower.

"We three ordinary folk were up against some powerful and really evil people but we managed to defeat many of them." Sebastian was thoughtful.

"Others like Vasko, Squibb and Mrs Milverton have got away with it for now."

"So what drives those who continue to grow the QPL consortium?" I asked. "Wealth? Power? Sex? The worship of the long dead Quincy Pitt? Black Magic? Satanism?"

"Their religion, if it is that, is confused. There is talk of Astorath the Crown Prince of Hell but Mrs Milverton uses paganism and Voodoo, hence the wax doll of your late wife. What they are doing is straddling the world between science and magic. In the old days, the two would have been indistinguishable." Sebastian spread his hands.

"London was one of the earliest international natural ports for shipping. The Docklands area became a melting pot for all cultures and all religions, good and bad, which blended and mixed, getting the best or worst of the different faiths. Somehow Blacksparrow Lane became a focal point for the bad religions."

"Like East Grinstead in Sussex, a focal point for the non-mainstream religions like scientology and so on," I put in. "Something to do with Ley Lines I believe."

"I don't believe in Ley Lines either. The one thing that seems to drive them all at QPL is this old and supposedly dead Victorian Quincy Pitt and I know less about him than any of the black arts. There are more questions than answers.

"There was a point when Felix Hoad seemed impossible to kill and I did wonder if he had found the secret of immortality. But no, in the end death would not be denied.

"I believe that there is so much more to the creation of life than we know but I also believe that the multitude

265

of organised religions we have on this planet are little more than superstition and ignorance. We need to look beyond them for answers."

"It is easier for me to know what I don't believe in than to know what I do believe in," I said. "But I have to have an open mind. The police believed much of what I told them but when it came to killer black sparrows, the death-defying Felix Hoad and a Victorian super villain, they thought what I had been through had unbalanced my mind. I was referred for analysis, you know. I am going through with it and telling the psychiatrist what he wants to hear. I have to say that after all the drugs the Leppards pumped into me I am still not sure for certain what was real and what was hallucination.

"Some of the truth has come out but not all of it. The media stories have been well orchestrated. Enough to stop people investigating any deeper.

"At least they closed down the Haven Hospital. None of the monstrosities we discovered in the cages there have been left alive. I don't know what happened to the head of Archbishop Augustus Ighodaro or the six fingered tank man and tank women but I have to believe that they were all destroyed along with all the other abominations."

"No, I hope the artificial man and woman survived in some way. They were living beings," Tipota put in.

"Perhaps they have. I am not sure what they were - genetically engineered – clones- or just monsters. They were too perfect. Perfect people given the one trade mark of a hidden extra finger to identify them," I said.

"If I were still a priest I would have to say that I don't think they were God's creatures," added Sebastian.

266

"Anyway the late Leppards have been exposed as vivisectionists but the full horrific story has been hushed up," I resumed my summing up. "The official line is that the Leppards were killed when the animals they were mistreating escaped and turned on them.

In fact, I'd read there was already an official line for every death:

Loveable rogue, Danny Stein, was killed in a gangland brawl.

Marquis Thorn and his pilot were killed in a tragic helicopter crash when they flew into a flock of birds.

Archbishop Augustus Ighodaro got caught up in the riots of New Cannon Town, which were put down to a new super strength drug with the power to make users go psychotic that was being dealt on the estate.

Felix Hoad is in hiding, and faces fraud charges.

Search as they might no one could find the underground church at Mercer Tower. The ancient foundations were buried in rubble and ruins and are said to be impossible to excavate. They said that I must have imagined the old underground church and all the old chambers, crypts and passages that lead off from it.

"We never found that wax recording of the voice of Quincy Pitt," I lamented.

"New Cannon Town is the subject of a regeneration programme that will be a monument to the work of the respected Archbishop Augustus Ighodaro," Sebastian volunteered, shrugging his shoulders.

"Is that going to work?" I was cynical.

"I hope so as I have taken up a post in the project." Sebastian surprised me. "I have a personal stake in it. When I was a priest my work was all about supporting the church. Now I am not a priest I am about supporting

267

and helping people who need it. I have also become a prison visitor, among other things. I might even call upon ex Detective Superintendent Ives from time to time. He might refuse to see me but I suspect that if you are incarcerated for a long time you welcome any visitors, even those you hate."

Tipota spoke in a hushed voice: "I just can't believe that Mercer Tower and the QPL Group survived. That horrible skyscraper is virtually finished and hundreds of people are working in there already. It was designed by mad men. Everything QPL builds is twisted and tortured. Mercer Tower is a devourer of lost souls."

"That vile building should be razed to the ground and the earth around it salted," Sebastian said. "The newspaper story says that Vasko is planning a big party for the official opening of the tower."

"I wonder if that will be when he plays that ancient recording and lets the world hear the testament of Quincy Pitt," I mused.

"If that happens it will be like a sermon from Satan," Sebastian shuddered.

"Has what we went through overcome your crisis of faith?" I asked him. "Do you believe in God again?"

"I don't know. But I certainly believe in the Devil now."

Chapter Twenty-Four
: Tea and Scones

I would often come to the top of Box Hill when I felt troubled and wanted to be alone and think. It was a short journey from where I lived but it offered an escape from the world around me. It allowed me to be in harmony with nature.

So there I was, sitting in the Box Tree café on top of the hill, with two cups of tea and a plate of scones and strawberry jam on the table in front of me.

She came into the café and sat down in the other chair at the table.

"I got us tea and scones. You used to like that," I said.

"Still do. You are drinking tea with milk. That is a first," Estelle said.

"So I am and it tastes fine."

"It is a message to you about change. Embrace change. Do not be frightened of it. Life has certainly changed for you. I see you remarried."

"Yes, Tipota has become Mrs Tipota Bell. She so wanted some stability in her life."

"I saw. It was a very small, quiet wedding. Not at all like our grand affair," Estelle smiled.

"It was just for the two of us, no one else. Plus during our marriage you drove all my friends and family away."

"It doesn't do to dwell too much on the past. It can destroy you."

"Indeed. How about you, Estelle? Are you happy now?"

"I am in a different place. In the same way that most people are not pure good or pure evil there is also no Heaven with people sitting on clouds playing harps and no Hell with damnation and pitchforks."

"So do you have an afterlife?"

"We all live on in other people. We are all One, made up of the bits and pieces of a thousand ancestors. Then what is us is sprinkled into the new generations. Billions and billions of us and no two people exactly the same. That is why few people are totally good or totally bad."

"Well I wouldn't agree with that after some of the people I have met recently."

"Your life will change again when you become a father."

"Yes. We should have had children. Things might have worked out differently for us if we had."

"I would have been a disaster as a mother. And becoming a father might be very different to what you imagine."

"After what I have been through, I can cope with anything."

"Life still has some new shocks in store for you. Be strong," she said.

"This is turning out to be a corker of a story," said Peter Wilde who sat at the next table bashing away at the keyboard of his laptop. "Still keeping an eye on you, old chum," he grinned at me. "You need friends to watch over you from this side as you have plenty of enemies over here who are also watching over you.

"As for you, you can't tell me what to write anymore." Peter waved to the next table where a charred and crushed Marquis Thorn glared at him, his broken arms dangling from his sides.

"This is all your fault. You are a shit pilot," Thorn barked at an equally charred and twisted Andries who sat opposite him.

"*Dom kop,*" Andries snarled back.

"It will take more than death to stop me," said Felix Hoad who sat at a nearby table and watched me from his one-eyed skull. "This is not over, Ronan Bell. I will beat death and destroy you yet." He tried to get up and launch himself at me but those goat legs buckled under him and he collapsed back into the chair.

"This time I control the dream, not you," I said. "Those goat legs – they are not working for you. They look ridiculous."

The decapitated head of Archbishop Augustus Ighodaro lay on the table before Hoad.

"I so wanted to be the next Archbishop of Canterbury," he gurgled. "Now the job has gone to that other bloke."

Danny Stein sat at a far table, arms folded and head split down the middle. He looked surly. Part of his brains were seeping out of the crack in his skull and he kept having to unfold his arms to poke them back in. "How can I put a Hit out on anyone here when everyone is already dead?" he complained.

Rick and Zoe Leppard sat together at further table, torn, mangled, kicked, chewed and mutilated. Great lumps of flesh had been bitten out of his face while she was covered in hoof prints. He eyed her with hatred while she could only glare at him through her one remaining eye.

"I thought that we might at least be separated in death," Rick Leppard sighed.

"Having to listen to you for all eternity is real Hell. I would opt for the pitchforks anytime," Zoe rolled her one good eye.

Mr Samuels lay across a chair at a far table, still as stiff as a board and unable to sit.

"They blame me for everything," Samuels told me. "If I had got to the auction on time and bought that statue of Pan, none of this would have happened."

It was good to see that Estelle and Peter had been restored in appearance. No signs of the wounds and damage inflicted at the end of their days. The rest seemed destined to carry their injuries with them beyond the grave.

"At least Mr Gilgeaous is not here," I commented.

"The birds and beasts are subject to the same rules as the rest of us," Estelle said. "If we have mistreated a species of animal during our lifetime it might be that we return in our next life as that that animal." She glanced across at the warring Leppards. Then she looked back at me and she was smiling. "Now I have to go." She stood up.

"Will I see you again?" I asked.

"Probably not but I cannot say for sure. Know that life will always surprise you. Remember where we are now for it will be very important."

"What? Box Hill?"

She blew me a kiss and I felt the chill of it on my cheek. The chill turned into a gale force wind.

Suddenly the whole café shook and I was being tossed around in my chair.

Estelle was lifted off her feet and carried by the wind out of the door.

Tables, chairs and people were being flung in all directions. I tried to hold onto something but suddenly I was flying through the air, gasping for breath.

I came to with a jolt, shivering and sweating. Tipota, in the bed next to me, was shaking me violently.

"Wake up! You seemed to be having a dreadful nightmare," she said.

"You have no idea and it was so realistic," I held her tight.

Tipota was only seven months pregnant when her waters broke and I rushed her to our local Surrey hospital.

She gave birth to a lovely boy, tiny, pink, hairless and premature. He had to be kept in a special care unit at the hospital for the first couple of weeks. However he grew fast, ate well and gripped my finger with a strength that belied the fact that he only weighed four pounds.

Tipota stayed in the hospital with the baby as she was breast feeding.

We were still arguing about a name. We couldn't agree on what to call our little miracle.

I was driving to the hospital to visit Tipota and the baby when it happened.

Firstly, I was passed by a familiar Passat Estate car with darkened rear windows going in the opposite direction. I recognised the registration number. I still had a note of it.

Then my mobile phone rang. I picked it up and it was a Tipota. She was hysterical.

"Our baby has been stolen!" she cried. "They told me a woman dressed as a nurse came and took him – they thought she was bringing him to me but he's gone! The whole hospital has gone into lockdown and the police have been called but it's too late. If you get here now they won't let you in."

My heart stopped. Our baby had been *stolen*? Then in a jolt I remembered the car I'd seen and burst into action.

"Tipota, I think it was Harriet Milverton." I paused and remembered my dream. "You must tell the police and say that Mrs Harriet Milverton was last seen going in the direction of Box Hill," I instructed Tipota. "I love you and I promise to get our baby back."

Then I turned my van around and raced it to Box Hill. My van was not built for speed but I pushed it as fast as I could.

The drive to the top of Box Hill was via a long winding road. The engine shuddered and screamed as I raced my van to the top. The one advantage of the road was that when it came to an end there was no other way out.

I reached the very top which was a car park and a National Trust shop and café. The Passat Estate was parked and empty.

I got out of my van which was billowing out smoke from the engine. There were a number of visitors milling around.

"Did anyone see an old lady with a young baby get out of this car?" I asked frantically. "Which way did she go?"

"She went that way." A concerned family pointed to a pathway through the woods.

I ran and followed the path that wound through the trees and bushes.

I stumbled through the trees in desperate frustration. My clothes ripped and my skin bled from crashing through the thorns. I did not know where to look. Something scurried through the undergrowth ahead of me. I had no idea what it was but I followed. It ran through the trees and bushes. I tried to see what it was but I couldn't.

Suddenly I felt I was back in the woods around Grimoire Priory and being stalked by all the unknown life forms that lurked in the dark undergrowth round there. What sort of creature was this and was it leading me somewhere or just fleeing from me?

I continued to follow the rustling leaves because I did not know what else to do.

I had almost given up when the crying of the baby alerted me. I followed the sounds, pushed through the trees and came out into the open.

Mrs Harriet Milverton stood there looking grotesque in a nurse's uniform. It seemed obscene that this vile woman should wear the uniform of those who nursed and cared. Half her face was still frozen and twisted as if she had had a stroke. She was holding my baby wrapped in a white shawl and lifting it high above her head.

She stood on the edge of a chalk quarry.

She turned and looked at me.

Behind her was a sheer cliff face of white chalk. It had to be about 300 feet from top to bottom.

"Don't do this. Give me my baby!" I didn't know whether to plead or threaten.

"I have to get revenge on you and your nothing wife!" Mrs Milverton screeched at me. "I will kill you both but not before you have endured endless suffering. You must pay for what you did and I planned to start with the death of your first born."

276

"Not the baby. Babies come into this world as innocents. Attack me but not a newborn. Are you without any conscience?" I asked.

"Oh I know what it is to be a mother. I had a baby once but it died."

Was she showing an unseen caring side?

"I'm sorry. Perhaps that explains a lot."

"Don't be sorry. I killed it myself. The old religion demands sacrifices."

The evil woman no longer shocked me. I tried to reach her another way: "Sorry about your face. Maybe some Botox could cure it."

She laughed and waved the baby in the air. At least my son had stopped crying but he was being dangled over a 300-foot drop.

"Oh I planned to visit you with all the Biblical plagues, the death of the first born being just one of them. However…" she paused and lowered the baby. "I can't do it because this is not your first born."

"What? My first wife Estelle and I never had children. This is my first!" I was confused.

There was a movement in the trees behind me. Detective Inspector Craven and Tipota, who was still in bed clothes, appeared and stood beside me.

"My baby. Don't harm him!" Tipota screamed.

"I am from the police," Craven bellowed. "Put the baby down before you make it any worse for yourself, madam. There are more police on the way."

"Trust me I will exact full revenge on you meddling pair of unbelievers. But not on the baby. Take him and look closely at him. Then you might want to kill him yourself," Mrs Milverton said.

Surprisingly, she handed me my baby. She gave me a malevolent smile as she did so. I did look at him. In spite of his ordeal he seemed contented. I looked for any injuries, lowering the shawl from his head, while Tipota watched beside me.

"Damn my hand," I said, looking at my left hand which had started to bleed. It was the first time that had happened since Hoad died.

"Perhaps he is not your first born because you are not the father!" Mrs Milverton threw back her head and cackled.

For a moment we were in silent shock. Tipota spoke first: "He is our baby. I will love him just the same."

Then I found my voice: "As I said before all babies are born innocent. I will love him like my own, whether he is or not." I hugged the baby to my chest to show that I meant it.

Mrs Milverton howled in rage. "What fools you all are!"

"Get out of our lives, bitch!" Tipota yelled.

Tipota left my side and before any of us knew what was happening, leapt up and kicked Mrs Milverton hard in the chest - so hard that the old crone was propelled backwards over the edge of the chalk quarry. Craven ran forward to try and catch her but was too late.

Screaming loud enough to shake all the leaves in the trees around us, Mrs Milverton hurtled downwards, her arms whirling and her legs kicking. Eventually a small cloud of chalk powder far below told us that she had reached the bottom of the quarry.

"No matter how much Royal Jelly she devoured she would not have survived that." I peered over the edge.

278

There was a loud squawking of birds high in the sky. I looked around me. An angry swarm of black sparrows was swooping down on to the upper branches of the trees around us. After a while, the birds quietened down, settled on the branches and glared down at us.

"Protect our baby." I gave Tipota the baby while watching the suddenly still birds. It was if they were preparing to attack.

"What is wrong with you, Bell?" Craven turned and then followed my gaze to the birds in the trees.

"Get ready to run," I said.

There came a loud meow and a black cat sprang up into the trees. It chomped its jaws over one of the black sparrows. The bird was quickly despatched in a flurry of black feathers and blood. The black cat then charged into the centre of the birds and sent them fluttering and squawking off in all directions.

We watched them fly away.

"Phew, just for a minute you had me believing your story about killer sparrows," Craven chuckled. "That cat sure saw them off. Cats and birds, historic enemies."

The black sparrows had gone and the cat scampered away into the undergrowth, running upright on its hind legs.

There was more movement behind us. We were joined by two uniformed policemen.

Craven spoke before anyone else. "I drove Mrs Bell here from the hospital and we arrived just in time to save the baby. Sadly the woman who stole the baby was so disturbed that she committed suicide by jumping off the quarry. We tried to stop her but we couldn't. Better get Forensics down there."

"Can you give me a lift?" I asked Craven. "I think I killed my van by racing it to get up here."

"Sure. You'll all need to come back to the hospital to get checked out and later I will need you at the station for a statement but I think we are all reading from the same page." Craven winked at us.

Tipota cuddled our baby and we walked back to the car park along the woodland path.

The baby was smiling broadly. He gave a little chuckle.

"He shouldn't be an only child," I said. "He needs a brother or a sister."

"Or both," Tipota smiled. "You'll need to buy us a proper car now. A family saloon with a child seat."

"No problem." I still had the cash Mrs Milverton had given me tucked away in my loft.

"Our baby will be fine," Tipota smiled at the bundle in her arms.

The baby smiled back. The face of an angel.

It was night when the black car drove up the drive and halted in front of Grimoire Priory.

The man in the car climbed out and stood looking up at the old building: a big old grey stone house with tall turrets, tall chimneys and dark windows hidden in the middle of an overgrown woodland area. Tangled ivy grew up every wall. The stone pond in front of the house was still filled with dead leaves and stagnant green water. A stone statue of a naked woman covered in green slime was wrapped around a broken fountain in its centre.

Many people found Grimoire Priory oppressive but he felt he belonged here.

280

As he surveyed his new property, he was unaware of the many glittering eyes that watched him from the depths of the deep dark woods behind him. Something shrieked in the woods. He spun round to see what it was but he could make out nothing but darkness. The scream ended abruptly.

He turned back, pulled a bunch of keys from his pocket and strode to the front door.

He was the new owner and he had such plans.

THE END

About the author

Alan Cork has spent a lifetime as an Editor and Managing Editor of obscure business and professional journals for different publishing houses. During his time working on specialist magazines, he travelled the world for his job. His final full time job was as Managing Editor at DMG World Media (Daily Mail Group). In semi-retirement he became a university lecturer and an NHS Trust Governor. Now he is just relaxing by writing stories to terrify all ages.

He is a widower with a son and daughter and three grandchildren and lives in London.

BV - #0074 - 021120 - C0 - 197/132/16 - PB - 9781912964499 - Matt Lamination